VIOLET BLOOD

LINDSAY MARIE MILLER

For my great-grandmother, Addie

I miss you every day.

~ ~

Preface

Addie

I'd always wanted a normal life.

Family. Parents who loved me. Children of my own.

Without them, happiness was a million miles away.

I walked to the river today. I knelt down on the bank and dipped my hand in the water. Then I rinsed off my face. I took a greedy drink and watched the sky through the trees.

I thought about Antoinette and everything she had endured. For love. For family.

For a good hour, I sat there and cried. Then I took off my shoes and eased into the river. It was so cold, but I dunked my head and plunged beneath the rapids anyway.

I opened my eyes underwater. And then I searched until I couldn't hold my breath anymore. I don't know what I was looking for. Some sign that my life wasn't over.

Just when I thought I had everything figured out, fate dropped a bomb on me. But this one was different. It had nothing to do with secrets and lies. Looking back, those had been easier to handle. Finding out I was adopted, that Daniel was my grandfather, Jimmy was my father, Josette was my mother, and I had a whole family living in Paris who loved me.

None of it compared to the heartache I felt now. It had ripped a hole right through me.

I came up for air and took a breath. Then I floated on my back and let the sun shine on my face. It had been so long since I'd done something as human as this.

I couldn't talk to Tom.

When I looked in his eyes, all I saw was sadness and pain. He hated the truth. But the truth is—it was all on me. This was *my* problem. *My* future. *My* destiny.

And I wasn't going to drag him under the water with me.

Like Ophelia. Like Antoinette.

I'd drown in my own misery, my own pain.

But he'd always have this *river*, these *woods*, this *place*.

And if I was lucky, he'd remember me.

Chapter 1

Tom

I never thought I'd live to see the day my wife died. As a man, I expected to be the first to go.

It was the way things were supposed to be.

When death came, I would be old and gray. Addie and I would have already experienced a long, happy life together. Blessed with children and grandchildren.

But we were just kids ourselves. It had only been a few months since Addie turned eighteen. And in a few more, I'd reach eighteen as well. The first mark of adulthood.

I never planned on watching her die in my arms. I was meant to die in hers.

There was so much blood. All over my hands. All over her.

It felt like my fault, because I was her husband. It was my duty to protect her. Had I been there in time, I would have taken both bullets for her. But I was too late.

Sitting in the hospital hall, I squeezed the emerald in my hand. On the inside, I wanted to crush the jewel to powder. I hated the necklace. Hadn't it been the catalyst of all this? For as long as I'd known Addie, the necklace had been her only source of danger.

Then again, without it, we might never have met.

Wasn't the necklace the only reason we'd struck

up conversation in the first place?

Sure, I'd been attracted to her. I'd wanted to get to know her for years. But it wasn't until Addie saw the lady in the painting—her grandmother, Antoinette, that a bond began to form between us.

It felt like fate. The way we'd been brought together.

In some ways, I had the necklace to thank. Without it, Addie never would have ended up in my arms. The threat of DeMilo had accelerated her trust in me from the start.

I shook my head. Maybe I'd been awake too long.

We would have met anyway. At school. It was just a matter of time.

She was mine. And I was hers.

We owed the necklace nothing. And I had no intention of putting it up on some pedestal. Maybe it meant a great deal to Addie. But that was only because of her family.

The hospital doors slid open and I looked up. There was a bloody man on a gurney. So I got up to make room and slipped the necklace in my pocket. As they flew past me, I met the man's gaze and the hairs on the back of my neck stood up.

It was Valjean.

They disappeared through the swinging doors and rounded the corner. My first instinct was to panic. Because they were taking him straight to Addie.

I went down the hall after them. Just a few short steps at first. But then my feet sped up, and I couldn't fight the beast inside me. I had to protect her. I had to keep him away. Before he killed her this time.

"Sir," a nurse called. "Sir, you can't go that way!"

I pushed through the double doors and rounded

the corner. But the nurse grabbed my arm and pulled me away from Addie.

"No, you don't understand." I jerked out of her hold. "My wife is back there. That man—" I stumbled back and ran into the wall. "He's a criminal, a jewel thief. He tried to kill her!"

"I understand, but you can't go back there."

"What about my wife?" I clenched my jaw. "She's back there. With him!"

"I can assure you that she is safe."

"Really? You don't treat gunshot victims in the same wing?"

She leveled her eyes at me and swallowed.

"Hey!" Ashton strode towards us. "What are you doing back here?"

"They took Addie back there with Valjean!" I pointed in the direction they had gone.

Ashton read the rage in my eyes and smiled at the nurse. "Why don't I take him off your hands?"

Feeling betrayed, I shot Ashton a sour look. The nurse left as Ashton escorted me into the waiting room. I'll admit my wife's cousin had been rubbing me the wrong way since we first landed in Paris. He hadn't done anything bad, so to speak. But the guy was just too nice, which made me question everything.

"Tom, I know you're worried about her. But you've got to calm down."

I ran my fingers through my hair. "He shot her! How do you think I feel? She could, she could—" I broke down crying and sank into a chair. Thankfully, there weren't too many people around. I guess everyone else was enjoying the Christmas holidays, while I'd watched my wife bleeding out in the snow.

"Tom." He crouched down and put his hand on

my shoulder. "Let me talk to the staff. I'll make sure Valjean is nowhere near her. All right?"

I nodded, planting my face in my hands.

"Why don't you get cleaned up?" he said.

I couldn't look at him, because there were tears in my eyes.

Ashton left me alone to talk to the nurse. I think it was the same one I'd argued with. I ran my hands over my thighs, taking a few deep breaths. How could he be so calm about everything? Even Edmond had been way too cool about his niece being shot, falling through the ice and nearly drowning.

Maybe they didn't care about her as much as they'd let on.

Then again, no one loved Addie like I did.

I escaped to the bathroom and shut the door behind me. It was a single room with a toilet and sink. Thankful for the privacy, I let my back slide against the door and sank to the cold linoleum floor.

Then I rocked back and forth, tugging my fingers through my hair. I wanted to rip it out. I wanted to hit somebody. I wanted to hold her. I wanted to go back in time. Before we'd ever met.

Maybe she'd still be alive.

I stood up and looked at myself in the mirror. Her blood was everywhere. All over my clothes, my skin.

I splashed warm water on my face and held on to the sink. And that's when it all came back to me.

* * *

"Hey." She touched my face. "What are you thinking about?"

I sat up with the sheet draped around my waist. "You."

6

Addie leaned into my body, running her fingers down my chest. I kissed her mouth. I kissed her neck. I kissed her everywhere. And as we lay together, I knew my heart had never felt so full.

It was overflowing. And when it came to our honeymoon suite, we hadn't even left the bedroom.

"So where are you taking me?" She fluttered her lashes and put those green eyes on me.

"It's a surprise." I rubbed her shoulders.

"You're no fun." She kissed my cheek. "Are you really not going to tell me where we're going?"

"You'll see tomorrow." I smiled and leaned into a kiss. Hers were always the sweetest.

"But, Mr. Sutton." She eyed the clock. "It already is tomorrow."

It was the middle of the night, but we had no plans to go to bed anytime soon. There was a view of the Eiffel Tower from our hotel room. I wished we could visit the landmark again. The day we'd taken a tour of the sights Addie and I had been fighting. It was my fault, and I regretted it now.

"Your family is pretty great," I said.

"Yeah," she smiled. "They really are."

"Addie." I held her in my arms. "You are my family."

Her emerald eyes ran over my face, and I saw something change in her. She turned out the light and sat down in my lap. She was wearing my shirt, the one I'd had on at the wedding today. It was a white dress shirt with a row of buttons down the middle. Most of them were undone.

She wrapped her hands around my neck and slanted her lips over mine. I felt her warm body through the shirt. It felt so good to have her near, to have her this close. She was finally mine.

I slid my hands beneath the shirt so I could feel her skin. She was so warm, so soft, so perfect. I'd spent years imagining what it must be like. To be alone and naked with her like this. The real thing was far greater than any fantasy my seventeen-year-old brain could have conjured.

"Did you know it would be like this?" she asked.

Times like these, I wondered if she could read my mind.

"Like what?" I held her waist as she kissed my neck.

"I had no idea it felt this good," she cooed.

I put one hand on her back so I could thread my fingers through her hair. We'd never made out like this. And Addie was really kicking the French kissing thing up a notch. Maybe it was in the air.

"Why do you think they call it sex?" she asked.

"What do you mean?" I trailed my fingers up and down her spine. Her skin was smooth as silk.

"*Sex*," she giggled, leaning back in my arms. "It sounds so provocative."

"That's because everyone knows what it means."

"Yeah, but would it sound as scandalous if people called it something else?"

"Such as?" I glanced up at her in the moonlight. Her hands were on my chest.

"I don't know." She looked off. "Church."

"What?" Now she had me cracking up.

"Yeah, what if church meant *sex* and sex meant *church*?"

"So going to church would mean?"

"Having sex," she answered.

"And having sex would mean?"

"Going to church."

I shook my head, not knowing what to make of her alternate universe.

"I mean, it is kind of spiritual." She pressed a kiss to my lips. "Wouldn't you say?"

I rolled us over so I was looming above her. And she yelped from being taken by surprise.

"Yeah." I rubbed my nose against hers. "I guess so."

We kissed and my heart kept pounding. At this rate, it could have easily exploded out of my chest. I'd worried that it might earlier, but it hadn't happened yet. I guess our bodies were built to handle this.

"I really love that we can talk to each other about stuff like this."

"Like what?" I kissed her collarbone. "*Sex?*"

She laughed as I tickled her with my scruff. I'd last shaved this morning. But it was the middle of the night, and my beard grew fast. Deep down, I knew she loved it. And I loved watching her squirm.

"Not just sex," she said on a serious note. "Everything really."

"Like the ten babies were gonna make together?"

"Ten! I thought you said five?"

"Who wouldn't want ten of you?" I asked.

She liked that.

"You have no fear do you?" She traced my skin as she lay beneath me.

"Sure, I do." I kissed the hollow of her throat. "I'm scared of lots of things."

"But you're not like most guys." She cupped my cheek. "You've never been. That's why I've always liked you so much."

"Oh really? I thought it was my Southern charm

and good sense of humor."

"You've got that, too." She stroked my arm. "But you're not scared of marriage, children. Most guys take decades to get as serious as you are. I've never met someone so young that was such a man."

"Maybe I'm not like most men," I said. "I haven't had the most normal upbringing."

Even as a boy, I felt behind. Like my parents had left without me. And it was my job to always be two steps ahead. Maybe I could catch them. Maybe I could prevent it from happening again.

"I'm sorry about your parents, Tom."

"Yeah, me too." I propped up on my elbow beside her.

"Why don't you ever talk about it?" she asked.

"I don't know." I toyed with the buttons on my shirt. "It happened so long ago. It makes me sad. I never even knew them really. I know things with your parents haven't been the best, but at least you had somebody. Grandpa was great, it's nothing against him. But it's just not the same as having a mom and a dad."

She ran her fingers down my back and then over my ribcage. It made me catch my breath.

"I want to have babies with you." She made it sound like a secret.

"Right now?" I joked.

"No, of course not. We need to finish high school first."

"And then there's college," I added.

"And then our careers."

"And then baby making time." I lifted my brow.

"Yeah," she said a bit breathlessly. "Somethin' like that."

"We're young, baby, really young." I folded my

fingers with hers. "We've got plenty of time."

"I know, but I'm really excited about it. About having a family of my own."

I caressed the back of her hand with my thumb. "So am I."

"All this adoption stuff, I don't know." She shook her head. "I just really want to have children that are ours, yours and mine. Biological children. Children who look like us and truly belong to us."

"With your hair and my eyes," I finished.

"Yeah," she nodded. "Let's give them something we never had."

"What's that?" I tucked a golden lock behind her ear.

"Blood."

* * *

There was a knock on the door. "Tom?"

It was Ashton.

"Yeah?"

"I found a shirt for you. Hopefully it's the right fit."

I opened the door and grabbed it. "Thanks."

It was rude to slam the door right back in his face. Especially when he'd gone out of his way to accommodate me. But I couldn't talk to anybody right now. Not even myself.

"Are you all right?" he asked.

"Yes, I'm fine. Thanks for the shirt. I'll be out in a minute."

They were curt replies. But I meant them.

I rinsed the rest of the blood off my face and changed shirts. Then I washed my hands and tried not to think about her. But memories of Addie kept racing through my mind, like a switch had been flipped. One that I had no way of turning off.

I felt her lips on my skin, the way she made my pulse race. But then I saw Valjean. He shot her. She screamed. Then there was fear, panic. The sheer will to get to her. Freezing water. Her blood. My mouth on hers in a desperate plea to get breath in her lungs. What if I'd been too late?

I found Ashton in the waiting room. He patted the seat beside him, so I plopped down. I'd been trying to get a handle on my worries. Like closing the lid on a pot. But they simmered and boiled, terrifying every part of me. So many things could go wrong. I hated being separated from her. What was happening?

"You need to make some calls," Ashton said.

I stared at the floor, holding my head in my hands.

"I would have done it already, but it's not my place."

I chewed on my lip to keep the tears at bay.

"Unless you want me to?"

"No." I forced myself to stand. "I'll do it."

I went outside and found a bench. Then I looked around to make sure no one was within hearing distance. I saw people from where I sat. But with the wind and snow, they were going inside as soon as the doors slid open.

I was a coward. So I called Jeanine first. She was my cousin, my friend. And I'd grown to trust her like a sister over the past year. When I dropped the bomb, she was speechless. Then I heard her crying, and I was crying too. She wanted to be here, but knew her parents wouldn't budge. With Addie in the hospital, who in their right mind would fly all the way out here to risk getting shot themselves?

Paris was a dangerous place for anyone who knew

about the necklace.

We got off the phone, and I dried my eyes. It was the middle of the night in Savannah. But I didn't even know if Jeffrey or Eleanor were home. They traveled so often, I couldn't predict the time zone.

But when it came to the news I had to bear, I guess it wouldn't really matter.

It was common knowledge that the Smiths didn't like me. Not that they hated me. But they'd never approved of our engagement. To top it off, Addie never even told them we were getting married.

Come to think of it, Jeanine didn't know that we'd actually done it. I hadn't bothered to tell her.

I called Jeffrey next, because he was more mild-mannered than Eleanor. It was a blessing when he actually picked up. Right now, I didn't know if I could bear the wrath of his wife.

"Hello?"

"Mr. Smith." I did my best to sound calm. "I don't know how to tell you this."

"Tom?" He sounded sleepy. "Are the two of you still in Paris?"

I closed my eyes as more tears came. "Addie's been shot."

Silence.

"Mr. Smith?" I heard him take a breath. "She's in the hospital. And they're doing everything they can." I was so close to breaking down again, the way I'd just done with Jeanine. "I-I'm sorry I didn't take better care of her."

"Stop it, Tom. I don't want to hear any of that."

I fought for air. It was so hard getting it in my lungs.

"Are you in Paris?"

"Yes." I told him the name of the hospital.

"We're getting on a plane right now. And we'll be there as soon as we can."

"Okay."

"Call me as soon as you hear something," he requested.

"All right. I will." I heard Eleanor in the background, asking what was going on. Then he hung up, and I was stuck in purgatory again. Waiting. Wondering. Wishing. Hoping. Praying that I'd see her again.

Edmond returned with Adeline and Juliette. They ran into Ashton's arms, huddling together in the corner. Edmond went to the front desk, using his position to leverage information. Last I'd been told, my wife was on the operating table in emergency surgery. And I couldn't be anywhere near her.

Jimmy ran inside like a mad man, screaming and shouting at the nurses. Edmond had to take him aside and calm him down. We all knew Edmond was the one with the power. It was in Addie's best interest to let him work his royal magic. For the better part of an hour, that's what we did.

Jimmy sat down beside me and whispered apologies. "I just got her back."

I wrapped my arm around his shoulder. "She'll be fine. I know she will. She's strong."

He gave me a fatherly hug. "You're a good kid, Tom. I couldn't have asked for a better son-in-law."

We waited together for hours that felt like years. I kept pushing worry away. It felt like playing football. And I was the one being tackled. Every minute. Every second. Just thinking about it was killing me.

But then Josette showed up. And that's when all

hell broke loose.

All seven of us were staring at her. Even Edmond's driver, who had been waiting it out with us inside. Now I understood why Edmond had spoken so harshly about Genevieve. Because she'd really been Josette. Living a secret life in Paris. For the life of me, I couldn't understand why she'd run away.

She may have been Addie's biological mother, but I despised her.

"What are you doing here?" Jimmy asked.

She clutched her purse in her lap. She didn't have the gall to meet his eyes.

"You changed your hair," he noted.

"Yes." She tucked a lock of it behind her ear.

"Are you ever going to tell me what happened? Or why the hell you even came?"

She pressed her lips together and stared at the ground.

"Well answer me!"

"Mr. Blake," Edmond scolded.

"Where have you been?" Jimmy drilled.

She raised her green eyes. They looked like Addie's.

"It's complicated," she murmured. "And if you would just let me explain it to you-"

"You drop right out of the sky after all these years." Jimmy stood up to face her. "I thought you were dead! I've been out of my mind without you. We had a life. We had a child!" He pointed towards the emergency room.

"For God's sake," Edmond said. "Calm down unless you want to get us kicked out of this place."

"Thomas?" A man in a white coat entered the waiting room.

I stood up and looked at the clipboard in his hand. "It's just Tom."

"Addie is your wife." He had a heavy accent, but I understood him perfectly.

"Yes." I showed him my wedding ring.

"Could I have a word with you in private?" he asked.

"Is she all right?" Jimmy butted in. "I'm her father."

"And I'm her mother," Josette said. "When can we see her?"

"I'd like to speak to her husband first, if you don't mind."

He led me down the hall without saying a word. I looked back at Jimmy and Josette. There was a sinking feeling in the pit of my stomach. I'd never felt fear like this before. I could taste it.

His name was Dr. Laurent. And he was nice enough. But my heart couldn't take the suspense.

"How is she?" I kept at his heels until he stopped in front of a glass wall.

Addie lay on a bed with her eyes closed. I saw her chest move. It looked like she was sleeping.

"We removed the bullets. There were two." He tucked his clipboard beneath his arm. "I don't think she'll have any problems with infection. But she lost a lot of blood, Tom."

I put my hand on the glass as my eyes filled with tears. She was alive.

"But she's going to be okay. Right?"

"We gave her a blood transfusion. And her levels are stabilizing. She should make a full recovery."

It sounded too good to be true. I almost couldn't believe it.

"Thank you." I hugged him close and probably squeezed a lot tighter than he liked. But I didn't know how else to thank him. He'd saved her life. And now everything could go back to normal again.

"There are some other things we should discuss, Mr. Sutton."

I let him go and took a step back. "She will be all right. Won't she?"

Laurent looked at her through the glass. "I've received your request about keeping her away from Valjean. He's been moved to a separate floor where he will be guarded day and night. He'll be taken to jail once he's out of recovery."

"You saved him?"

He looked me in the eye. "It is my job, Mr. Sutton."

I clenched my jaw and smoldered, then glanced at Addie again.

"It's not my place to judge," he said. "I don't get to decide who lives or dies."

"He shot my wife. He could have killed her."

"I understand. But you must let justice take its natural course."

I crossed my arms and nodded. I could live with it. I didn't like it. But I could live with it.

"I'd like to see her now."

"Your wife needs rest," he said. "I've given her something to help her sleep."

There was a pane of glass between us. But it felt like we were worlds apart.

"Please. We just got married. I need to be with her."

He nodded. "Only you. And only if you'll do your best not to wake her."

I'd agree to anything at this point. "All right."

"We're moving her into a private room. You can see her then."

"Okay." I was so excited I felt like a kid high on sugar.

"But I'd like you to come with me first. We need to talk."

"About what?" I looked back at Addie before he led me to his office.

When we arrived, he shut the door and leaned against his desk. "Have a seat."

"I'm not sure what this has to do with-"

"Have a seat."

I sat down.

"I've been thinking of the best way to tell you this, Mr. Sutton. Especially now that you tell me you've just gotten married." He took off his coat and walked around to the chair in front of his desk.

Just seconds ago, it felt like my prayers had been answered. She was alive, stable, breathing.

"Your wife is very young."

I caught on to his tone. He hadn't told me everything yet.

"I hate to be the one to tell you this, Tom."

My mind went numb. His words were all garbled in my head, like I didn't want to accept them. So my body was rejecting every syllable. Expelling them back like vomit.

My palms were sweaty. I couldn't breathe.

"I thought you said she was fine," I accused.

"She is fine. There is no reason why she can't live a long, healthy life."

I broke down and cried. I was drowning. All of the oxygen in the room had been sucked away.

"I've never had to deal with something like this before," he said. "Not with these circumstances. I thought it would be better to tell you first. And then I'd let you decide."

"Decide what?" I sobbed.

"How you want her to find out. Would you like to tell her? Or do you want me in the room?"

"I don't know." I wiped the tears off my face. "Do we have to tell her today?"

"Not if you don't want to. You're her husband. The choice is up to you."

I nodded. "Could you let me think about it?"

"Of course. Let me see if she's been moved into her own room. Would you like to see her now?"

"Yes." I stood up, hurting all over. I hated knowing something she didn't.

He put his hand on my shoulder. "I'm sorry."

I walked out of his office and felt like I was living someone else's life.

Because this damn sure wasn't mine.

We rode the elevator in silence. And then I talked to the nurse assigned to her room. They left and shut the door behind them. So I opened the blinds to let in a little light and pulled up a chair beside her.

I wanted to touch her so badly it burned. She was in a deep sleep, but I couldn't risk waking her. So I made myself behave and kept my hands to myself. Even though I longed to hold her hand, caress her face, tuck the golden lock of hair behind her ear that always seemed to fall out of place.

I sat there for hours, just watching her breathe. A nurse stopped by occasionally to check on her. During one of those visits, I went downstairs to tell everyone the good news.

Addie was fine. She would live. But they wouldn't be able to see her today.

I felt bad for Jimmy. I would have been going out of my mind if I hadn't seen her already. But I respected Dr. Laurent, and I wanted to follow his wishes. So the rest of the family went back to the castle, and I promised to call with regular updates. But I wasn't about to leave her side. I was spending the night.

When the sun went down, I closed the blinds. Then I stared at her until it made me cry. She was the most beautiful thing I'd ever seen. And I just wanted her to be all right. I wanted her to be happy.

But when she found out, that might not even be a possibility anymore.

Chapter 2

Addie

T om." His name was the first word on my lips. Something hurt. My head, my back, my arms. I wasn't in pain. It was discomfort. A hollow ache.

"Tom." Opening my eyes was a struggle. Like the world was too bright, and I wasn't quite ready for it yet. I felt someone touch my hand. And that was what let me know that I had survived.

I fluttered my lashes until the blurry face beside me turned clear. It was him. *Only* him.

"Hey." He took my hand tenderly in his. "I'm right here."

He sat in a chair by my bed. There were tears in his eyes.

"What happened?" I asked.

He pursed his lips and brushed the back of his knuckles against my cheek. "You were shot."

My memory bank may have been fuzzy, but I hadn't forgotten everything. "I remember."

"You lost a lot of blood. But they took good care of you. And you're going to be fine."

I squeezed his hand with the strength I had left in mine and whispered, "I missed you."

He moved closer and held my face in his hands. "Baby, I missed you too."

"How long have I been in the hospital?" I admired

his amber irises, sweet like honey.

He took a breath and dried his eyes. "About a day, I guess. It happened just before dawn."

I nodded and tried to stretch my legs. But I felt so stiff. And this bed was nothing like the one at home.

"You feel so far away." I ran my fingers through his hair—shiny black locks that had gotten longer in the winter.

He opened his mouth several times, his eyes racing over my face.

"What is it?" I asked.

He cradled my face in his hands and then buried his face in my lap. "Tell me if I'm hurting you."

"You're not." Confused by his actions, I kept petting his hair as he wrapped his arms around me.

Tom pressed his cheek to my stomach and cried. The kind of tears that shake your whole body. I couldn't imagine what he must have gone through, waiting to see if I would die. So I rubbed his back and soaked up every emotion. When he lifted his head to meet my eyes, I stroked the stubble on his face.

"I dreamed about you." I shed a few tears myself. "And the way you touch me."

"So it was a naughty dream?" he sniffled.

"No." My lower lip trembled as I raised his chin. "It was nice."

He gave me one of those ear-splitting grins. More like a smirk than a smile. I'd always been attracted to his boyish good looks. But he was beginning to look like less of a boy and more of a man.

Then again, he always had.

I furrowed my brow, hating to break a fragile moment of intimacy. "I'm cold."

"Okay." He caressed my face while I admired him

in appreciation. "I'll get you a blanket."

He walked into the hall, where I heard him talking to a nurse. I looked around the barren hospital room. The blinds were closed, so it would have been dark as a cave in here, if not for the lamp. There was a picture of roses hanging on the wall, and it looked like I had my own bathroom. Unless that door led to a closet instead. I couldn't remember the last time I'd been to the bathroom and it not only scared me.

It made me feel sick.

"They had a spare blanket." Tom returned with the blanket in question and cracked the door behind him. I was propped up in bed with pillows behind me, so it didn't take much for me to sit up.

He spread the blanket over my body, carefully tucking me in. I hadn't said anything before, but he'd gotten a little too close to the wounds surrounding my hip. I'd have to speak up next time, even though I might hurt his feelings. It was really my fault anyway. I'd wanted him to hold me so close it hurt.

"How's that?" He leaned over me and adjusted the blanket, trying to make it perfect.

"Better." I waited for him to say something else. But he just kept standing there, staring at me.

"What is it?" he asked.

I reached out and stroked his arm. "I'm hungry."

He looked at the bedside table. "They brought you some water."

I felt like a whiner. But I was *starving*. It was making me irritable.

"It's after ten. But let me see if they can fix you something." He handed me the cup of water. It was thin plastic—the clear kind with a rim around the top. "Why don't you sip on that first?"

I looked at the water and it slipped right out of my hand, soaking my new blanket.

I hung my head and burst into tears. I had no idea I was so weak. I couldn't even hold a plastic cup.

"I'm sorry," I whimpered. "I tried to... I couldn't..."

"Addie, I'm so sorry." Tom collected the empty cup and set it on the table. "I'm sorry, baby."

I broke down and touched my throat. There was a lump burrowing its way at the back. And it hurt. I wasn't really crying for any particular reason. I was tired. I was hungry. I was weak.

I looked into his eyes, and he put my head on his chest. He rubbed my back and threaded his fingers in my hair. In that moment, it felt like all I really needed was for him to hold me.

"I thought I was never going to see you again," I whispered.

He leaned back and cupped my cheek in his hand. Then he pressed his forehead to mine, tracing my jawline. "I'm never going to let anybody hurt you again."

I shut my eyes and squeezed him tight. "It's my fault. I shouldn't have run away like that."

"Addie." He stroked my hair.

"I almost died," I sobbed. "I almost left you alone. And it's my fault."

"Baby, no." He cradled my head in his hands. "You didn't do anything wrong."

"But I did." I brushed his arm. "I betrayed you. How can you even look at me?"

He sat down and pulled me in, locking my body in his arms. I cried on his shoulder and then buried my face in his chest. It was a way to hide from all the damage I had done. If only I'd stayed inside...

"*Addison*," he spoke near my ear. "I won't have you blaming yourself. Do you understand me? I don't want to hear it." He rubbed my back and sighed, slowly coaxing the life back into me.

"Yes." I looked up and met his gaze. He was tired, worried, scared. But he had me.

If survival had taught me anything, it was to never look back. I'd struggled with my past for so long, it felt like a monkey on my back. Maybe it was time to let it go. And finally live my life.

I kissed him. Softly at first. But then I was burning for him.

Desire rippled beneath my skin as I pulled him closer. He held my face and touched his lips to mine. But he was careful, too careful. So I let out a strangled sob and leaned back, exposing my aching neck.

He trailed kisses down the column of my throat, sliding his hands around my waist as he did. I shut my eyes and forced myself into the moment. It was worth blocking it all out—the pain of the past.

He grabbed my hip and I flinched. My eyes shot open as I gazed into his, so hopelessly disappointed. I felt tears brewing on the inside, but he caressed my face and smiled. Then he kissed my forehead.

"It's okay," he whispered. "We have the rest of our lives for that."

I bowed my head and nodded.

"Why don't I get you something to eat?" he said.

"Yeah, I am hungry." And thankful for the diversion.

He squeezed my hand and left a kiss on the back of it before he left. I lay back and closed my eyes. I'd forgotten about spilling the water until now. I was freezing without him in the room. So I awaited his return and sent a request into the universe—that whatever he brought back for dinner was *warm*.

Fifteen minutes later, he walked into the room with a tray. There was a nurse with him who checked my vitals and made sure there were no complications. She had an excellent bedside manner, but I was happy when she left. And even more delighted that she shut the door behind her.

"Well." Tom pulled up a chair. "I got you chicken breast, steamed vegetables and fettuccine."

"I knew there was a reason I married you."

He chuckled, and it was the best sound I'd heard all night.

"Here." He put the tray in my lap with tender care. "I went ahead and cut the chicken for you. I thought it'd be easier."

"Thank you." I picked up a fork and twirled it in the fettuccine. Craving the noodles was easy. Getting them in my mouth, on the other hand, was a different story.

"Do you need some help?" he asked.

I huffed and puffed, because I hated feeling helpless.

"Let me." Tom cut the fettuccine into bite-sized pieces. Then he cupped my chin and slid a morsel into my mouth. I put my hand on his shoulder—a way of grounding myself in his strength.

"What happened to Valjean?"

He averted his eyes and fed me a piece of chicken.

"Is he dead?"

"Your uncle shot him." He speared a piece of broccoli. "And umm, he went down."

"Okay?" I furrowed my brow. "So he's dead?"

"He's in protective custody," he said. "I'm sure he'll end up in prison."

Relief washed over me. "Thank God they got him."

"Yeah." He offered me more fettuccine. "Thank God."

"What about the necklace?" I had a hard time reaching his eyes.

He took his time looking at me. "It's safe."

"Good." I ate in silence, happy to hear the good news.

"Want some water?" he said.

"Yes." I let him help me drink. "Thank you."

He fed me what was left on the plate, and it was such a relief to have food in my stomach. I nestled against the pillows as he set my drink down and put the tray on the bedside table.

"I guess I'm cashing in on those wedding vows pretty early, huh?"

"What do you mean?" he asked.

"In sickness and in health." I smiled, but he wouldn't meet my eyes.

He took my hand and held it between both of his.

"So I'm really okay?" I wondered. "The doctor said everything's fine?"

He lowered his face and pressed his cheek to mine. Then he smelled my hair, running his nose over my shoulder. He put his head on my chest and listened to my heart, wrapping his arms around me.

"Tom?" I heard him crying. "Is everything okay?"

"Yes." He toyed with my shirtsleeve. "I was just so scared of losing you."

"Well, I'm right here." I lifted his chin with my hand. "I'm not going anywhere."

The look in his eyes was electrifying. He covered my face in kisses then lay down beside me. I ran my fingers through his hair as he rested his head on my breast.

I couldn't imagine what he must have been through. Then again, I'd thought Tom was dead last summer. And it had been the most god-awful, gut-wrenching time in my life.

For me, purgatory had lasted for minutes.

For Tom, it must have felt like a lifetime.

Hours of waiting in the hospital, wondering if I would make it out alive, if this was the end, if we'd already shared our last kiss, our last touch, our last everything. When we'd only just begun...

"I love you, Addie," he sobbed. "I love you so much."

A lonesome tear skirted down my cheek.

"And nothing has to change."

"What are you talking about?" I asked.

He sat up and dried his eyes. "I mean, we can go back to living a normal life."

I touched his cheek, and he placed his hand over mine. Then his touch drifted up my arm and back down again. I grabbed his wrist and saw the wedding band on his finger. Mine, however, was missing.

"Where is my wedding ring?"

"Oh, I forgot." He pulled it out of his pocket along with my engagement ring. "They took them off when they did surgery. Sometimes, your fingers can swell. And they asked me to hold on to them for you."

"Why don't you hold on to them for me a little longer? Until they let me out of here."

He laughed. "Okay."

"When do you think that will be anyway?" I asked.

"I don't know. Days, I guess. But I'm staying here with you. I won't leave you alone."

We held hands and I took a breath. He was so good to me. I couldn't remember a time when he hadn't been. It was one of the many reasons why I loved him so much.

"I called your parents," he said.

"Which ones?"

"Uhh, Jeffrey." He paused, gauging my tolerance. "And Eleanor."

"What did they say?' I asked.

"They said they're on the first flight out of Savannah."

"Who did you talk to?" I played with the hospital band around my wrist.

"Jeffrey."

"Did he sound concerned?"

"Yes. I think they're both very concerned. They care about you, Addie."

I rolled my eyes.

"Even if they have a funny way of showing it."

"Did anything else happen while I was unconscious?" I said.

"Yes, your family came by. Everyone's been very worried about you. But I've been checking in regularly with updates. They're very happy to hear that you're in stable condition."

Something was eating at me on the inside. But I closed that door in my mind. I didn't want to think about her and what she'd done to me. The past twenty-four hours had been enough.

"Josette came by," he said. "She was very worried. I think—"

"I don't want to see her."

"Addie, she's your mother. All this time, you thought she was dead."

"And whose fault is that?" I steamed. "I don't want anything to do with that woman."

"What about Jimmy?" he asked. "You didn't have a problem letting him into your life."

"That's different," I said. Tension was building inside me. So much for a good night's sleep.

"How?" he said. "He knew about you. He could have made contact and—"

"Jimmy wasn't living a secret life in Paris. He wasn't hiding from his daughter."

He looked down and sighed. I let go of his hand and he slid back in his chair.

"Maybe there's more to it than you think. If you'd just give her the chance to explain—"

"I don't owe her anything. And I *don't* want to see her."

"Addie, I think you're making a mistake," he said.

"Can we not talk about this?" I snapped. "Do you think you could let me recover first?"

He waited a beat. "Yeah, baby. I'm sorry. I didn't mean to make you upset."

Tears burned the back of my eyes, but I wouldn't let them loose.

His cell phone vibrated and he checked it. "I should get this. I'll only be a minute."

I watched him step into the hall and then released the emotion I'd been holding in.

To be honest, I did want to see her. Eleanor had always felt more like a wicked stepmother to me. But I'd grown to accept that it came with her personality. Even if I'd been her biological daughter, I think she still would have treated me that way. Some people just aren't cut out for parenting.

But Josette had been waltzing around the castle for the past week. The whole time, she'd known that her long lost daughter was right there. I thought about the brief conversations we'd had. Since we met, I'd been sure she was my cousin, the same relation I shared with Ashton.

It was simply too much.

I'd already had enough family secrets for a lifetime. Would it ever end?

With Tom gone, I closed my eyes and tried to relax. All of these worries could be dealt with tomorrow. Right now, I needed to rest. It was the only way I'd recover faster, so I could get out of this place.

I dozed off for a little while. When I woke up, Tom was still gone. So I turned the light out and made myself as comfortable as I could. This time, sleep came hard and fast. It almost felt strange.

I heard a noise and grumbled. It must have been Tom. But I was too tired to talk.

He brushed his fingertips across my forehead. It made me smile. I was on the precipice of a dream.

But when I opened my eyes, he was standing by the window. "Tom? What are you looking at?"

He turned around and it was Valjean.

I felt paralyzed. Unable to move. There was nothing I could do.

He covered my mouth with his hand and held a knife to my throat. "Don't make a sound," he said. "Where is the necklace?" He moved his hand but kept the blade where it was.

"I don't know," I breathed. The words came out shaky.

He nicked my skin. "Of course you do. Where is

it?"

"I don't have it."

There were bandages around his neck. He could hardly talk.

He picked up my hand and teased the blade with my wrist. "Where?"

I looked at the door and gasped. He turned his head to look and I grabbed the knife. It took less than a second for me to turn it over in my hand and stab him in the heart.

Slowly, the life and soul drifted right out of him. He bled all over the hospital bed. Then he collapsed on the floor and I got out of bed to see what I had done. I checked his pulse, and Valjean was dead.

Two nights ago, I'd gotten married, I'd made love, I'd counted my lucky stars.

But even good things—no matter how pure of heart—come at a price.

Yesterday, I'd had the world in the palm of my hand.

And now, I'd killed a man.

Chapter 3

Tom

I hated leaving her. But I had three missed calls, countless text messages and a voice mail from Jimmy. He was waiting downstairs in the lobby. Even though I'd specifically asked them all to go home.

But I'd never been a father. I had no idea what it felt like. The worry.

Jimmy loved Addie. And he'd always been supportive of my intent to marry her. What could I say?

"Hey there." I took a seat beside him. "You know visiting hours are over."

"I just couldn't do it," he said. "I'm not leaving until I see her."

"You mean, you've been here this whole time?" I asked.

He nodded.

I put my arm around him. "She's fine. Really. She's in stable condition. She just had something to eat."

"Can I see her?" He stared me down. "Tom, I want to see my daughter."

"Okay." I held up my hand. "It's not me. The doctor was pretty strict about the number of people in her room. I think he doesn't want her feeling crowded so soon. Do you understand?"

"I'll only be a minute, I swear."

"You don't have to convince me, Jimmy. I'm her husband, and I've been going crazy."

"Well, let's go." He got up and made a bee line for the elevator. We rode to her floor in silence, while I thought about what Dr. Laurent had said. It had been eating away at me like a festering wound.

Maybe we didn't have to tell her. I hoped I never had to.

I knocked on the door to give Addie some warning. But when I came in, she was squirming and moaning. Her eyes were closed, but tears were streaming down her face. She'd been having nightmares for as long as I'd known her. Sadly, the older she got, the worse they were.

I shook her awake, and her body jerked with a sharp intake of breath.

"Hey." I cupped her cheek in my hand.

She looked into my eyes and swallowed. There were beads of sweat on her forehead. It must have been a violent dream. As I ran my fingers through her hair, she dove into my arms and cried.

"It's okay," I whispered. "It's okay."

Jimmy took one look at us and stepped out of the room. Maybe he understood her fragile condition now.

"I was so scared," she said. "And you were gone."

"Well, I'm here now. I'll never leave you."

She leaned back against the pillows. "Could I have some water please?"

"Yeah, I'll get you some." I grabbed the cup by her bed. "Are you all right?"

"Yeah." She took a deep breath. "It was just a dream. I'll be fine."

"Okay." I stood up and froze on the spot. "Jimmy is outside. But I can tell him to leave."

"No," she smiled. "I want to see him. Let him come in."

I opened the door and nodded. He looked so happy that I didn't want to disturb their time together. So I got Addie some water and waited in the hall. I let about ten minutes go by before I popped back in.

"Hey." I handed her the water. "How are you feeling?"

"Much better." She sipped from the straw. Jimmy had been holding her hand.

"Well, I better go and let you get some rest," he said.

"No, it's fine," Addie insisted. "You can stay."

"I know." He patted her cheek. "But you need to rest." He kissed her hair. "I'll see you tomorrow."

"Okay." She looked disappointed, so I sat down on the edge of the bed to comfort her.

"Mr. Sutton," he called. "You take good care of my girl."

"Yes, sir," I said. "I will."

He nodded on his way out and shut the door behind him.

"I didn't expect him to leave so fast," she said.

I tucked a fallen lock behind her ear.

"I'm really glad you're here."

I bit my lip and stroked the back of her hand. "Are you gonna tell me what that dream was about?"

She covered her eyes with her hand. For a second, I thought she'd fallen asleep. But she was just breathing.

"It's stupid," she said. "It was about Valjean."

My pulse quickened. "What about him?"

"I had a dream he was here in the hospital." She looked down. "And I killed him."

I ran my fingers through my hair.

"Isn't that crazy?" she asked.

"No." I avoided eye contact. "I don't think so."

Sighing, she rubbed my hand and moved over. "Will you sleep with me?"

"Is there enough room?" I saw the narrow space she'd opened up. "I don't want to hurt you."

"Please," she pouted. "I don't want to sleep alone tonight."

"All right." I took my shoes off and lay down beside her.

Addie loved to cuddle. So she draped her arm across my stomach and put her head on my chest.

I held her close, as she quickly drifted off in the night. I may have been exhausted, but sleep evaded me. I kept thinking about the doctor and what he'd said. What would Addie do when she found out?

I shut my eyes and cried. Just a little bit. I didn't want to wake her up.

But more importantly, I didn't want her to know the truth. Not yet.

I wasn't ready for that.

* * *

Sunshine came bright and early the next morning. I didn't remember leaving the blinds open. But when I saw the nurse frowning at the sight of Addie tangled in my arms, everything became pretty clear.

I stepped into the hall to give them some privacy. Addie was in good spirits this morning. For that I was thankful, because there was no way to prepare her for the bad news coming.

It had kept me up most of the night. I hated keeping secrets from her. But I just wasn't ready yet.

I bumped into Dr. Laurent on the way back from the cafeteria. A sickening feeling spread through my chest as soon as I saw him. I knew what he was going to say. And I didn't want to hear it.

"I've just checked on your wife," he said. "Her vitals are good. She's doing very well."

"Yeah." I held a bottle of apple juice from the cafeteria. "I think so."

"Tom, I know you're trying to protect her. But at some point—"

"Not now," I growled. "She's just starting to feel like herself again. Can't you give her a break?"

He looked displeased. "I'm taking the week off to spend time with my family. I had to work Christmas this year. What I'm saying is, I won't be here much longer. So if you want me to tell her—"

"When does your vacation start?" I asked.

"I go off duty tonight at six. If you want me in the room, you need to let me know before then."

It felt like I was having a panic attack. I dropped the juice and slid down to the floor.

"Breathe," the doctor said. "It's okay, Tom."

My shoulders heaved as I dried my eyes. "No, it's not. You don't understand."

"I know this is hard for you. But hiding the truth won't make it any easier on her."

I sniffled and wiped the tears off my face.

"I'm just not ready," I said. "I'm not ready to let her go."

"I'll stop by tonight before I leave. If you want me there, we can tell her together. If not, I'll just make sure she's recovering nicely and then I'll leave you

37

alone with her. And it can be between the two of you."

"I don't know what to do." I tried swallowing, but it hurt too much.

"These things are never easy," he said. "But your wife is a remarkable fighter. We nearly lost her many times."

I looked up at him. "Why are you telling me this?"

"Because your wife is stronger than you think."

I looked at the wedding band on my finger.

"I'll give you some time to think about it."

He walked away and I sat in that hall for a long time.

I didn't want to do it. But I guess the decision had already been made.

When I came back in the room, she looked so happy to see me.

"Hey, baby," she grinned. "Come here."

I sat down and held her hand. I had no words.

"Are you gonna kiss me or do I have to beg?"

I had a heavy heart. But I leaned in and pressed my lips to hers.

"I'm guessing you didn't sleep well last night?" she said.

I shook my head. "Not really."

"I'm sorry. Was I a bed hog?"

I stroked her cheek. She had such soft skin. And those gorgeous emerald eyes.

"Is everything okay?" she asked.

"Yeah," I lied. "Everything's fine."

Jimmy burst through the door with flowers and balloons. Edmond was right behind him. Followed by Adeline, Ashton and Juliette. With five more people in the room, it was a bit much.

"Addie!" Adeline rushed over to give her a hug.

"Be careful," I said.

Jimmy tapped me on the back. "How was she last night?"

"Fine." I crossed my arms. "But I don't think she's ready for this."

"Let me see my beautiful niece." Edmond hovered by the other side of her bed.

The next thing I knew, so many people were talking at the same time that I had a migraine. I stepped outside as my phone went off. "Hello?"

"Oh my god! You got married in Paris without me?"

I cringed at the sound of my cousin's voice.

"Jeanine." I tried to think of a way to explain.

"Yes?"

"I'd say I'm sorry, but I'm really not."

When she didn't say anything, I thought we'd been disconnected.

"It was last minute, but something we had to do. I'll explain later."

"I'm not mad, especially since..." she paused. "Well, I just wish I could have been there."

"I know," I said. "We do, too. But that's just the way it had to be."

"How is she?" she asked.

"Better. She's expected to make a full recovery. That's what the doctors say."

"Well, I'm glad. Also... *Excuse me! Could you move please?*"

"Where are you?" I asked. I kind of felt sorry for whoever she was yelling at.

"JFK."

"What?" I must have heard her wrong.

"It's just a stopover on my way to Paris."

"What? Jeanine, you're coming here?" I said.

"Yeah! You thought we were just gonna sit around and wait for you to come home?"

"What do you mean *we*?"

"Oh, Eric is with me."

"And your parents are okay with this?" I checked.

"Well, Daddy doesn't actually know, but—"

"Jeanine! You get back on that plane and go home."

"I'm sorry, I can't hear you."

"Jeanine!"

Eric grabbed the phone. "Look man, I tried to stop her. But she has a will of iron."

"And your parents don't mind you going out of the country?"

"Nope, they let me use their frequent flyer miles. And we kind of have chaperones."

"Yeah," Jeanine said. "We're on the same flight with them and everything."

"With who?"

"Addie's parents," Eric said. "They were totally cool with it."

I was about ready to pull my hair out. By the time everyone got here, there would be an army of relatives in her hospital room. Would Dr. Laurent have to break the news in front of all them?

"Hey, we gotta go," Jeanine said. "But I'll see you tomorrow in Paree!"

She hung up and I took a breath. It felt like I hadn't slept in days.

"I was hoping we could talk."

I looked up to find Josette standing in the empty hallway.

"What are you doing here?" I asked.

"I'd like to speak to my daughter. But I have a feeling she doesn't want to see me."

"How did you figure that out?" I said.

"Because she's just like me."

"I don't know." I ran my hand over my face. "There's a lot going on right now."

"You think I don't know that?"

"What did you come here to say?" I asked.

"I love my daughter more than anything in this world. All I'm asking for is a chance."

I stood up and slid my phone in my pocket. "I believe you."

"I'd like to see her," she said.

"I don't know if that's such a good idea, right now." I led her down the hall where we could talk more privately. "There are already too many people in there as it is."

"I won't let you keep me away from my daughter."

I saw fire in her eyes. She'd never revealed this side of her personality before.

"I'm not trying to. Believe me, I want her to let you in. For her benefit."

"Maybe it would help if I explained everything to you first," she suggested.

I raised my brow, wondering why she cared what I thought.

"You could tell me if it's too much, or help me with how to explain things. I may be her mother, but I don't know her like you do. I can see that you love her. And I know she loves you."

"How?" I asked.

"Because I remember what it felt like. And I know the things you do for the one you care about."

"Well, lay it on me." I took a seat on a bench. "I'm

not sure how this week can get any worse."

For the next twenty minutes, she told me the story of her life. Some parts were fascinating, others funny. But when she got to the worst of it, I could hardly bear to listen. It was just a tragedy.

"Do you think she'll understand?" she asked.

"Yes." I rubbed the nape of my neck. "The trouble is getting her to listen."

Jimmy saw us in the hall, and I heard Josette gasp.

"Does he know?" I wondered.

"No." She lowered her head. "He hasn't given me the chance to explain."

"Well, why don't you try telling him next?" I stood up. "I need to go check on my wife."

Jimmy approached her as I walked away. I saw him take a seat next to her. Even from a distance, I recognized the glow of love in their eyes. Despite the years apart, it had yet to fade.

Edmond was the only one left in Addie's room. Everyone else had gone to the cafeteria. That's all he talked about before he left me alone with her. She sat up in bed with her arms crossed over her chest.

"Hey." I touched her arm and she pulled away from me.

Her rejection hurt me immediately. She turned her head my way and gave me a death glare.

"What's wrong?" I asked.

She lifted her chin and looked out the window, ignoring me.

"Addie, come on. For God's sake. Don't shut me out now."

"You said Valjean was in protective custody," she said.

I closed my eyes and regretted not being totally

honest with her.

"Edmond just told me that he's been moved."

I hated that she was mad at me.

"Moved out of this hospital," she said. "Which means he was here last night!"

"I'm sorry, but I knew it would upset you. That's the only reason I kept it from you."

"You *lied* to me!" Her face was rigid, solid as stone.

"Yes, I lied. But it was to protect you. I'm just trying to do what's best for you."

She set her sights on the window again. "What else haven't you been telling me?"

"Addie," I said. "He's not even here anymore. Why does it matter now?"

"Because we made a promise to each other! No secrets. No lies. You're my husband!"

"And you're my wife!" I took a step towards her. "You think I liked keeping it from you?"

She lowered her pretty green eyes.

"No! I didn't! I've never liked lying to you. But I did it to protect you. Because I thought if you knew he was here, it would be too much. And don't act like you've never kept me in the dark before."

"Tom."

"I've been going out of my damn mind worrying about you! But you're here and you're alive." I got down on my knees and took her hands. "So please don't shut me out now. I can't take it."

Moisture filled her eyes. "I'm sorry. Tom, I'm sorry."

I cradled her face and put my mouth on hers. She inhaled and kissed me back, running her nails down my back. I groaned and kissed her some more. The kind of kissing that got her good and weak in the knees.

I leaned my forehead against hers, and we were both gasping for air. She cupped my cheek and ran her thumb over my bottom lip. "Do you think we could do some more of that when I get out of here?"

I looked into her eyes with a laugh. "Yes."

"I'm sorry I got so mad," she whispered.

"I'm sorry, too." I folded my fingers through hers.

"Was that our first big fight as a married couple?" she asked.

"I hope so," I said. I also hoped it was our last.

"What?" She saw the speck of worry in my eyes. "Is there something else?"

"Yes, I just talked to your mother. Josette, I mean. She had a lot to say."

"About me?" she wondered.

"Please don't get mad, but I really think you should give her the chance to explain."

She looked off. "I'll think about it."

"Okay." I'd take it. "Thank you."

I breathed a sigh of relief. Maybe she wouldn't fight me on this forever.

Someone knocked on the door. I looked up to find Jimmy walking in.

"You still feeling all right?" he asked.

"Yeah," she smiled. "I'm feeling better."

"Listen." He shut the door. "I just had a conversation with your mother."

"What, are the two of you tag teaming me now?" she joked.

I looked at Jimmy. "I really think you need to talk to her," he said.

"My husband seems to think so, too."

I held my breath and waited for her to explode again.

"Thanks for your concern, both of you," she said. "But I just don't think I'm ready for that right now."

"Why?" Jimmy pressed. "After all this time. She's finally here. And she wants to be your mother."

"Well, I already have a mother," she snapped.

"Addie." I furrowed my brow. It was so unlike her. She'd never gotten along with Eleanor.

"I understand," Jimmy said. "But if you would just let her come in here and talk to you."

"I don't trust her," she said. "Okay?"

"All right," he backed away. "I understand. I'll give you space."

Once he left, Addie shook her head at me. "If I could just have five minutes of peace."

"I know." I held her hand and stared at her.

She looked like she was thinking about something. "What?"

"You told me the necklace was safe," she said.

"Yes."

"Well, where is it?"

"You want to see it?" I reached into my pocket, but it was empty. The other one was, too.

"Tom, what's going on?" She was on the verge of really losing it this time. So was I.

"Just hold on a second." I stood up. "I'll be right back."

I ran into the hall, but there only Jimmy. "Where is she? Josette?"

"She left," Jimmy said. "Why? Did you need to tell her something?"

I bit my tongue and put my fist through the wall.

Chapter 4

Addie

I looked out the window and thought about her. I'd wanted a mother for so long. My whole life, Eleanor was the one who'd left me feeling betrayed. Why wouldn't she talk to me? Nurture me?

Why didn't she *want* me?

Tom was the first human being to ever make me feel wanted. Romantically, of course.

I hadn't felt like part of a family until Edmond had welcomed me into his. Not to dismiss, Jimmy, but he was only one person. I'd been so neglected that the sudden interest of a long lost relative wasn't enough. I'd needed a whole family to finally feel like I belonged.

But Josette? She'd been late to the party. Hadn't I already done this enough?

How many more long lost relatives could one person possibly have?

Deep down, I wanted to punish her, shut her out of my life for the way she'd left me behind.

But Tom had a point. How was that fair when I'd forgiven Jimmy so easily? Not to mention, accepting the Beaumonts right off the bat. I'd been thrilled to meet them. Every last one.

With my mother, it was something entirely different. She had given birth to me, carried me inside her womb for nine months. I'd been told she died after my birth. I thought it was my fault she'd been taken away from me.

To learn, eighteen years later, that she had not only survived, but she'd been living a secret life in Paris. One that had nothing to do with me. Was she ashamed of me? The love child from her past?

Tom knew I was being stubborn. Sometimes, he was the only one who could break down my walls. He knew me like no one else. The real Addison. I wasn't even sure what my maiden name was anymore. Beaumont? Blake? Smith? It made me happy that I had Tom's name now. I didn't have to worry about it.

I may have resented her. But that didn't mean I hated her.

It's just that betrayal had become such a common occurrence for me. Without Tom, it would have been too much to bear. I'd reached a breaking point countless times. But this was different, the last straw.

When Tom returned, I patted the bed and he sat down beside me. "You're right."

He looked perplexed. "About what?"

"Josette." I put my hand in his. "I know what I just said. I've been very angry at her. But I think I'd at least like to give her a chance. I mean, she did give birth to me. Don't I owe her that?"

He gave me an ear-splitting grin.

"What?"

"Could you say the first part again?" he asked.

I blushed when I understood what he was saying. "You're right."

"What was that?" He put his hand behind his ear.

"I said you're right," I repeated.

"That's what I thought you said."

"Don't be smug." I lifted his chin. "I don't like it."

He leaned over me with a smirk, sealing his lips over mine. I ran my hands up and down his back, wishing we could have gone on that honeymoon. Since the wedding, we'd hardly had a second to enjoy the perks of married life.

"What happened to your hand?" I touched it tenderly. "You're bleeding."

"I know." He looked at his knuckles. "I'll put some ice on it."

"Why is it bleeding?" I asked.

He took a breath, running his fingers through my hair.

"Tom."

"I'll be fine," he said. "I just needed to blow off a little steam."

"By doing what?"

"Punching a wall," he winced, then laughed.

"Baby." I rubbed his shoulder. "Do you think the universe will ever give us a break?"

"God, I hope so."

I hugged him and put my head on his chest. "I'm sorry I've been so difficult."

His fingers trailed my neck. "I'm sorry I let you out of my sight."

"It's not your fault." I took his face in my hands. "Stop blaming yourself."

"Do you need anything? Water? Are you hungry? I can let you rest."

"Some water would be nice." I adjusted my position to get more comfortable. "Actually, I'd like to talk to Josette. It's making me nervous. I'd rather just get it over with so I can rest."

"Okay, but she already left."

"What? I thought you said she was just here," I said.

"Well, I did. She was. But she's gone. Jimmy is out looking for her."

I saw tension in his neck. "Is there something else?"

"Yeah. I can't find the necklace. It was in my pocket and then—"

I pulled it out from under the covers and set it in my lap.

"You've had it this whole time?" he asked.

"No," I smiled. "I found it when you went in the hall. It must have slipped out when we were sleeping last night." I ran my thumb over the emerald stone. "Give it to Edmond. He'll keep it safe."

"Are you sure?"

"Yes. I trust him. He can keep it locked up in the castle until we decide what to do with it."

"All right." He watched me. "Why don't you give it to him when he comes back?"

I nodded, distracted by every fleck of green.

"What are you thinking about?" he asked.

"I don't know if I'll ever be able to really let it go. It feels like such a part of me now."

"All it's ever brought into our lives is danger," he said.

"I know that. But it's part of my heritage, my identity."

"The only identity I've ever had is wrapped up in you."

I looked at him. "Tom." Times like these, I saw the little boy inside.

I felt awful for complaining. I had two sets of parents. He had none.

How could I gripe about my biological mother to him?

He was an orphan. And I was a spoiled brat for venting my frustrations to him.

"Tom, I'm so sorry." I touched his arm. "If anyone deserves a family, it's you."

He hung his head and looked like he was about to cry.

"You need ice on that hand." I pressed a button for the nurse.

"I'll be all right." He forced a smile. "As long as you're okay."

"I am, Tom." I brushed my fingers through his hair. "I'm more than okay."

The nurse arrived to check on me. She was happy to tend to Tom's hand. So he left with her while I looked at the necklace. Even now, it felt cool to the touch. I'd never been able to figure out the strange temperature. No matter what, it was always cold. Like there was a tiny block of ice inside.

Someone knocked on the door. "Come in," I said.

It was Dr. Laurent. I slid the necklace under my blanket and grinned.

"How are we feeling today?' he asked.

"I'm still pretty tired," I said. "But better, I think."

"Good." He marked something off his clipboard and sat down.

He'd been patient and kind from day one. I couldn't have asked for a better doctor.

Empathy was his middle name. I'd be indebted to him for eternity. He'd saved my life.

Not to mention, he was easy on the eyes.

"I'm just going to check your vitals," he said.

"All right." I gazed into his pastel eyes. They were

the color of a robin's egg.

He checked my temperature and pulse. "Let's have a look at your hip."

I hid the necklace behind my back as he turned the covers down. He opened my gown enough to expose the bandages along my hip. I'd been shot twice. By some miracle, he'd managed to remove both bullets. When Valjean shot me, there had been no clean exit. If Dr. Laurent hadn't extracted them, I would be dead.

"All right." He lowered the gown. "There doesn't seem to be any sign of infection."

I sat against the pillows as he covered me with the blanket.

"I'd like to keep you here for a few more days. Just to make sure."

It already felt like I'd been here for a year. "Okay."

"I'm not sure if your husband told you, but I'm going off duty tonight at six."

My heart dropped. "Oh."

"I'll be in town. But I worked Christmas. And I need to spend time with my family."

I saw a wedding ring on his finger. "I understand."

"I'm leaving you in the charge of Dr. Rousseau. I've already gone over your file with her. You don't need to worry. She's one of the best. I wouldn't trust anyone else. Do you have any questions?"

"No." I shook my head.

"I'll be by before my shift ends tonight. In the meantime, why don't you get some rest?"

"I will." I watched him walk away. "And Dr. Laurent?" He turned around. "Thank you. For everything."

"You have your whole life ahead of you, Addie.

Don't forget that." He let himself out.

Before I could really think about what he'd said, Edmond popped his head in the door. "There's my beautiful niece." He stood by the bed and patted my hand. "How are you feeling?"

"Fine," I giggled. "Same as when you last saw me."

"Your husband seems to have injured himself."

I laughed and regretted it immediately. "I know. Poor Tom. I feel bad."

"Don't you worry about him. He'll be just fine."

"Can I ask you something?" I said.

He nodded and took a seat.

"Were you and my grandmother very close?"

"Incredibly close. I've missed her very much. I still miss her. Every day."

"Did you keep in touch? After she left France?" I wondered.

"Yes, we spoke on the phone. I think she was happy with your grandfather. But that happiness came at a price."

"Do you think that's just how it is? Life, I mean?"

"Yes." He touched my cheek. "You can't have God without the devil."

"But why?"

"That's just the way it is. You have to take the good with the bad."

"I wish life could be like a fairy tale," I said.

"But it is. Without pain, you'd never know how it feels to be content."

I shot him a puzzled look.

"You're young." He patted my arm. "One day, you'll understand."

I grabbed the necklace behind my back. "I'd like you to take this."

"I gave it to Tom when you were in surgery. I think it helped him cope."

"I'm glad," I said. "But you know it's not safe to have it here."

He took the necklace and slipped it in his breast pocket. "I'll take care of it."

"You never told me, how did my grandmother get the necklace in the first place?"

"That's a story for another time," he said. "But I promise to tell you one day."

He had an air of mystery about him. A wall I thought I'd already knocked down.

"I wish I could go back to the castle," I whined. "I'm so sick of being here."

"I know, but you need to get better first. How many days until you can come home?"

"Two or three, I guess. I wish it was sooner. I feel like I'm in prison," I said.

He chuckled. "You'll get through it. And we'll gladly welcome you home."

Adeline burst through the door, rushing to my side. "They had ice cream."

Edmond patted her back and stepped into the hall. But Ashton caught the door and came inside with Juliette. Adeline sat down on the edge of my bed, while Ashton lingered at the foot.

"Mmm. What kind?" I asked.

"Just chocolate and strawberry," Adeline said. She was eating a scoop of the latter.

"I don't think I'm up for ice cream just yet." I smiled, happy she was here.

"Your friend called," Ashton said.

"Who?"

"A girl from Savannah. I think her name was—"

"Jeanine?" I asked.

"Yeah," Juliette answered. "She was so worried about you."

"I haven't had the chance to talk to her, but Tom did. She's his cousin, actually."

"No wonder she was pissed." Adeline licked ice cream off her spoon.

"About what?" I asked.

"Well." Ashton looked at his wife. "She was so worried about you being in the hospital. I didn't realize she hadn't already been informed about the wedding."

"Ashton, you didn't," I said.

"I thought she already knew."

"She's going to kill me," I exhaled. "I guess this means Eric knows, too."

"Eric?" Adeline asked.

"Her boyfriend," I said. "His parents are friends with mine." I thought about it and froze.

"What?" Ashton said.

"My parents don't know Tom and I got married."

"Why not?" Adeline said.

"It's complicated." I gnawed the inside of my cheek. "I was going to tell them."

Everyone was quiet, looking at me.

"I would have rather told them myself."

"You still can," Juliette said.

"I mean, told them *first*. By now, I'm sure Eric told his parents. And his mother probably called mine. I'm sure they already know. There are so many ways they could have found out by now. I just wish it could have been through me. I wanted to keep it private. And *I* wanted to be the one to break the news."

Tom walked in the room holding his arm. His hand was wrapped in gauze.

"What happened to you?" Ashton asked.

"I punched a wall," Tom said.

"Have you talked to Jeanine lately?" I asked him.

"Yeah." He came over and stood by my bed. "She was at JFK."

"What?" I couldn't believe it.

"Yep," he said. "Eric was with her. Your parents, too. They're all on the same flight."

"Wonderful." I twisted my hands in my lap. "I'm sure they know by now. That we got married."

"Yeah. Jeanine wasn't too happy about not getting an invitation."

I sighed.

"Why don't we let you have some privacy?" Ashton said. "We'll be back tomorrow."

"You don't have to leave," I said.

"I know, but you need your rest." Ashton smiled.

"Feel better soon, Addie," Juliette said. "Come on, Adeline."

"Bye, Addie." She gave me a gentle hug. "I hope you feel better soon."

"Thanks, Adeline." I watched her leave with her parents.

Ashton waved to Tom and shut the door on their way out.

"How is your hand?" I asked.

"I'll never do that again," he said.

"Come here."

He put his head in my lap so I could run my fingers through his hair.

"So I guess Jeanine and Eric will get here tomorrow. With my parents."

He closed his eyes and put his hand on my leg.

"Who knew we were so popular?" I joked.

"It's not me they're coming here to see." He looked up at me. "Everyone loves you."

"I don't know about that," I said. "I doubt Jeffrey and Eleanor are thrilled."

"Well, you know what? They can get over it. This is *our* life. It's not up to anyone else but you and me."

Surprised by his grouchiness, I pulled back on his head. "You must have hit your hand pretty hard."

"You could have died." He gazed into my eyes. "So when it comes to us getting married, I don't care what anyone thinks. You're my wife now. And everyone else can just get over it."

I grinned, running my fingers over his fresh beard. "I love you."

"Good, because I'm not giving you up. Ever." He took my hand. "No matter what happens."

"That's good to know." I rubbed his head as he shut his eyes again. "Dr. Laurent stopped by."

"Oh. Really?"

"Yeah, he's taking a week off for the holidays. So I'll be getting a new doctor."

He didn't say anything.

"It's fine, but I really like *him*. I mean, he saved my life."

"I know."

"But I understand. It is the holidays. He'll be by tonight before his shift ends."

"Oh."

"So at least he's checking up on me before he leaves. That's nice. I've been so lucky to have a doctor like him."

He swallowed.

"Are you tired?" I asked. "I think I want to sleep."

"Okay." He sat up.

"You don't have to go."

He lay down beside me and pulled the covers up to keep me warm. Then he caressed my cheek and looked like he was about to cry. I nuzzled his neck and whispered against his lips. "Hey."

He threaded his fingers through my hair.

"Everything is gonna be okay," I whispered.

He nodded, drawing me into his arms. I smiled and buried my face in his chest. It felt so good to have him here. Despite everything, I had the love of so many people around me.

For the first time in my life, I had faith that everything would work out. Believing in a future with Tom had been the only thing getting me through my hospital stay. Once I got out, we could start our new life together. I was determined to find happiness in my marriage and whatever the future might hold.

So I closed my eyes and relaxed, drifting off to the fantasy of our own happily ever after.

Chapter 5

Tom

The nurse came by with Addie's dinner at 5:30. I sat in the corner and watched her eat. She was watching a game show on TV, laughing along with whatever was happening. She looked beautiful, happy. And I couldn't place the reason for her sudden shift in mood.

Ever since this afternoon, she'd adopted a positive outlook. I guess she'd overcome so much, that she chose to be grateful for her life. And the happily ever after kind of future she thought we had together.

As the minutes passed, I grew more unsettled. I kept my eyes on the door, anxious for Dr. Laurent to stop by. He had warned me out in the hall. I knew what would happen. He was going to tell her himself.

Was I a coward? That's how I felt.

But I just couldn't break the news to her. Not when she finally seemed so brave.

I wasn't sure what had inspired her thankful demeanor.

Maybe she'd been through so much anxiety, that her body simply couldn't take it anymore.

And seeing the bright side had been her only way out of the darkness.

"That was delicious." She set her dinner tray aside. "Hey. Are you okay?"

"Yeah." I leaned forward in my chair. I was on the other side of the room.

"Why are you so far away?" she asked.

I forced a smile.

"Are you sick of me already?"

There was a mischievous look in her eye. I got up and sat down beside her.

"That's better." She grabbed my hand and caressed the side of my face.

I bowed my head and felt like breaking down. But I held it in for her sake.

"What's wrong?" she said. "You're being so quiet."

"I'm just tired." I couldn't look at her. "I have a lot on my mind."

There was a knock on the door. And I knew. My whole world was about to come crashing down.

"Hi." Addie smiled. She was always happy to see Dr. Laurent. She liked him.

"Hello, Addie." He approached her bedside. "How are you feeling?"

"Fine," she said. "I'm ready to get out of here though. I missed my honeymoon for this."

He chuckled, and I felt the walls closing in. There was an echo in my eardrums.

I got out of the way so he could check her vital signs. She made small talk with him as he looked over the gunshot wounds. Then he assured her that his replacement was going to take good care of her.

For a moment, I thought he had gone back on his word. It sounded like he was about to walk out the door. And I wondered if he had left me to do the heavy lifting myself. But then he pulled up a chair.

"Before I leave, there is something we must discuss." He slanted a glance at me.

I crossed my arms and looked out the window, turning my back to them.

"Okay."

I heard the confusion in her voice. Had we blindsided her?

"When you were shot, there were some complications internally."

"But you said I'm healing fine," she said. "No sign of infection. Right?"

"Right. And you should be able to live a perfectly normal life."

"Then what's the problem?" Her anxiety went through the roof. I could feel it.

"I'm afraid there is a high probability that you may never be able to bear a child."

I shut my eyes as tears stained my skin.

She audibly gasped. "What are you talking about?"

"Even if you became pregnant, and you carried to full-term, I don't think you'd survive the birth."

"No," she whimpered. "No. No. No."

I turned around and looked at Dr. Laurent. I think it was even hard for him to tell her.

"I know how hard this is to hear," he said. "You're so young. But there is no reason why you can't live a long, healthy life."

"What are my chances?" she asked. "Of having a baby?"

"If you became pregnant, I'd put your mortality rate at 98%."

She burst into tears and hid her face with her hands.

"I can't tell you how sorry I am," Dr. Laurent said. "We did everything we could."

"I know you did," she croaked. "But it's just too

much. It's too much."

"Your husband thought it would be best if we told you together," he said. "I'm leaving you with my phone number if you ever have any questions. I'm so sorry, Addie. Truly, I am."

She nodded. "I think I'd like to be alone with my husband."

"Yes, of course. Best of luck to you, Addie." He looked at me. "Tom."

He left the room and closed the door behind him.

"Can you turn the TV off please?" she asked.

I turned it off and approached the bed.

"How long have you known?" She wouldn't look me in the eye.

"Since you came out of surgery," I said.

She nodded. And then she sobbed so uncontrollably that she lost her breath.

I knelt down by the bed and took her hand. "I'm sorry I kept it from you." I tasted tears in my mouth. "But you'd already been through so much. And there have been so many people coming by. I didn't know when the right time would be to tell you. And I wasn't ready. I didn't know what to do."

She cried so hard her whole body was shaking. "It's too much. I can't take it."

"Baby, listen to me." I took her face in my hands. "I don't care about that."

"But I do." There was an ocean of sadness in her eyes.

"Listen to me." I got in bed with her. "You're gonna live a long, healthy life. And we're gonna be happy. Okay? And when it comes to kids, we can always adopt."

"No! No, Tom. I don't want that kind of life. I

want kids of my own!"

"They will be our kids," I said.

"No, they won't! I want to make babies, not buy them. This is the one thing I wanted most in this world. And now it's gone! Don't you understand that?"

"Baby, we can make this work," I said.

"How can you even want to be with me now? I can never give you a family. A *real* family."

"I don't care about that! You're my family. Just you, Addie. That's all I need."

She gritted her teeth as her sadness turned to rage. "No. This is not my life."

"Baby, please. It broke my heart when I first heard. But can't you look at the bright side?"

"What bright side? There is no bright side!"

"You could've died," I said.

"Yeah," she nodded. "And I wish I had."

"You don't mean that."

"You don't know how I feel! You have no idea how this feels!"

"Addie, we're in this together."

"But I'm the one who can't have children!"

I gave her a minute to calm down. It was really too much to bear. But life is like that sometimes. If experience has taught me anything, it's that pain was designed to make you stronger. I'd had some time to process how cruel fate could be. But I wasn't giving up on her or us. *Ever.*

"I love you," I said. "And I'll never leave you. This changes nothing for me."

"Not me." She looked depressed. "This changes everything."

I furrowed my brow.

"It's not fair," she sobbed. "It's just not fair."

I didn't know what to do. What could I say?

"You think adopting a child can fill this hole inside of me? It would turn out just like us."

"What's so bad about us?" I asked.

"Do you honestly have to ask that question?"

"I know this isn't easy. It's the last thing you want to hear."

"I wish I'd died in your arms."

"Addison!" I pulled her into my arms. "Don't say things you don't mean."

She cried on my shoulder, but she wouldn't wrap her arms around me.

"I do mean it," she said. "I mean every word."

"You still have a life."

"You're seventeen. What the hell do you know about life?"

"I mean, you have a life with me," I said. "Or do you not want that anymore?"

"I don't know what I want," she whispered. "Not this. Not this."

She put her head on her pillow and didn't talk for three hours. I went out in the hall and sank down to the floor. Then I ran my fingers through my hair and cried for the life I'd been so sure we'd have.

Was I disappointed? Anguished? Heartbroken? Of course.

I'd wanted a family, too. I'd dreamed of Addie pregnant and barefoot in the kitchen.

I'd imagined making babies together, watching them grow, having a family of our own.

But life had never dealt me a fair hand. Why should I expect it to now?

I could accept this. As long as she still loved me. But I wasn't sure if we even had that anymore.

In the blink of an eye, she'd gone from hopeful to broken.

I dried my eyes and thought about her blood in the snow. She could have died in my arms. That's the only thing that had gotten me this far. The fact that she had almost slipped away. But she was here now. She had lived. And I would take her anyway I could have her.

When I returned, she was awake. I shut the door and hesitated, eventually sitting down.

She looked at me. "I'm sorry." Her eyes filled with tears. "I'm sorry for what I said."

I sat on the bed, sliding her head on my chest. "It's okay. I understand, you're angry."

"I'm so mad," she confessed. "I hate this. I hate it, I hate it, I hate it."

I rubbed her back and smelled her hair. I just wanted to hold her forever.

"I don't know how to handle this." She leaned back, and I brushed the fallen locks out of her face. "It feels like I've been robbed. Like my whole life, my future has been taken away from me."

"I know." I held her hand. "But I want to find a way to work through this."

"I don't know what I want anymore."

I cupped her cheek. "Do you still want me?"

Her eyes lifted to meet mine. "Yes. Do you still want me?"

"Baby, of course." I squeezed her in my arms.

"Why?" she whispered.

"Because I've wanted you for as long as I can remember."

"Tom." She shook her head. "You'll never have the life you planned with me."

"The only life I ever counted on is one with you."

She rested her head against mine. "Really?"

"Yes, baby." I kissed her and ran my fingers down her spine. "I want you. Nothing else matters."

"You really think we can get through this?" she asked.

"Yes." I covered her face with kisses. "Just try."

She kissed me back and threaded her fingers in my hair. Then she tilted her head back so I could trace the column of her throat. I lay her on the bed and put my lips all over her.

"I just want to be happy," she breathed.

"You'll be happy with me. I know you will."

"Maybe you're right. But I can't let it go just yet."

"I know. But I promise we'll get through this. Together."

She was crying as she stroked my cheek. "They don't make 'em like you anymore."

"I know," I said. "But they don't make 'em like you either."

Tears were running down her face. "Do you think we can still go on that honeymoon?"

"Yes. I'll find a way. I'll make it work."

"I need time," she said. "To figure all this out."

"Take all the time you need. I'm not goin' anywhere."

"I'm sorry you had to deal with all this by yourself. That must have been unbearable."

I broke down suddenly. "I hated keeping it from you."

"I'm sorry I was so angry," she said. "I don't want things to be like this."

"We have the rest of our lives to argue with each other. I just want you to be okay."

She giggled. "It feels like a dream. Because you're

here. But now it's just a nightmare."

"We'll get through it," I promised. "We'll get through this. You can be happy."

"Are you happy?" she asked.

"As long as you're in my arms."

"Come here." She wrapped her arms around me, and we cried together.

"We can make it through this," I said. "I'll never give you up."

"Hold me," she begged.

I held her tight and whispered sweet nothings in her ear. Then I kissed all of her tears away. We lay together and talked about our future into the night. I was so thankful she hadn't shut me out.

It was tragic, but her death would have been so much worse.

I made a vow to pull together all the good in our lives.

That's how we would make it through this.

I'd love her until the day I died. Until then, I'd do everything I could to make her happy.

Even if it meant that one day, I'd have to leave her alone.

Chapter 6

Addie

I lay in the dark, thinking about all the things I'd done wrong.

Was God mad at me?

Was I damned?

Tom was asleep beside me. I ran my hand over his face and kissed him. He smiled in his sleep but didn't wake. I buried my face in his chest and cried quietly. No need to disturb him again.

Of all the bombs Dr. Laurent could have dropped on me, I wasn't expecting this one.

There was a hole in my heart. An empty space that could never be filled. I'd never know what it was like to truly be a mother. Carry life inside you. Give birth to a living, breathing being.

It was almost enough to make me not want to go on.

While Tom slept, I sat up in bed and checked the wounds on my hip. They were fine. But they also weren't fine. Because weren't they the reason why I could no longer bear a child?

Internal permanent damage. What was that? How can you describe how that feels?

I felt hollow. Like the breath had been knocked out of me. And there was fire in my lungs.

But I would have to deal with this. I still had Tom.

And God, he loved me. I don't know why.

My whole life was ahead of me. That's what people kept saying. But they were wrong. My whole life was over. Because there was no way it could ever bring me what I wanted. A family of my own *blood.*

I got up and walked down the hospital halls. It was the middle of the night, so the place was a ghost town. I ended up in the nursery of all places. There were rows of newborn babies sleeping quietly.

I pressed my hand to the glass and watched them flutter their eyelashes. They looked so small. Baby hands and feet. Tiny fingers and toes. It brought tears to my eyes, because I wanted one so bad.

"Which one's yours?" someone asked.

I looked up at a tall Frenchman with greying hair. He was easy on the eyes.

"Oh." I dried my eyes. "I was just looking."

"That one." He pointed to an infant dressed in pink. "She's ours."

"Congratulations." I forced a smile.

"It was a young couple," he said. "Not ready for a child or able to care for it."

"You're adopting her?" I asked.

"Yes. My wife and I. She's with the mother now."

I gritted my teeth. "I can't imagine anyone who would give up a child."

"Maybe they think they're unable to give her what she needs."

"So they just give her up instead?"

"It's not out of malice. They want a better life for her. It's a sacrifice of love."

I didn't agree with a word he said, but I couldn't yell at him.

"Will this be your first child?" I wondered. "You

and your wife?"

"Yes." He grinned at the little girl through the glass. "Finally."

I felt awkward standing there. I didn't want to talk anymore.

"We've waited a long time for this moment."

He looked mesmerized by the tiny creature, so I took the moment to slip away. I went to the bathroom and cried. I didn't know if I could handle this. A whole life ahead of me, but no child of my own.

What kind of future was that? What did I have to look forward to?

I rinsed my face off with warm water and trudged back to my room. Tom was still asleep. So I shut the door and climbed in bed beside him, resting my head on his chest. I wrapped his arm around me and snuggled under the covers, knowing the past few nights had been sleepless for him. Now that the weight of keeping this secret from me was off his shoulders, he could finally rest.

But I was restless as ever, tossing and turning. I winced when it felt tender around my hip. Then I gave up fighting it and lay against Tom, shutting my eyes. I did my best to find sleep, but it wouldn't come.

The next morning, a nurse came in to check up on me. I should be able to leave in another day or so. That's what she said anyway. But I wasn't counting on anything. Life wasn't made of promises.

Tom was bright eyed and bushy tailed, and I was happy. He'd finally caught up on his sleep last night. But I would need the whole day to rest. So I went to sleep and he stayed by my side, making sure I had enough water.

I nibbled at lunch. I'd hardly touched breakfast.

All I really wanted was to lie in bed and never wake up.

But then there was a knock on the door. And Jeanine came bursting in. Eric was right behind her.

"Addie!" She rushed to my bedside, but Tom held her back.

"Be gentle, cuz." He gave her a hug and then shook Eric's hand.

"I've missed you," she whined. Her blue eyes were just as bright as I remembered.

"I've missed you, too." I winced when she gave me a hug.

"Jeanine," Tom warned. "That's enough hugging."

"Sorry." She sat back and looked around the room. "How are you feeling?"

I shared a look with Tom. He narrowed his eyes, like he was trying to see right through me.

"Fine." I faked a smile. "It's good to see you." I looked at Eric. "You too."

"Hey, Addie," he said. "You had us worried."

"I'll be happy when I get out of this place."

"How much longer are they keeping you here?" Eric asked.

"Another day or so, I guess," I said. "I'm just ready to get home."

"I don't blame you," Eric said.

I saw a gift bag in his arms.

"What is that?" I asked.

"Oh." Jeanine stood up, and he handed it to her. "We got you something."

"Y'all didn't have to do that." But it made me feel all warm and fuzzy inside.

"Do you want to open it now?" Jeanine asked.

I furrowed my brow and tried to sit up. "Tom."

He sat down on the edge of my bed. Jeanine set the gift bag in his lap.

"Will you open it for me?" I asked.

He stroked my cheek and squeezed my hand. "Yeah, baby."

I sat back and tried to relax. I felt colder today. But maybe that was just the weather.

Tom pulled the tissue paper off the top. Then he picked a small basket out of the bag. It was filled with bubble bath, shower gel, soaking salts, an aromatherapy candle, two bath bombs and a home spa kit.

"Jeanine, you didn't have to do all this," I said.

"I know. But I thought it would be a nice way for you to relax while you recover."

"Thank you. Both of you."

"Hey." Eric wrapped his arm around Jeanine. "That was all her."

"I guess we should go. I know you need to rest," Jeanine said.

"You don't have to leave yet." I was sad to see my friends go.

"Yeah, but I think you have a lot more visitors on the way," she said.

"Where are you staying?" I asked.

"We've actually been invited to stay at the castle," she said.

"Edmond?" I smiled.

"Yeah." She nodded. "When I called to check on you, he told us we could stay with him."

"I'm glad." I missed my family. "You'll really like him. Edmond's great."

"Umm." Jeanine looked nervous. "There is something else."

"What?" I put my hand on Tom's back.

"I kind of let it slip that the two of you had gotten married."

"You mean, to Jeffrey and Eleanor?" I asked.

She nodded.

"What did they say?" I asked.

She turned to Eric. "They were just so worried about you."

"Where are they?"

"Downstairs."

I leaned my head on Tom's shoulder.

"Congratulations, by the way," she said.

"Yeah. Congratulations!" Eric said.

I eyed Jeanine. "What? You're not mad at me?"

"Not now! I'm happy for both of you. Right now, you just need to focus on getting better."

"Okay."

"Later, I can harass you about not inviting me," she joshed.

"Deal," I laughed. "Thanks for flying all the way out here."

Jeanine hugged Eric and circled her arms around his waist.

"We were really worried about you." He rubbed her back and held her tight.

"Believe me," I said. "So was I."

"We'll see you later, Addie," Eric said.

"Thanks for stopping by." I smiled.

Tom stood up to see them out the door.

Jeanine turned back. "I can't believe we're getting to stay in a castle!" she squealed.

I laughed as they went out into the hall. It was good to see them. For a second, I felt like the old Addie. Before the shooting and the knowledge that my dreams of having a family were over.

When Tom returned, I patted the bed. "Come here."

He sat down and touched my face. I rubbed his arm and sighed. "You're pretty."

"And you're medicated." He kissed the end of my nose. "I think you're pretty, too."

"Really?" I giggled. I was drunk on sleep deprivation.

He nodded and I tugged at the back of his neck. He leaned in and slanted his mouth over mine. I murmured something unintelligible and ran my fingers down his back. Then I kissed him and pressed his body down on mine. He held himself above me, so he wouldn't brush my wounds.

We were making out, and I loved it. He covered my neck with kisses. And I cooed in appreciation.

Someone cleared their throat. Eleanor was standing by the bed. Jeffrey was behind her.

Would they ever learn to knock?

"Tom." I pushed against his chest.

"What?" he smirked. Then he saw them and froze for about five seconds.

"Mom. Dad. What are you doing here?" I asked.

Jeffrey pulled up a chair for Eleanor to sit down in. She gracefully slid into it and lowered her head. Then she burst into tears. I'd never seen her show this much emotion in my entire life.

"We were so worried about you," she sobbed.

Jeffrey put his hand on her shoulder. "How are you feeling?" he asked.

"I'm better." I couldn't stand the sight of her crying. Eleanor didn't cry. Somehow, it made me feel bad. I'd been the one to shatter her walls and get her to finally be human and show some emotion.

"They've been taking real good care of her," Tom said.

"I'm going to be fine," I said. "Really."

I draped my arm over his stomach, leaning on him. He put his left hand over mine. And I settled my head in the crook of his neck.

Eleanor's eyes dropped to our wedding rings. Soon, Jeffrey's followed.

We sat there awkwardly, while they stared at the platinum bands.

"There's my beautiful niece." Edmond let himself in with a big fat grin on his face.

Adeline filed in with a dozen balloons. And then Ashton brought a fresh bouquet of flowers with Juliette on his arm. Jimmy waltzed in next with Josette staring into his eyes. I saw her and held my breath.

"Addie!" Adeline handed the balloons to Tom and then gave me a hug. "How are you?"

"Fine." I smiled. "You didn't have to bring me more balloons. I already have too many."

"Yeah, but those are from your dad. You need some from us, too."

"And flowers, Ashton," I directed at him. "I already have too many."

He smiled and set them down by the window. "You can never have enough flowers."

Edmond kissed me on the forehead and patted my hand. "You look well today."

"Thank you." I caught the looks on Jeffrey and Eleanor's faces. "Umm."

Everyone was so busy carrying on with each other. And they were all so happy to see me. I loved my new family, and the lengths they went to each and every day, just to make sure I was all right.

"Well, hello." Edmond noticed Eleanor. "I'm Edmond Beaumont. Nice to meet you."

Jeffrey and Eleanor shook his hand, but failed to say anything.

"He's a count," I bragged. "Don't let him fool you."

"Papa, I think we've intruded," Ashton announced. Tom had whispered something in his ear.

"Yes, we didn't mean to interrupt. It's just that Addie is very dear to us, you see," Edmond chimed.

"Addie is very dear to us as well," Jeffrey said.

"I see." Edmond gave me a small smile. "Well, we won't intrude any longer."

"No." I looked at my new family in longing. "You guys don't have to go."

Edmond kissed the back of my hand. "I believe we must."

"I can't wait to see you back at the castle." Adeline gave me a hug and followed Edmond out.

Ashton and Juliette looked back and then headed out the door. I hated that they felt like they had to leave. I wanted to see them. They were my family. I grabbed Tom's hand and forced him to sit.

"What did you say to Ashton?" I whispered.

"Just that now wasn't a good time." He looked into my eyes.

I saw Jimmy and Josette over his shoulder. They were the only newcomers who hadn't left yet.

"How are you feeling today?" Jimmy sat down on the other side of my bed.

"Much better." I grabbed his hand. "I'm really glad you came."

"My little girl getting married? I wouldn't miss it

for the world."

"He was at your wedding?" Jeffrey asked.

I looked at Jeffrey. He was fuming. I'm talking daggers in his hazel eyes.

"Yes," I said.

"It was a surprise," Jimmy said.

"Yeah, well, it was a surprise for us, too," Jeffrey snapped.

I looked up at Josette. She hadn't said a word.

"Who is this woman?" Eleanor asked.

"Probably someone Jimmy picked up at the airport." Jeffrey glared at Jimmy.

Eleanor huffed. "Well, I don't think—"

"She's my mother," I said. "My real mother."

Eleanor touched her chest. "*I'm* your mother."

I shut my eyes and ran my fingers through my hair.

"You believe some stranger is your mother?" Eleanor probed.

"Was she at the wedding, too?" Jeffrey asked.

"No, I didn't even know who she really was then."

"Yes," Josette said. "I was."

I stared at her. "What?"

"I watched from the banister."

I couldn't believe her. "Why didn't you tell me? Why didn't you tell me then?"

"I was scared," she said. "I'm so sorry." Her lower lip trembled as she shed quiet tears.

Jimmy went to her side, taking her hand in his. "It's okay."

Eleanor stood up and crossed her arms. "Do you mind if we have a moment alone with her?"

"I don't want them to leave," I protested.

"You're *our* daughter!" Eleanor yelled. "I've had you since you were a baby. We've provided for you.

We've taken care of you, given you everything you could ever need."

"What are you talking about? You've never spent a day with me in your life!"

"Addison," Jeffrey scolded. "Listen to your mother. You are our child. No one else's."

My face turned red. "She's *not* my mother. And I'm *not* your child."

"Addie," Jimmy said.

"No!" I pointed at him to silence him. It worked. "I don't belong to anyone but myself."

"We are your legal guardians, Addie," Eleanor hissed. "Should I show you the paperwork?"

"I'm eighteen now! And I'm married! And there's nothing you can do about it!"

"Is that why you didn't invite us to the wedding?" Eleanor asked. "You invite everyone else!" She motioned towards Jimmy and Josette. "I had to find out about my own daughter's wedding from Jeanine on the plane. Do you know how embarrassing that was? That I was excluded from my own daughter's wedding?"

My chest rose and fell. I knew my blood pressure was rising.

"You betrayed us!" Eleanor said. "You chose them over us! The people who abandoned you!"

"Well, I love them!" Tears filled my eyes. My shoulders shook, and I couldn't breathe.

Tom pulled me into his arms and ran his fingers through my hair. "Baby, it's okay."

"I guess you've chosen another family," Eleanor snipped.

"That's enough!" Tom growled. "Addie is my wife, and you won't talk to her like that ever again!"

Silence filled the room.

"You have no idea what we've been through in the past few days! This is our life, not *yours*. If you want to remain a part of Addie's life, then I suggest you shut your damn mouth and leave her alone! Stop making her feel guilty for marrying me. She wanted to! And this was our decision. You got it?"

Tom glared at my adoptive parents. I hardly recognized him.

"Tom," I whispered. "You don't have to do that."

"No, I do! It's about time someone starts standing up for my wife." He was panting.

"Maybe this is not the best time," Eleanor said. "We'll wait outside."

The minute she left with Jeffrey, it felt like I could breathe again.

"I'm sorry," Josette said. "I didn't mean to—"

"It's not your fault," I said. "They've always been assholes."

"Addie!" Jimmy scolded, wrapping his arm around Josette.

"What? It's true!" I laughed.

"I'll remember never to get on this one's bad side," Jimmy teased.

Tom released the breath he'd been holding. His whole face had turned red.

"Come here, baby." I put his head in my lap. "Thank you for sticking up for me."

"Always." He stroked my side and breathed me in.

"I am ready to talk to you," I said to Josette. "Just not right now."

"I understand. I never meant to interfere with your family."

"You're my family," I said. "And whatever

happened, I forgive you."

"Why?" she asked. "You haven't even let me explain yet."

"Because I've missed you my whole life. And I love you. Unconditionally."

"I love you, too." There was longing in her eyes. "I never wanted to let you go."

"I believe you." I ran my fingers through Tom's raven locks.

"I think Addie needs to rest," he said. "I hope this hasn't been too much for her."

"I'm right here," I said.

"I know."

"Then why are you referring to me in the third person?" I asked.

"We'll come back later," Jimmy said. "You just rest, Addie. Okay?"

I nodded and looked at Josette. "Bye."

"Bye, Addie." She blew me a kiss and waved goodbye.

The door shut, and Tom moaned. "I need to stop complaining about being an orphan."

"Why?"

"Because you've got four parents now. And I'm kind of worried they might kill each other."

I laughed. "It will be fine. I hope. It's just a lot to take in all at once."

"Hasn't it always been?" He got up to shut the blinds and then sat down beside me. "Are you getting hungry? You haven't had much to eat today. I think you should eat a big meal for dinner."

I touched my stomach. "I kind of am starving."

"Let me find the nurse." Tom left me alone in the room.

A few moments later, there was a knock on the door. "Hello, Mrs. Sutton?"

"Yes." I sat up in bed.

"Hi. I'm Dr. Rousseau." She pulled up a chair beside me. "I'll be taking care of you while Dr. Laurent is out."

"He told me about you. He had a lot of nice things to say."

"Well, he's kind of biased," she said.

"What do you mean?"

"He's my father."

"Oh." I searched for a resemblance but couldn't find one. She must have looked like her mother.

"So." She took a seat. "How have you been feeling today?"

"Fine. I've been getting asked that question a lot."

"Sorry about that. Why don't we check everything out?"

When she was done, I looked at her dark hair and brown eyes. She had olive skin.

"I've been feeling kind of depressed," I confessed.

"Well, you were shot twice. And you've been cooped up in this hospital for days."

"It's not about that." I met her eyes. "Dr. Laurent said I may never be able to have children."

"Yes, I know." She patted my arm. "And I can't tell you how sorry I am."

"I don't know what to do." I stared at the ceiling. "It's all I can think about."

"Then try not to think about it." She looked at my chart.

"My husband wants to adopt. Not now of course. But later."

"I think that sounds like a great idea," she said.

"I don't want to adopt."

"Why not?"

"I was adopted. And he was, too. We've never had a real family."

"What makes you think it wouldn't be real?" she asked.

"They won't be my kids."

"You'll be the only mother they've ever known."

"True." I looked away.

"It's not any different, Addie. You can still have the life you want."

"No." I shook my head. "I don't know."

"It's love, Addie. Not nature, but nurture. Blood is just blood."

"What are you saying?" I asked.

"I was adopted."

"Really?" I asked.

"Yes. My birth parents died in a car accident when I was three months old. Dr. Laurent and his wife adopted me. She'd been diagnosed with endometriosis as a teen. They gave her a full hysterectomy."

I widened my eyes in terror.

"I needed a family. And they needed a child. We needed each other."

"I didn't know," I whispered.

"Life has a way of working out when you least expect it to."

I felt a sudden surge of hope. It came over me like a tidal wave.

"Life can be wonderful." She patted my cheek. "If you just give it the chance to be."

I watched her get up to leave.

"I'll be checking in on you every day. Let me know if there is anything you need."

I nodded as she headed for the door. "Dr. Rousseau?"

"Yes, Mrs. Sutton."

"Thanks."

"Get some rest." She smiled and shut the door behind her.

When Tom returned, I was so happy to see him.

"Hey. How are you feeling?" He sat down on the bed, taking my hand.

"Good." I touched his cheek.

"Sorry I was gone so long. They are bringing you a huge dinner."

"That sounds great. Dr. Rousseau stopped by. I really like her."

"I'm glad." He held my hand. "Everything is gonna be all right, Addie."

"I know." I rubbed the back of his neck.

"You do?" He sounded relieved.

"Yeah." I smiled up at my beautiful husband. "I do now."

"Oh, baby." He pressed his lips to mine and lay down beside me. "I'm sorry I lost my temper."

"It's okay. I think Jeffrey and Eleanor are in for a rude awakening."

"Why?" He toyed with my wedding ring.

"Because it's not about them anymore."

He kissed my head and held me close. "What do you want to watch?" He turned the TV on.

"Anything's good. We need to work on our French anyway."

Tom flipped channels, searching for something.

"Thanks for standing up for me today."

He turned his head towards me, wrapping his arm around my shoulder. "No problem, baby."

A photo of Valjean flashed on the screen. I tensed immediately, clinging to Tom.

He turned the TV off and held me in his arms. "I'm sorry. You don't need to be afraid of him anymore."

"He's going to prison, right?" I asked.

Tom hesitated. "Yes. Of course."

"Thank God." I nuzzled his chest and closed my eyes.

"You're safe now." He rubbed my back. "I'll make sure no one ever hurts you again."

I smiled and drifted off in his arms. He was my rock, my fortress. My way to shut out the world.

I knew that Tom meant every word. Because it felt like a promise.

Chapter 7

Tom

Addie dozed off after dinner, so I went to the cafeteria in search of comfort food. When I got there, my eyes were on the TV screen. It was a news report about Valjean. I couldn't understand what they were saying. But I could feel the mood of the piece. Something was wrong.

My appetite ran off like a scared dog. I hated leaving Addie alone in her hospital room, but I had to find out what was going on. It would drive me crazy not knowing. And while I loathed keeping secrets from her, I had a feeling that—once again—I just might have to.

"What's going on with Valjean?"

Edmond sighed on the phone. "Well, Mr. Sutton, you get right to the point."

"Come on, what's going on?"

"Are you sitting down?" I heard the burn of his cigar.

"Yes." I wasn't.

"I don't know how to tell you this, Tom. But it looks like he might get off."

"What!" I shouted. Everyone in the cafeteria stared, so I stepped into the adjoining corridor.

"You can't be a jewel thief for twenty years without having some connections."

"What does that mean? He knows the judge? He bought him off?"

"You have to understand the position you're in, Tom. I love Addie. She's my niece. But you're outsiders here. You're Americans. And you're not in America anymore."

"He shot my wife!"

"And it would be easier to convict him if he had killed her," Edmond said.

I clenched my fist and considered throwing my phone against the wall.

"Why can't you help? Aren't you royalty over here or something?" I asked.

"I'm only a count. It's more about nobility than politics."

"So you're telling me, after all the hell he's put us through, that he's just going to walk?"

"If you could prosecute him on US soil, it would be an entirely different story. But he is a citizen of France. And you're in France, his homeland. You don't understand how the courts operate over here. You can't even speak French. You're foreigners. Do you understand?"

"He shot my wife! Since when does that not hold up in court?"

"There's more, Tom. I'm just not at liberty to discuss it with you."

I scowled. "You told me he's a notorious jewel thief. You're telling me the public doesn't hate a common criminal? What about the Louvre? What about all the homes he's robbed in France?"

"Tom, you're treading in deep water."

I ran my fingers through my hair. "Addie has lost more than blood from all this."

"Was there a child?" he asked.

"No. But now the doctors say there may never be one."

"Oh God, it's worse than I thought. I had no idea."

"Well, now you do. So are you going to do something or not?"

He hesitated.

"Can you help me?" I begged.

"I'll see what I can do." He cleared his throat. "In the meantime, you may want to get out of France."

"But Addie is still in recovery. I don't know when Dr. Rousseau will release her from the hospital."

"Well, you may just have to leave early," he said.

"And go where? Back to America?"

"I don't know. Maybe not just yet. You need to come up with a plan."

"A plan for what?" I asked.

"A plan for getting your wife out of this country alive."

* * *

The next morning, Addie woke up with a smile on her face. "Hi," she crooned.

"Hi." I kissed her forehead and smoothed her hair back. "I have a surprise for you."

"Mmm." She rubbed my arm, sleepy and beautiful. "I like surprises."

"Good." I opened the door and Dr. Rousseau stepped inside.

"Good morning, Mrs. Sutton," she said. "How are you feeling today?"

"Fine." She sat up on her elbows. "Better, actually."

"That's great. Well, I have some good news for

you."

Addie raised her brow. "Really?"

"I think you might be able to go home today."

"Really?" Addie looked like a little girl.

"Yeah." Dr. Rousseau took a seat. "You've been cooped up in here for far too long. And we've kept you to make sure there are no complications. But you've been recovering beautifully. As long as today goes smoothly, I'm prepared to discharge you later today."

She looked at me. "That's great."

Dr. Rousseau went through the routine of checking her vitals and bandages. Then she returned her attention to Addie's chart. "Everything looks good. I'm thinking this afternoon. How does that sound?"

"Wonderful," Addie mouthed. I thought she was about to start crying.

"Well, a nurse will be in with your breakfast shortly. In the meantime, let me know if you need anything else." Dr. Rousseau patted her arm. "I'm proud of you. Everything is going to be all right."

"Thank you." Addie watched her leave, then gaped at me.

"You're going home, baby." I pulled her into my arms.

"I'm so happy." She nuzzled my chest. "It will be so nice to be back at the castle."

I leaned back, holding her at arm's length. "Actually, I had something else in mind."

She cocked her head like a cute little puppy.

"Remember that honeymoon we missed?"

She nodded. Her eyes were glued to mine.

"Well, what if we go on it now?" I said.

There was an entire week of Christmas vacation

left. We wouldn't be missing school.

"But I thought you said it was too late," she remembered.

"Don't worry about that." I cupped her cheek. "I took care of it."

"And you already talked to Dr. Rousseau?"

"As long as we take it easy," I grinned. "You should be fine."

"What about the plane tickets? You rebooked them?"

I tucked a lock of golden hair behind her ear. "We're not going to the airport."

She gave me a funny look. "So we're going to swim there?" she teased.

"Did you know your uncle has a private jet?" I asked.

Her eyes lit up like the Emerald City.

"Well, he's going to let us use it."

"And we're still going to Italy?" She curled her arms around my neck.

"Rome. Naples. Florence."

"What about Venice?" she asked.

"Yep."

"And fair Verona?"

"You're such a romantic."

"I know." She kissed me. "But so are you."

"Yes," I said. "Whatever you want."

"Oh, Tom." She wrapped her arms around me. "It sounds wonderful."

I lay down beside her and held her close. "Everything is gonna be all right."

"Okay." She kissed me and I buried my face in her neck. "Tom!" she giggled. "Wait, we're not even out of the hospital yet." She pushed back on my chest. "And remember, I'm a delicate new bride."

"Is that so?" I caged her in my arms.

She nodded as I kissed her neck, trailing my nose along her collarbone.

"You're gonna have to be gentle with me," she sighed.

I traced her jawline and looked into her eyes. "I'm always gentle with you."

She caressed my face and stared right back. "I know."

* * *

It was dark by the time we made it to the castle. Edmond's driver, Fernand, parked by the front steps. When he opened the back door, I got out and lifted Addie in my arms. She was light as a feather.

"It's cold," she shivered, snuggling into my chest.

Fernand grabbed the front door, and I thanked him. He'd been a huge help to us. Even going so far as to wait in the hospital with the family when Addie was shot. I'd never forget his kindness.

"Thank you, Fernand," I said.

He bowed his head and smiled.

"Addie!" Jeanine came barreling down the staircase. "Addie's home!"

Adeline ran down the steps next. Followed by Jimmy and Eric.

"Hi." Addie smiled and then shut her eyes.

"Is she all right?" Jimmy asked. "How is she feeling?"

"She's fine," I said. "She just needs rest. Let me put her to bed."

They let me take her up to our room alone. I lay her down on the bed and tucked her in.

"Tom?" She reached out for me.

"Yes? Are you in pain?"

She shook her head. "I'm thirsty."

I brought her some water and put it by our bed. But by the time I got back, she had already dozed off. Dr. Rousseau had given her some pain killers. I was seeing firsthand just how strong they were.

"I'll be right back," I whispered, even though she couldn't hear me. I left a kiss on her forehead.

I shut the bedroom door and found everyone downstairs. "How have y'all been?"

"Fine." Ashton stood up and patted my back. "How is she?"

"Better," I said. "She's glad to be out of the hospital."

"I'm sure," Juliette smiled. "We're glad to have her back home."

Adeline and Jeanine were sitting together in front of the fireplace. Now that I thought about it, they had a lot in common. And they both adored Addie. It made sense that they'd become fast friends.

"They left," Adeline said.

The room fell silent.

"Who left?" I asked.

"Mr. and Mrs. Smith," Jeanine answered.

"Well where did they go?" I asked.

"They went to stay at a hotel," Eric said. "It's nothing personal. It's just—"

"Don't worry about it. I think I know my mother-in-law well enough by now."

That was just like Eleanor. Everyone else was here for Addie. All Eleanor could think about was herself, what she wanted, how the situation made her feel. I rolled my eyes and made an effort to forget about it.

I saw Jimmy take Josette outside for an evening stroll in the snow. There was so much Josette and Addie needed to clear up as mother and daughter. Maybe they could have that talk before we left for Italy. It would probably help Addie have a better time on our honeymoon. She deserved a clear head.

I'd only been talking to Eric and Ashton for a few minutes before Edmond appeared.

"I'd like to speak with you in my study. Alone."

I followed him down the hall. He shut the door behind us.

"Is everything okay?" I asked.

"How is Addie?" He lit a cigar.

"She's fine. How many of those have you been smoking a day?" I asked.

"That's not your concern now. Is it, Tom?" He exhaled a stream of smoke.

"What's this about? Valjean?"

"I don't know what's going to happen. But it looks like he's going to get off. I know for sure now."

Here we go again.

"How? He shot my wife!"

"Keep your voice down, Tom." He put his cigar out. "It's not like he killed her."

I stood up as he turned his back to me. "Whose side are you on?"

"It's not about picking sides, Tom. Valjean has connections. He knows people."

"Who? Are you telling me he paid off the judge? What do you know?"

"I'm not at liberty to say. Just trust me. I'm doing everything I can."

"What happened to justice?" I plopped down in my chair.

"This is the law, Thomas. It has nothing to do with right and wrong."

"What am I supposed to do?" I buried my head in my hands.

"I already told you." He looked back at me. "Get her out of France."

"When?" I had no intention of rushing Addie in her fragile state.

"As soon as possible."

The conversation was over. So I left his study and found Addie's parents outside. Jimmy must have sensed that I needed a moment alone with Josette. Because he headed inside and gave me a nod.

"Hello, Tom." Josette hugged my neck. "How is she?"

"She's sleeping. But I think she's happy to be home."

"I'm glad." She gazed up at the stars. "It's beautiful tonight."

"Listen, I think you need to have that talk with your daughter. And I think it needs to be soon."

She nodded. "I understand. How about tomorrow?"

"Yes." I saw my breath. "That sounds perfect."

"I'd ask you to take care of my little girl, but I can see you've already done that."

I watched her walk away and then went upstairs to take a shower. I dried off and pulled my boxers on, slipping in bed beside Addie. She mumbled in her sleep and put her head on my stomach.

I ran my fingers through her hair as she snored. It was so cute. My wife was asleep in my arms, alive and snoring. We were in a French castle with her royal family. Even now, it still felt surreal.

I relaxed and wrapped her in my arms. It was amazing to be back in a normal bed. After everything Addie had been through, I shouldn't have been complaining. But I hadn't slept well at the hospital.

I rubbed her back and dozed off with a sappy grin on my face.

"Tom," someone hissed, jabbing my arm. "Tom!"

It had only been moments since I'd shut my eyes. That's what it felt like anyway.

"What?" I opened them and winced, holding Addie close.

She groaned and hid her face at the juncture of my shoulder and neck.

Edmond stood by our bed. It looked like he hadn't slept all night.

"You need to get Addie out of here!"

"What are you talking about?" I grumbled.

"Valjean posted bail. He's out. Come on. Let's go!" Edmond ordered.

Fernand ran in to collect our things, already packing the car.

"Tom?" Addie sat up with the sheet draped around her waist. She was wearing my shirt.

"Good morning, baby." I needed to keep her calm. "How are you feeling?"

"What's going on?" She rubbed the sleep from her eyes.

"It's time to get dressed." I pulled her to the edge of the bed. "Just hold on to me."

She clung to my shoulders as I helped her into her jeans. I put her socks on for her and then guided her feet into her shoes. I eased her arms through the sleeves of her jacket and pulled the hood up.

"Tom." She winced and leaned back in bed.

"Are you hurting?" I asked, putting my own shirt and jacket on.

She nodded.

"Here." I gave her two pain pills and a glass of water. "Come on. Let's go."

I jumped into my jeans and tied the laces on my boots. She tried to stand and almost collapsed on the floor. Panic flushed my veins of any exhaustion. I was pumped full of adrenaline now.

"Fernand!" I lifted Addie in my arms and motioned for him to grab our remaining bags.

It was the crack of dawn, so the rest of the house was still asleep. We hurried down the stairs and into the car out front. Edmond slammed the back door as Fernand sped off to the rising sun.

Addie lay down across the back seat and put her head in my lap. I was 100% sure that she had no idea what was going on. Because my heart was beating a mile a minute. I was excited for our honeymoon. But I never imagined we'd depart like this.

When we reached the airport, Fernand pulled up beside a private jet. I carried Addie up the steps in my arms as Fernand followed with our luggage. There was just the pilot and us. I didn't know how I felt about that. Didn't you need co-pilots to keep you from crashing the plane?

Fernand started yelling in French and shut the door. I held Addie in my arms as the plane took off. Fernand went up front to join the pilot, which made me think something was wrong. He was supposed to drop us off and go straight back to the castle. So why wasn't he?

I covered Addie with a blanket and looked out the window.

VIOLET BLOOD

Valjean was standing on the tarmac.

Chapter 8

Addie

I woke up feeling like I was in a dream. My hip was tender and my head hurt. It felt like I'd been jerked out of bed and thrown into a car. When I opened my eyes, I realized the reason why.

"Tom?" I looked up and he was there. But he also wasn't.

He sat next to me, stoic and tense.

"What's going on?" I looked around and froze. I had the window seat in a private plane.

"Umm..." He drummed his fingers over the arm rest. "I thought we'd get a head start on the honeymoon."

"By leaving at the crack of dawn? What time is it anyway?"

"A little after nine." He rubbed his jaw and stared straight ahead.

"Tom."

He was in his own world.

"Tom!"

He flinched and turned to me. "Yeah. What's wrong?"

"You're acting weird." I shifted in my seat and winced.

"Are you okay?" he asked.

I shut my eyes and sighed. It was frustrating,

because I felt blindsided. He wasn't telling me everything. And I hated being babied, which was his favorite thing to do—since I'd been in the hospital anyway.

"Is something wrong?" I said.

"No." He couldn't meet my eye. "Everything is fine."

"Yeah, sure." I unbuckled my seatbelt and got up.

"Where are you going?" He gazed up at me, driving me crazy. It was like dealing with a mother hen.

"Tom, I have to go to the bathroom. And I don't need you preening and poking and prodding!" I walked around him and found a door at the back. It led to a master bedroom suite with a private bathroom.

Breathing a sigh of relief, I went straight to the bathroom and splashed water on my face. I looked in the mirror and saw how tired I was. It would have been nice if he'd given me a little more warning.

I took a hot shower and washed my hair. It felt so good to get clean. There were complimentary bottles of shampoo and conditioner. I thought about the gift basket Jeanine had given me. Tom probably didn't think to pack it, but I would have. It would have been the perfect spa treatment for our honeymoon.

I got out and slipped into a cotton robe. I'd seen our luggage in the bedroom. Thankfully, Tom had packed all of my things. But I would have rather been the one to do it. Not to mention, say goodbye to everyone at the castle. Why had Tom taken me away when everyone was asleep?

I couldn't find my toothbrush in my suitcase. Maybe it wasn't that big of a deal, but even the smallest thing set me off today. So I tossed Tom's bag onto the bed and started going through it.

There was nothing in the pockets. So I unzipped the bag and rifled through his clothes. He hadn't even bothered to fold his shirts properly. And it was sending me over the edge in a very melodramatic way.

My hand froze when I saw what lay at the bottom. *Thousands in cash.*

I picked up a set of bills. It was nothing but hundreds. Stacks that lined the bottom of the bag.

And then there was a gun. I'd never seen it before. And I was too stunned to touch it.

Someone knocked on the door. I knew it was Tom. So I put his clothes back in the suitcase exactly as I'd found them. Then I zipped it shut and slid it across the bed. When the door opened, I was sitting on the edge with my eyes down. Now I knew the secrets he'd been keeping.

"Hey." His voice was soft as he shut the door. "You okay?"

I nodded.

He knelt down in front of me, taking my hands. "What is it?"

I met his amber eyes and then looked away. He hadn't told me about the cash or the gun. And I hadn't revealed that I'd found both. We were both lying to each other, and I hated it.

"I'm just tired." I gnawed on my lip. "We left so suddenly."

"Yeah, sorry about that." He massaged my hand. "I wanted it to be a surprise."

"Well, it worked." I got up and dried my hair in front of the mirror. I felt his eyes on me. "I can't find my toothbrush. I guess you forgot to pack it."

"Oh, I'm sorry."

"You know, I could have packed my own

suitcase." I turned around. "You don't have to treat me like a child."

"I wasn't."

"Well, it feels that way." I gave him a stern look. "I'm older than you."

He crossed his arms over his chest. "And your point is?"

"I'm your wife. I want to be included. I don't like it when you keep things from me."

He crept up behind me and touched my shoulders. "I'm sorry."

"Well, sorry isn't good enough." I turned around and pushed him away. "Not when it comes to things like this."

"What are you talking about?" he asked.

"I found the money, Tom," I hissed. "And the gun."

He blinked at me like I'd lost my mind. "What?"

"Don't act like you don't know."

"Addie, I have no idea what you're talking about."

"Oh, really?" I put my hand on my hip. "So there's no reason why you're acting weird?"

"Yes but—"

"You have to stop hiding things from me." I plopped down on the bed. "I don't like it."

"It's only for your protection," he said.

"I don't care! I want to know!" I saw the pain in his eyes and burst into tears.

"Addie."

"Stop." I held my hand up. "Please. There's been too much going on lately."

"I know." He sat down beside me and rubbed my back. "Baby, I know."

"What haven't you been telling me?" I looked into

his eyes as he caressed my face. "Please, just tell me the truth. I want to know what's going on. Otherwise, I'll just go crazy."

He sighed, but gave in. "Valjean is out on bail."

My instinct was to start shouting. Especially since he'd originally told me that my attacker was headed for prison.

"I don't know what happened, but somehow he got off. Your uncle knows the particulars, but he wouldn't tell me. He said he couldn't. But he's doing everything he can to keep you safe."

I took a deep breath. It was better that I hadn't lashed out. That was something I needed to work on—letting Tom fully explain before I lost my cool. He loved me, and I needed to remember that.

"What about the money in your suitcase?" I searched his eyes. "And the gun?"

He furrowed his brow and opened his suitcase. For the first time, I realized why his clothes were such a mess. Because Tom hadn't packed his bags. He hadn't packed mine either. Someone else had.

Tom looked at the money and froze, turning to me.

"The gun's at the bottom," I said.

He pushed the money aside and found a pistol.

"Addie, I didn't know about any of this." He stood there looking bewildered.

"Edmond must have slipped it in your bag," I guessed. "Who packed for us?"

"Fernand."

"So this morning, Edmond found out about Valjean getting out of jail," I assumed.

"Yeah." Tom nodded. "And he got us out of there immediately."

Worry covered my thoughts like a heavy blanket. "Now I see why you kept it from me."

He squeezed my hand. "It's just that you've been through so much over the past few days. I didn't want to put any more stress on your shoulders. I just wanted you to be able to rest and relax."

I nodded, accepting his reasons. "So now what?"

"I'm getting you out of France. We're going somewhere no one can find us."

Right then, the way he said those words did something to me. I saw him as the protector. He just wanted to keep me safe. I felt warm and breathless, fresh from my hot shower.

"Did you lock the door?" I kept my eyes on his.

He took a step back and twisted the lock. "Yes."

My heart was pounding in my chest, and my mouth went dry.

He came towards me and leaned over the bed. I wrapped my arms around him and tilted my head back. He left one tantalizing kiss after the next, slowly lowering me onto the bed. Then he blew over the pulse point in my neck, softly tracing the line of my jaw with his thumb.

"Don't tease me," I begged. "Not now."

Smiling, he gave me a hungry kiss and lifted my body with one arm. My head hit the pillow and he pulled the covers back, making room for us both. I closed my eyes and ran my hands down his back so I could untuck his shirt. He buried his face in my neck, kissing his way down my sternum.

When I opened my eyes, he was struggling to get his shirt off. "Let me," I whispered.

He watched my face as I slid my fingers under the material. I palmed his chest and pushed his shirt over his shoulders. But my man was impatient. So he pulled his shirt the rest of the way over his head and tossed it on the floor.

I hummed and ran my hands down his back. "That's better."

He grinned and kissed me. And it was all so good. The way he touched me. Even the way he smelled. I craved him like a junkie, and when he loosened the tie on my robe, I threw my arms over my head.

He kissed his way down my body, leaving feather light kisses on my ribs. I ran my fingers through his hair and squirmed, ready for wherever he was going to take me. He nipped at my earlobe and brought his mouth to mine. Then he peeled my robe all the way off and finished getting undressed.

I sat up in bed with the duvet covering me. He draped my robe over the chair and threw the rest of his clothes on the floor by his shirt. When he climbed back in with me, I curled my arms around his neck and made room for him.

"We have to be gentle." He kissed me. "Okay?"

"I don't want you to be gentle."

"Addie," he groaned.

"Tom." I stared up at him and batted my lashes.

He held himself up with his arms. "You're gonna kill me."

I giggled and stroked the back of his neck.

"But I love the way you laugh."

"I love you," I sighed.

He kissed my cheeks and pinned my hands to the mattress, hovering above me. Then he whispered in my ear, "I love you more."

He made love to me slowly. I tried to keep quiet, but the strangest noises were coming out of my mouth.

I clawed his back and held on, never wanting this moment, this connection to end.

Maybe I was greedy and desperate. But I couldn't help myself from wanting him as badly as I did. I tried hooking my calf around his back and ended up hurting my hip. I gasped and dug my nails into his shoulder.

"Tom." I ran my fingers down his arm.

"Yeah." He cradled my face and peered down at me. "What is it, baby?"

"It's my hip." I read the look in his eyes. "No, don't stop. Just..." I covered my face with my hand.

"I'm not gonna hurt you," he said.

"You're not hurting me."

He bowed his head and exhaled.

I turned his face towards me. "You're my husband. And I need you."

"I know. But I can't stand to watch you in pain." He got up and covered me with the duvet. "Especially when I'm the one causing it." He grabbed his clothes off the floor and went into the bathroom. He shut the door, and I heard the shower come on. That's when I realized the moment was gone.

I rolled over in bed and cried, hugging the pillow to my chest. I'd never imagined being a newlywed would feel like this. We'd almost been married a week, but I'd hardly had the opportunity to enjoy it.

I buried my face in the sheet, shaking with grief. In a matter of days, I'd lost everything.

The ability to bear a child. Safety. Intimacy. Strength.

I felt so weak. I'd waited a lifetime for Tom's love. Now he wouldn't even share it with me.

To be honest, I was just so frustrated. *Physically. Emotionally. Sexually.*

I wondered how many newlyweds had started off a marriage like this. Surely, not many. The honeymoon I'd fantasized was no more. In my condition, Tom wouldn't lay a hand on me for weeks. And no matter the destination, I wouldn't feel safe. That's what paralyzed me—the thought that I may never feel safe again.

When Tom got out of the shower, I kept my sobbing to a soft whimper. I looked out the window, and it was overcast outside. I wondered if it might rain. Tom walked around the bed and pulled down the shade, forcing the room into darkness. It felt like we were in a cave.

I closed my eyes and tried to fall asleep. But it was no use. I felt rejected and betrayed.

"Baby." He sat down on the bed. "Please don't cry. I don't want to hurt you."

I looked up at him in the dark. "You didn't hurt me."

He took my hand, and his touch sent me over the edge. "Yes, I did."

The tears poured out like a broken dam, and it was happening all over again. I just couldn't hold it in anymore. I needed something good in my life for a change, instead of all the pain from the last week.

I wanted to feel good. In a way that only Tom's touch could make me feel. And he was taking it from me, robbing me of the pleasure and passion I'd felt in his arms.

"It's okay if you don't want me," I sobbed. "I know I'm a mess right now."

"Addie." He slipped in bed beside me. "Is that what you think? That I don't want you?"

"Of course! If you felt the way I do—if you wanted

me as badly as I want you..." I couldn't finish that sentence. It hurt too much to imagine.

"Addie, baby." He caressed my cheek. "You have no idea how much I want you."

"Yeah, right," I sniffled, wiping my nose. "You're just saying that to make me feel better."

His touch drifted down my neck. "If you only knew what I want to do to you right now..."

Breath hitched at the back of my throat. Blush stained my cheeks. I felt excited and nervous all at once.

"What do you want to do to me?" I asked.

He kissed the pulse point in my neck and whispered in my ear, "I want to love you forever."

"Tom." I dug my fingertips into his naked back. "Don't tease me. I can't take it."

He kissed me. But it was soft, gentle, innocent. Like something you'd do in a church.

"Why don't you get some sleep? We have the rest of our lives to do that," he said.

"Do we?" I put my hand on his chest. "We can't count on forever."

He threaded his fingers in my hair. "Everything is going to be fine. All right?"

I sighed.

"You're tired and so am I. Let's just get some sleep," he suggested.

I was so happy that he was going to stay in here with me. "Okay."

I ran my fingers over the contours in his back and watched him fall asleep. Once his eyes were closed, I pulled the sash off my robe and slipped back in bed. He rolled onto his back and talked in his sleep. I couldn't make out what he was saying, but I could've sworn I heard my name.

I leaned up on my elbow and touched his hair. It was getting longer, but I liked it. I brushed my knuckles against his cheeks, loving the rough texture of his beard. He was such a real man. Even at seventeen. And I couldn't get enough. Looking at his body was like being stuck on the other side of a glass wall.

I yearned for him like a smitten school girl. He was the one thing I wanted but couldn't have.

My heart pounded with desire. He was the most beautiful man I'd ever seen. Just looking at him got my blood pumping. He was a life size aphrodisiac. My husband. My stubborn, sexy man of a husband.

I sat up and pulled the covers back. Then I took a deep breath. He'd given me no choice.

I was going to have to seduce my husband. How hard could it be?

I touched his arm and shivered with delight. He was so warm, so strong. And he was *mine*.

I kissed his face and neck, running my hands down his chest. He muttered something in the dark and I straddled his waist, hoping it wouldn't wake him. His hands slid up my thighs and it thrilled me. Even in his subconscious, he wanted me. But he was too stubborn to indulge in all the love I had to give.

"Addie." He was half-awake as he looked up at me.

So I jumped at the opportunity and planted my mouth on his. He wrapped his arms around me and pressed his hands into my back. I was so happy that I was about to start crying. But I couldn't let the moment slip away. Especially when he sat up with me in his lap.

He tasted my neck and stroked my arms. "I want you so bad."

"You have me," I kissed him again. "I'm all yours."

"Addie—"

I interrupted him with a hungry kiss. I could feel him pulling away. So I pushed him to the flat of his back and pinned his arms above his head. He gazed up at me, his breaths matching the beat of my heart.

"Addie, we can't."

"I want to." I leaned over him so my hair covered his face. "I want you."

As we kissed, I tied his wrists together with my sash. He pulled at the double knot and I giggled.

"Addie." He sounded angry. "What have you done?"

"Please." I kissed his cheek. "I want to be with you."

"You drive me crazy, woman."

"Good." I kissed my way down his torso and he let me. "You're not gonna fight me on this?"

"No." He captured my bottom lip when I put my mouth on his. And I got so caught up in him that I didn't even realize he was breaking free. I heard the fabric rip, and he tossed my torn sash on the floor.

"Hey! I really liked that robe," I whined, though I was only teasing.

He sat up and put his hands on the small of my back. "You mess with the bull, you get the horns."

Then his mouth was on mine, and we were chest to chest. I combed my fingers through his thick hair and hugged him close. He kissed the hollow of my throat and cradled my back in his arms.

"I love you," I whispered in the dark. "So much."

"I love you, too." He traced his fingertips down my spine, and all of my troubles went away.

* * *

"Mmm." I snuggled up against his warm body, feeling blissfully sated.

"I can't believe you tried to tie me up," he said, circling his hand over my back.

"Well, you were being stubborn." We lay together in bed, tangled up in the sheets.

"How do you feel? You're not in pain, are you?"

"No," I sighed, putting my head on his chest. "Quite the opposite."

He chuckled, and the sound rumbled in my ear. "Mrs. Sutton, what should I do with you?"

I smiled and bit my lip, cooing when he leaned down and gave me a sultry kiss. But then the plane dipped and swerved. I screamed when it felt like I was sliding out of bed and couldn't hold on to anything. The mirror crashed into the floor and glass shattered, as the plane spun out of control.

There was a knock on the door. "Monsieur?"

"Get dressed." Tom leapt up and put his clothes on.

I was wrapped in the duvet. And when the plane swerved again, I fell on the floor.

More knocking. "Monsieur?"

"What?" he shouted.

"There is a storm. You need to come out and put your seatbelts on."

I winced as Tom helped me up.

"Your hip?" he asked.

I nodded, and he looked enraged.

"We'll be right out!" he yelled.

"Tom." My feet were slipping. "I'm scared."

"I know, baby." He grabbed some clothes out of my suitcase. "Hold on to me."

I sat down on the bed as he pushed a t-shirt over

my head. He helped me into my underwear and jeans next. But the plane was out of control. It was hard to keep my footing, even with Tom's help.

When my socks were on, he eased my feet into my boots. Then he tugged a sweatshirt over my head and put his jacket on. He looked back at his suitcase and grabbed the gun, tucking it into his pants.

"Tom." I couldn't understand.

"Take this." He handed me a stack of hundreds and took one for himself. "Hide it."

He zipped the money up in his jacket pocket and I stuck mine in my jeans. Now would have been a good time to have a bra on. But I wasn't wearing one, so it wasn't like I could hide the money there.

"Tom." I felt sick.

"Come on." He grabbed my hand. "We're fine. Everything is fine."

I swallowed and leaned on him. He took a few more stacks of cash and then slid his suitcase under the bed. He hid the extra money in his clothing and then took my hand, pulling me into the cabin.

The lights were flickering over head as Tom buckled me up in a seat. Fernand sat down in the aisle across from me and fastened his seat belt. But Tom went into the cockpit to check on the pilot.

"Tom!" All the lights went out as the plane teetered. "Tom!"

The wind was howling and it frightened me. I felt like Dorothy.

"Tom!" I tried to unfasten my seatbelt, but it was stuck. "Tom!"

The plane dropped, and I felt us falling through the sky. Fernand started shouting. I saw him taking the oxygen mask overhead. There was one dangling in front of me. And a second where Tom should have been sitting. But I didn't want the oxygen mask. I wanted my husband here with me.

"Tom!" I screamed.

It all felt like a nightmare. I wanted it to be.

I watched Fernand. It looked like he was praying.

That's when something hit me in the head and I was gone.

* * *

When I woke up, we weren't moving. I looked out the window, and there was snow everywhere. The storm had passed. My body was shaking, as I struggled to unfasten my seatbelt. I stood up and lost my balance. I hadn't expected to be so dizzy. But I had to get to the cockpit. The pilot was covered in blood.

And Tom was missing.

The door had been ripped away during the storm. A patch of air was all that remained.

I crept down the staircase and into the snow. He couldn't have just disappeared. He had to be somewhere.

"Tom!" I turned in a circle. "Tom!"

And then I saw a body lying face down in the snow. *Oh God. Oh God, no.*

"Tom!" I cried and fell to my knees.

Then I took a staggering breath and rolled him over.

Chapter 9

Tom

Addie was calling my name. And it made every part of me go into a panic. I'd already strapped myself into the co-pilot's seat. The pilot was straining to control the plane. He was covered in sweat.

It didn't help that he looked scared to death.

"Hold on!" I yelled to Addie. But everything was so loud, maybe she couldn't hear me.

The pilot said something, but I wasn't wearing headphones. I looked for the co-pilot's headset and wished the co-pilot in question had been here. He was probably enjoying the holidays like everyone else.

We flew out of the storm, but the sky remained cloudy. I saw trees in the distance. Then I figured out the pilot's plan to land the plane manually. It might have been the only option, but it terrified me.

The pilot grabbed my arm when I tried to unstrap myself. But I had to get to Addie. I couldn't leave her in the cabin by herself. I already regretted doing it now, even though I'd been trying to save us all.

As the plane lowered, trees ripped away the left wing. We dipped and shuddered, while I held on for dear life. The pilot swerved and my head hit the window. I saw a crack in the glass and felt woozy.

We were flying directly over a forest. I felt sick, knowing tree tops could destroy the engine—or what was left of it. I looked at the dashboard in the cock pit, and it didn't take Einstein to figure out that malfunctions were running rampant. So I ducked my head as the plane dropped faster and faster, shooting through the trees. It was a miracle we hadn't crashed into one already.

I kept my hands over my head as we went down, because I couldn't look. The plane slammed into the ground and rolled a few hundred feet before jerking to a halt. My head started spinning and didn't stop.

My hands were shaking when I looked up. I saw the pilot and couldn't comprehend why his face was in the control wheel. That's when everything started pounding. I couldn't think straight or even hear.

I fumbled with my safety belt, jerking and tugging to get out. When it released, I fell down on my way to the cabin. I couldn't tell if Fernand was alive or dead. And when I saw Addie, my heart concaved.

She was lifeless, sitting there with her head slumped over. I couldn't breathe.

My knees buckled and I smashed into the wall. The door to the plane was wide open. I looked out at the snow. Then I crawled forward to get some air. But I lost my balance and toppled down the stairs.

It knocked the breath out of me. Not that I'd had any to begin with.

I used my elbows to gain traction. I was trying to find shelter under a tree. But my strength gave out before I got there. I saw blood in the snow, and it took a few seconds for reality to kick in.

The blood was mine.

I gave up and lay down. Face first in the snow. It was so cold, but I felt hot all over.

It was a paralyzing shock. Addie was gone. And I'd

left her to die alone.

I shut my eyes, because it was easier. Then I prayed that I would see Addie soon.

* * *

"Tom!"

I groaned.

"Tom!"

What was that noise?

"Tom!"

Someone put their hand on my shoulder and rolled me over.

And then I saw her, looking up from the flat of my back. It was the voice of an angel.

"Tom." She buried her face in my chest, running her hands over my body.

"You're crying." I felt her shaking when I pressed my hand to her back.

"Oh God, Tom." She squeezed my ribs. "I thought you were dead."

It was hard for me to sit up, but she forced my torso into an upright position.

"Don't you ever do that to me again!" she yelled, slapping my arm.

"Ow." I furrowed my brow. "Why are you so mean?"

"Tom, you're bleeding." She touched my head. "Can you hear me?"

I nodded and held on to her arm.

"Stay awake." She shook me, because I felt like dozing off. "Tom!"

"I'm okay, I'm okay." Was she always this loud?

"We have to get help." She hauled me to my feet. "The pilot, I think he's dead."

I hugged her close, even though I could hardly keep my balance. "Where are we?"

"I don't know," she said. "But this doesn't look like Rome to me."

There was a reason for that. Because we never made it to Italy.

We'd crash landed in Switzerland instead.

Fernand and the pilot survived. But it took hours for us to get a signal in the plane. And when that failed, even longer to climb down the mountain in search of help. Turns out, we weren't far from the Swiss Alps. No wonder it felt like I was freezing to death.

The pilot was an American named Frank. And he had connections in every part of the world.

All thanks to Edmond of course—the perks of flying a private plane for a wealthy aristocrat.

Everyone received medical attention. Addie had minor injuries—despite hitting her head—just like Frank and Fernand. But I was mildly concussed from smashing into the window. It all left me feeling strange.

There was a private chalet waiting for us under a fake name. After brief communication, Edmond had stressed something important. *No phone calls.* Which was fine by me, but had Addie going crazy.

"I want to call Edmond. I want to call Dad. I want everyone to know we're okay."

I followed her into the chalet. It was a luxury cabin with enough room for ten guests. But Fernand was staying in the guest house next door. And Frank had a friend who lived nearby. So we had the place to ourselves.

"Edmond will let everyone know we're safe," I said.

She went straight to the master bedroom and

dropped our bags. I walked into the room and she turned around. The shades were drawn since it was night time. We hadn't even eaten dinner yet.

Addie gave me a look that made my heart race. I took a step and she was in my arms. Our tongues tangled in the dark as we slammed into the wall. She hooked her legs around my waist and whimpered.

I kept my mouth on hers, sliding my hands under her sweatshirt. She leaned back and took it off, wrapping her arms around my neck. It was so good to feel her warm skin. So soft. So smooth. So right.

I still couldn't believe she was mine.

I walked toward the bed and set her on the nightstand. The lamp fell over and she laughed, tugging my shirt over my head. I pulled her pants down and she took care of mine, peppering kisses on my stomach.

"Tom." She ran her hands down my back.

I picked her up and lay her down on the bed. She kicked our luggage until it toppled to the floor. Then she wrapped her limbs around me, running her nails down the back of my neck. I heard her groan.

"Tom, please," she begged. "Hurry."

I hovered above her and thought about kissing her neck.

She blinked up at me. "What is it?"

"We have to be gentle."

She cupped the back of my head and rubbed her nose against mine. "Screw gentle."

I laughed as she teased my lower lip. Her mouth was soft and sweet. I was glued to the kiss.

So I cradled her body in my arms and gave in to the wife I adored. She was perfect.

* * *

Addie put her head on my chest, running her hand down my torso.

I caught my breath and rubbed her back. She was lying on top of me.

And I was loving every minute of it.

"Wow." I looked at the ceiling. "It's never been like that before."

She leaned up and kissed me. I felt her grin against my lips. "I know."

Times like these, I was glad we'd waited. If we'd been having sex already, I wouldn't have been able to function. School would've been nearly impossible. Especially during the classes we had together.

How could I focus around her?

I would have needed her every minute.

When school started back, I didn't know what we were going to do. At least I'd have her in my bed every night. We probably wouldn't be getting much sleep. But it would be worth it.

I'd just have to make sure we didn't flunk our last semester of high school.

She pressed kisses into my pecs and then lay against me. I pulled the sheet over us and held her close. She fluttered her lashes against my skin, and I closed my eyes.

We'd never been so quick and frantic before. But sex was new to us. And if I'm being honest, it felt like we'd been cheated out of our honeymoon all over again. Couldn't we just enjoy each other for a change?

Why did someone always have to be chasing us?

"You're quiet," she said. "What are you thinking about?"

"If I tell you something, will you promise not to

freak out?" I asked.

Her body tensed. I massaged her shoulders, but it didn't help.

"You said you're tired of me keeping things from you. And you're right. You should know everything that's going on. But I don't want it to paralyze you, baby. You've already been through more than enough."

"What is it?" she asked.

"Promise me you won't freak out," I said. "We're perfectly safe."

"Okay."

"When we left the airport in Paris, I saw Valjean on the tarmac."

She sat up with the sheet draped around her. "What was he doing there?"

"I don't know." I leaned against the headboard. "But the plane malfunctioned."

She chewed on her lip. "Do you think he did it? Tampered with the engine or something?"

"I don't know." I kissed her shoulder. "I don't know."

She turned to me with a tender look. There was fear and innocence in her eyes.

"I want you to trust me." I touched the wedding ring on her finger. The one I'd given her. "I'm your husband now. I need you to believe in me. I can take care of you. Of us. No matter what happens."

"I believe in you." She curled her arms around my neck. "It's him I don't trust."

"I know, baby." I kissed her forehead. "But all this stress isn't good for you."

"I know."

I tucked her head under my chin and bundled her

in my arms. "You're safe with me."

"I really wanted to enjoy tonight," she murmured. "Just the two of us."

"Let's enjoy it then." I caressed her skin. "Are you hungry?"

"Yes." She kissed my stubbled jaw. "Very."

"Let's find the kitchen." I helped her out of bed and watched her get dressed. She put on sweatpants and the same sweatshirt she'd worn on the plane. But she might as well have been wearing a gown on the red carpet. Because she looked gorgeous to me.

"What are you looking at?" She pulled her hair back in a ponytail.

I got dressed and stood behind her in front of the mirror. "You."

She smiled at our reflection as I wrapped my arms around her stomach. I kissed her neck and she sighed, holding on to my hands. "If you keep doing that, we're never going to eat."

"Fair enough." I took her hand and led her into the kitchen.

There was a gift basket on the island with gourmet snacks. But I wanted to cook my wife a meal. The kitchen was stocked with a week's worth of food. Even on such short notice, Edmond had thought of everything.

I cooked wild salmon with brown rice and asparagus for dinner. Addie wanted to contribute, so she made a salad. There was a bottle of white wine, but we were both on pain meds. So we drank water instead, eating at the bar and talking about everything we could do while we were in Switzerland.

"What's for dessert?" Addie set her napkin down.

"I saw some ice cream in the freezer."

"Yum." She stretched her legs in my lap.

I got up and gave her a piggyback ride to the freezer. She found the ice cream and grabbed two spoons. Then I set her down on the counter and stood between her legs.

She opened a pint of mint chocolate chip ice cream and let me have the first bite. I took the extra spoon and fed her, kissing the corners of her mouth. But then I got distracted kissing my way down her neck.

"Tom," she gasped. "Your lips are cold."

I grabbed her legs and kissed her again. She dropped her spoon on the counter and I let mine go. Her arms went around me as I pulled her body into mine. She tilted her head back when I buried my face in her neck. I hadn't shaved, so I knew it tickled. But she wasn't laughing.

Addie sighed and put her forehead to mine. Her fingertips touched my lips.

"Do you want to take a shower?" I asked.

"Mm-hmm," she whimpered.

I picked her up and carried her to the master bathroom. There was a walk-in shower with frosted glass. I'd thought of running a bath. But with her hip, she couldn't be submerged in water. She had a bandage over it now, and I knew the area was tender. As always, I'd have to be careful with my new bride.

I walked into the shower with her in my arms. She leaned around me to turn the water on. As she adjusted the temperature, I planted kisses down her neck. She looked up at me and touched my cheek.

"I hope I get to do everything with you," she said.

I looked her in the eye. "You will."

We made love, and I wanted to do it everywhere. I

never wanted this feeling to go away.

As we got ready for bed, I really felt like a husband. She took care of my injuries from the plane crash. And I looked over her hip and any bruises she had left. It felt like we were a team. And I'd always thought that's what a marriage should be. Two people working together who really love each other.

Addie was looking through her suitcase when she froze. I sensed her anxiety from a mile away.

"What is it?" I touched her back, loving the feel of her wet skin. She was wrapped in a towel.

"Is there something else you forgot to tell me?" she asked.

"What?" I furrowed my brow.

"Edmond put something in my bag, too."

"What?" I pulled her arm until she turned around.

"This." She was holding the necklace in her hand.

Chapter 10

Addie

T om widened his eyes. They even turned dark, which scared me. He snatched the necklace up and looked closer, just to be sure it was really there. Then he squeezed the emerald inside his fist.

"Why would he put this in your bag?" he growled.

"I don't know. I thought it was at the castle."

"We've had it this whole time." He wound his arm back and threw the necklace at the mirror.

"Tom!" I screamed.

The necklace put a sharp crack in the mirror, and I heard the glass split.

"Why did you do that?" I picked the necklace up off the floor. "Now you broke the mirror!"

But when I turned the necklace over to inspect the stone, all I felt was *shock.*

"Look at this." I faced Tom. "The emerald, it's not even scratched."

It was true. The mirror was broken. But the necklace was unharmed.

"How is that possible?" I sat down on the bed. "And it's cold. Why is it always so cold?"

"I'm so sick of this." He put his hands behind his head. He was pacing. "Can I not have one damn night alone with my wife? That necklace follows us everywhere! It never leaves us alone!"

"I think you need to calm down." I touched his arm. Unlike the necklace, he felt *very* warm.

"*You* are telling *me* to calm down?"

That hurt, so I couldn't help lashing out. "I was trying to get better at that."

"That's it." He dug into his suitcase. "I'm calling Edmond."

"He said no phone calls."

"I don't care what he said. He slipped that necklace in your bag without asking first! That puts a target on our backs. Even if no one knows we have it but us. He should know better than that."

I stared until he looked at me.

"Well, shouldn't he?" he yelled.

"He said no phone calls," I repeated.

Tom pulled out his cell phone anyway.

"No!" I tackled him onto the bed and his phone hit the floor.

"Would you stop being so stubborn?" His face was red. Veins were popping out of his neck.

"You're the stubborn one," I said. "We're supposed to be in hiding, remember?"

"I don't care." He tried to sit up, and I tightened my grip.

"I do." I wrapped my hands around his wrists and squeezed.

"You want to keep it. Don't you?"

"Edmond must have put it in my bag for a reason," I said.

"He said it could get us killed." He squared his jaw from the flat of his back.

"He also said it would keep me alive. When I was in the hospital bleeding to death. Or have you already forgotten about that?" I asked.

He gave me a blazing smolder.

"My uncle isn't stupid. The only thing we have to worry about is Valjean."

He rolled his eyes.

"In the meantime, you're going to stay put and keep your mouth shut."

His lips lifted a little.

"If this was our last night on earth, I sure wouldn't want to spend it arguing."

He pursed his lips and relaxed. But his eyes stayed with me.

"You asked me to trust you and believe in you. Now it's time for you to believe in me."

He watched me and still managed to look smug.

"What?" I snapped, because it felt like he was mocking me.

"Nothin'," he grinned. "You're pretty cute when you're mad."

"Tom." I slapped his chest without realizing that it would free his arms.

He grabbed my wrists and sat up, while I balanced on his lap. I didn't know whether to hiss or laugh. And I was still mad at him, so I turned my head away. He ran his nose down my neck and whispered, "I'm sorry."

I looked at him and tried not to smile.

He hugged my waist and flashed me those doe eyes. "Do you forgive me?"

"Yes," I grouched.

"Good." He kissed my neck and reached the hollow of my throat.

I leaned my head back and started talking softer, slower. "But you are the most frustrating man."

He laughed and rubbed his beard on my throat. I

clung to him and yelped, nearly falling off his lap.

"You know, this necklace does look beautiful on you." He took it off the bed. Then he looked into my eyes. His were burning gold again, glistening with sweet desire. He slid the towel down my waist and laid the necklace against my chest. I held on to the stone as he fastened the clasp behind my neck. "There."

I ran my fingers over the silver chain. It felt cool to the touch. Just like the emerald.

He looked up at me and touched my hair. "I just want to keep you safe."

"I know." I leaned my cheek into his hand. "But you need to let me keep you safe, too."

He tugged at my earlobe and held my gaze. It might be the longest we'd ever shared.

We met in the middle, his lips crashing into mine. And I surrendered to every kind of ecstasy.

* * *

I woke up the next morning to an empty bed. Hearing voices in the kitchen, I slipped into a robe and ran my fingers through my hair. It was so dark in our room, like a cave, but I left the curtains closed.

Tom was talking to Frank and Fernand in the kitchen. Last night in bed, I'd mentioned inviting them over for breakfast. I must have slept in really late, but I was thankful Tom didn't wake me. I needed the rest.

"Good morning," I chimed, happy to see our guests.

Frank sat at the bar, while Fernand poured himself a glass of orange juice. There were waffles and bacon on the stove. And I saw a pan of scrambled eggs. But Tom sidestepped me and grabbed my arm.

"What the hell?" He adjusted the collar of my

robe so it hid the necklace.

"Sorry." I closed my eyes with a breath. I'd forgotten I was wearing it.

When Tom turned back around, Frank and Fernand greeted me. I made small talk and fixed a fruit salad. Since we'd arrived, a salad of some kind was all I'd been able to make. But I wanted to contribute something.

Frank was ex-military, and he'd been honorably discharged from the air force. It felt like a string I needed to pull, but I left it alone for now. In his mid-thirties, he had a wife and daughter who lived in Paris. He'd been working for Edmond for five years and sounded grateful for the job.

"I'm sorry we took you away from your family during the holidays," I said.

"It's okay." He had black hair and hazel eyes. "It was an emergency."

"So where are you from?" Tom handed Frank a cup of coffee.

"Dallas, Texas," he replied.

"I thought I heard some twang," I grinned, giving him a high five.

Tom slanted me a look in the kitchen.

"I met my wife while I was in the air force. France is her home."

I forced a smile and nodded. Tom stood so close our shoulders brushed.

"How about you, Fernand?" Tom asked. "Have we kept you away from your family?"

"No, monsieur. My wife, well, she's been gone a very long time," he said.

"Do you have any children?" I wondered.

"No. We never had children."

"I'm very sorry." I held on to Tom's arm. "I can't imagine."

"Edmond has looked out for me. I've been with him for forty years. His family feels like my family."

That explained a lot. Forty years. No wonder Edmond trusted him so implicitly.

"We're grateful that Edmond sent you here to look out for us." Tom put his arm around my shoulders. "But he's put you both in danger. Did he warn either of you about what's going on?"

Frank spoke for both of them. "We know more than you think."

"It's been all over the news," Fernand said. "Valjean and the stolen necklace."

I put my arm around Tom, and he pulled me closer.

"I saw him on the tarmac," Tom revealed, "when we left Paris."

"So did I," Frank confessed.

"I did, as well," Fernand said.

"What?" I snapped. "So everyone knew but me."

"Edmond warned me that this could be dangerous," Frank said.

"Then why leave your family?" There was no malice in my voice. Just blatant curiosity.

"I'm being paid *very* well."

"Do you think he could have tampered with the plane?" Tom asked.

"It's likely," Frank said. "I thought the same thing myself."

"Is there any way to know for sure?" I asked.

"Not right now," Frank said. "Someone would have to look into it."

"You put your lives on the line for us. At

Christmas. How can we ever thank you?" I said.

"Just doin' my job, ma'am," Frank said.

"As am I." Fernand looked serious.

Edmond had a good group of people surrounding him. People we could trust.

"What about the storm?" I asked. "Could that have been the reason we almost crashed?"

"The storm was rough," Frank said. "But I have a funny feeling it would have happened anyway."

That meant he believed someone had tampered with the plane. A chill shot down my spine.

Tom touched my back. "I'd actually like to go over it with you more. Maybe after breakfast?"

"Sure," Frank agreed. "I don't mind at all."

We ate breakfast in the den. And it was the first time I really looked at the place. The wood work was marvelous, like something only a seasoned architect could design. There was a stone fireplace large enough for the lobby of a hotel. But what had me distracted was the panoramic view. Windows stretched from floor to ceiling, exposing snow-covered mountains and tree tops. The glass was so clear that I was mesmerized, enchanted. I wanted to reach out and touch the skyline.

"Addie." Tom touched my shoulder. "You okay?"

I blinked and looked at our guests. They were both waiting for me to say something.

"Umm, yeah." I saw an atlas on the coffee table. Tom had marked the place we landed with a red marker. There were black dots denoting the original flight plan from Paris to Italy. "I think I'm gonna go take a shower."

"Okay." He rubbed my back. "I'll be right back," he said to the men.

I told Frank and Fernand goodbye, thanking them for all they'd done.

Tom put his arm around my waist and led me to the bedroom. "You feelin' okay?"

"Yeah." I closed my eyes. "I'm just a little tired."

He caressed my cheek. "Give me a few minutes, and I'll join you."

"Sounds good." I blushed when he kissed me. Even now, it made me tingle all over.

He left and I walked into the en suite bathroom. There was a garden tub against the far wall and a walk-in shower that we'd used last night. I bit my lip and blushed at the memory of my hand pressed against the frosted glass.

Sex was unlike anything I'd ever imagined. The reality surpassed the fantasy ten times over.

I stood by the mirror and looked at my reflection. Even my appearance showed that something had changed. I glowed where I used to shy away.

I was happy.

I took my robe off, and it pooled at my feet. I hadn't examined my naked body in so long. Maybe not ever like this. I was wearing the necklace and nothing else. It glimmered beneath the skylight as I studied every fleck of green. Had my grandmother ever worn it like this? How about Josette?

Maybe it'd been the same for Daniel and Antoinette, Jimmy and Josette, as it was for us.

Was it too much to believe that three generations of women had shared the same kind of love?

A trifecta of stubborn blondes falling for tall, dark and handsome over and over again?

I turned the shower on and the sun disappeared. Confused, I looked up and saw someone standing on the skylight. I backed into the wall and they kept walking. I'd seen the intruder's boots and nothing else.

I put my robe back on and ran into the den. Tom jumped up when he saw me, taking my hand.

"What? What is it?"

I could hardly catch my breath. "There's someone on the roof."

"Monsieur!" Fernand yelled.

There was a masked man scaling the window outside. He pulled out a gun and shot through the glass.

"Ah!" I screamed.

Tom pushed me behind the bar and lay on top of me. I heard bullets flying as glass shattered on the floor. Then there was silence. The kind that made me shake. Tom rose up and put a finger to his lips.

I didn't want him to go. I was too scared something might happen to him.

He draped his arm over my stomach and got on his knees. I clung to his arm and watched, searching for truth in his eyes. There were footsteps and then a loud thwack. Enough to get Tom on his feet.

"Stay here," he whispered, squeezing my hand.

He left me on the floor. But I couldn't just shut my eyes and wait. Not with all the noise.

I peered around the bar, but Fernand was standing in my way. He moved to grab a chair, and then Frank tied the intruder to it. Tom paced the den with a pistol in his hand. I'd never seen him like this.

"Who are you?" Frank said. "Did Valjean send you?"

The intruder was wearing a ski mask. When he didn't answer, Frank ripped it off.

Everyone took a noticeable breath, and my blood

ran cold.

It was Valjean.

Frank punched him in the face. "You could have killed us!" He kicked his legs. "I'm the pilot. Their lives were in *my* hands! And you did it! Didn't you?" He hit Valjean until he turned over in the chair.

"Frank." Tom touched his shoulder. "Take it easy, man."

Frank hit him again. Valjean was lying awkwardly on the floor. There was blood on his face.

For some reason, I couldn't bear to watch. Especially when he saw me.

Caught in the act, I came out from behind the bar. Fernand and Tom put his chair right side up while Frank stood at a distance. When I walked in the den, Valjean was still watching me. Tom tightened the restraints.

"What did you tie him up with?" I asked.

"Sheets," Frank said, catching his breath. "We found them in the hall closet."

I spotted an open door down the hall. There were linens spilling out on the floor.

"Are you okay?" Tom slipped his arm down my back.

I nodded and turned into him. We were standing dangerously close to Valjean. It surprised me.

He spit blood on the floor. "You stupid Americans. You let her walk around with it."

I touched the emerald on my breast. It had slipped out from the robe again.

"Is this what you want?" I asked.

His eyes ran up and down my figure. Then they settled on the stone in my hand.

"I thought I did," he admitted. "Once."

"It's not my place, Mrs. Sutton," Frank said. "But after everything he's done to you, I see no reason why this man has a right to live."

Valjean shifted in his seat. But his eyes stayed with me.

"I wanted you to die," I said. "But I just don't think you're worth it."

"You can't leave me tied up here. You can't hold me against my will."

"You're the one who broke in," Tom said. "You shot the glass with your gun."

There was bloodlust in his eyes. Not the kind Frank had. Tom was slow and deliberate.

"Whatever happens here, no one will believe you. If you even live to talk about it."

"I don't want to play a part in this game anymore," Valjean said. "I'm just here to take the necklace to the scientist."

"What scientist?" I asked.

"Gustav Lehmann."

Frank cocked a pistol and aimed it at Valjean. "Talk."

"Who is Gustav Lehmann?" I asked.

"A German scientist," Frank gasped. He actually looked afraid. "He believes there is a chemical compound in your necklace. He wants to extract it and test it."

"Test it for what?" Tom asked.

Valjean exhaled. He was sweating bullets. "He believes it will cure any ailment."

"Like a miracle drug?" I said.

"Yes," Valjean hissed. "Precisely."

"Where does Gustav live?" Tom asked.

"Munich."

"What's the address?" I grabbed a notepad and a pen.

Valjean was shaking in his boots. Especially when Frank put the pistol to his stomach. "Tell her!"

My pulse was racing, because I never thought I'd live to see the day. We had Valjean like a mouse in a trap. Maybe we could finally get some answers. And end the danger in our lives for good.

Valjean spouted off an address, which I wrote down as fast as I could.

"How did you come in contact with Tony DeMilo?" I asked.

"He hired me to steal the necklace. He was going to take it to the scientist. Tony believed Gustav could cure him."

"So what—you were only in it for the money?" I asked.

"In the beginning, yes." He was still shaking.

"And then what?" I said.

"I have a daughter. She's very ill. I thought if I stole the necklace, he could heal her."

"Don't believe him, Addie," Frank said. "He's lying."

I grabbed Tom by the arm and led him behind the kitchen counter. "I think we should call the police."

"So do I," he said. "He's a wanted thief. They should expedite him to France and lock him up."

I nodded, holding on to him for support. "But what happens then? Does he get off?"

Tom thought about it.

"What are we going to do with the necklace?" I asked.

He covered it with my robe. "I don't know."

"Maybe we should wait."

"What are you talking about?" he asked.

"Let's keep interrogating him. We need information, Tom. If this is ever going to end."

"How can you trust a word he says?" He looked at the notepad in my hand. "I'm sure he just fed you a fake address. You really believe he would tell us the truth?" He squeezed my arm. "Baby, this is the man who tried to kill you."

"I know." I looked over his shoulder at Valjean. He was sitting in the same chair, watching me.

"Let's just call the police and get him out of here. And maybe we should just go home."

"Okay," I said. "You're right. I'm sick of this. It's gone on long enough."

Tom kissed my forehead and went into the other room to make the call. I walked back into the den where Frank and Fernand were keeping a close eye on Valjean. He stared me down as I entered.

"You're a beautiful woman, Mrs. Sutton."

Frank clenched his jaw, and even Fernand looked uncomfortable. I chose to ignore the compliment.

"You look so much like your mother," he said.

I froze completely. He'd struck a chord.

"You knew my mother?" I asked.

"Yes." He smiled. "We were close. *Very* close."

"You're lying," I said. "You don't know my mother. You've never even seen her."

"I could tell you things," he teased. "Lots of things."

He'd gotten in my head. One minute, he was scared. The next, confident and relaxed.

I left and found Tom in the back. "Don't call them."

"What?" He hung up his cell phone.

133

"Did you talk to the police?" I asked.

"Not yet. I couldn't get a signal."

I took a breath. "I think we should wait."

"Wait?" He thought I was crazy.

"Keep him here, make him answer questions."

"Addie, he's already told us everything we need to know."

"Valjean knows my mother. My real mother."

He blinked. "What?"

"I want him to tell me about her."

"You don't think he's lying?"

"I don't know why, but I believe him."

He tilted his head back and took a breath.

"It's just a delay," I said. "We can report him later."

"I don't like this."

"I don't either." I touched his arm. "But I don't know what else to do."

He pulled me into his arms and we shared a warm hug. One that I could've gotten lost in for days.

But we had a jewel thief in the den. So you could say that the honeymoon wasn't going exactly as planned.

Chapter 11

Tom

I'll be the first to admit it. I wasn't too excited about Addie's plan to keep Valjean around. But I couldn't tell her no.

In her eyes, I saw innocence and beauty. She wanted so badly to believe he was telling the truth. But I had no doubt in my mind that it was a trap.

Hours later, after some serious questioning, Addie hadn't gotten the first answer out of him. He'd been quiet for most of the interrogation. And I felt like he'd only said Josette's name to string Addie along.

We ate dinner and let Valjean starve. But he had a will of iron. There seemed to be no way of getting words out of him. I felt like he had all the right cards. And he knew how to play them. But I didn't want to tell Addie that she'd been duped once again.

It was getting late, and Valjean had gone mute for hours. Frank and Fernand volunteered to stay up and watch him, so Addie and I could get some sleep. But I didn't like the idea of leaving them to fend for themselves. They'd already put their necks out for us enough this week.

"Listen to me." Frank pulled me to the side. "I learned tactics in the military. I know how to get it out of him. But that's not going to happen when your pretty little wife is in the room."

I sighed, because I knew he was right.

"Get some sleep." Frank patted my back. "We can take care of him."

"All right," I said. "I just don't want to leave y'all holding the bag."

"You're not." Frank eyed Valjean across the room. "Trust me. I was born for this."

Addie looked displeased, but I didn't know what else to tell her. She left the den and went straight to our bedroom. I flinched when she slammed the door. Her anger wasn't directed at me. But I had a feeling I'd be the one absorbing the full effects of everything Valjean had put her through.

I came into the bedroom and shut the door. She sat on the edge of our bed, brushing her hair.

"Do you want to take a shower?" I asked.

"No." She pulled the brush through her hair in quick strokes. It looked like it hurt.

"What do you want me to do?" I moved closer but was too afraid to touch her.

"Nothing." She set the brush down and sighed. "There's nothing you can do."

"I've never thought he was someone we could trust." I took my shirt off and tossed it in the closet. "You shouldn't feel bad about—"

"Just say it," she hissed.

"Say what?"

She kept her back to me. "That I'm wrong and you're right. I'm sure you've been dying to say I told you so."

"No, I haven't."

"Well, you must think I'm stupid!" she yelled.

I saw her shoulders heave and knew she was crying.

"Baby, I don't think you're stupid." I crawled across the bed and touched her back. "Come here."

She turned around and looked at me. "I feel like an idiot."

I pulled her close and ran my fingers through her hair. "You're not an idiot, Addie."

"I really thought he was going to tell me something," she sobbed. "How could I believe him?"

"Because I think you want to believe that everyone is good. But they're not."

"I know." She wrapped her arms around me and squeezed. "You're right."

"That doesn't mean you're stupid. Okay?" She nodded. "You're the smartest girl I know."

"You really think so?" She looked up at me in that adorable way—her eyes like emeralds.

"Yes." I rubbed her back as she trembled in my arms.

"I think you're pretty smart, too," she whispered.

"Oh yeah?" I shot her a grin.

"Yeah." She nuzzled my neck and kissed my shoulder.

I lifted her chin and kissed her back, pulling her body into mine. She cooed and lost herself in the moment. I lay her down on the bed and turned out the light. And she pulled me on top of her.

* * *

"I love you," Addie whispered.

We lay tangled in each other's arms, and I didn't want to move. We'd been staring at each other in the dark for a long time. And it felt like paradise.

"I love you, too." I ran my fingers down her back. It made her look sleepy.

"Tomorrow, we'll get it out of him." She yawned and closed her eyes.

"I have to brush my teeth." I kissed her forehead. "I'll be right back."

She dozed off as I looked for my clothes in the dark. I pulled on my sweatpants and went to the bathroom. My hair was a mess, and I looked totally worn out. But I grabbed the toothpaste and brushed my teeth, dying to climb back into bed and go to sleep with Addie.

But then I heard something that sounded like a gunshot, and the toothbrush slipped out of my hand. I spit in the sink and heard shouting as I hustled towards the den.

"Tom." Addie crashed into me, and I wrapped my arm around her.

"Come here, baby." I held her close as we walked together.

Fernand was lying on the floor, but he didn't appear to be injured. And Frank was nowhere to be seen.

"What happened?" I helped Fernand to his feet. He was so shaken he had to take a seat.

"It's Valjean. He got away."

"What do you mean?" Addie asked.

Fernand pointed at the wall of broken glass. So I approached the edge and looked out. It was pitch black, and the ground was covered in snow. Even from here, I could make out blood in the tracks.

"Where is Frank?" I asked.

"He went after him."

Addie shot me a terrified look. So I grabbed her hand and pulled her into my arms.

"Poor Frank," she whispered. I rubbed her back as

everything sank in.

Without Frank, I had no idea how to protect her from Valjean. We could fly back to Paris. But it wouldn't be on a private plane. And I hated putting Fernand's life in jeopardy yet again.

"I heard a gunshot," she said.

"I did too."

"Do you think it was Frank or Valjean?"

I lifted her chin. "I don't know."

There were tears in her eyes. And I didn't know what to say, what to do. Addie put her head on my chest, so I held her tight and tried to think. So many times, I'd been afraid it was our last night. But what if all this had finally caught up with us? Maybe we should get rid of the necklace once and for all.

We had each other, but that came at a steep price. Addie had lost so much recently, and I didn't want to keep putting her through that. It was time to go home and start a new life together. One where she would be happy and safe.

"Baby." I leaned her head back. "I think it might be time for us to go home."

She furrowed her brow and stared into my eyes. "Okay."

"I can't lose you." I cupped her cheek. "I couldn't live with myself."

She squeezed my back and cried into my chest. "I thought it would be different."

"What?" I tucked her head beneath my chin.

"Eloping in Paris."

"Best laid plans?" I said.

"Something like that."

"Monsieur," Fernand said.

At the sound of footsteps, I turned around. Frank

walked into the room. He looked rough. But he was alive.

"Frank!" Addie helped him to a chair. "You're alive. Thank God. What happened?"

"Water. Please." He could hardly keep his shoulders up.

I grabbed him a glass of water. But sipping it was a struggle for him.

"I was interrogating him. And he got his hands free. I don't know how."

Addie gave him more water. He was so weak, she had to help him drink.

"Then what?" she asked.

"He jumped." He pointed at the broken glass. "So I went after him."

"Did you find him?" I asked.

"I tried. Believe me. But he's good. Really good."

"So he's..."

"Gone." Frank looked defeated.

"It's okay, man." I patted him on the shoulder.

"No, it's not."

Frank pulled a strip of paper out of his pocket. "I found this."

Addie stood up, and he handed it to her. She opened the message. I leaned over her shoulder to read it.

I won't return. I'm not the one looking for you now.

"What is that supposed to mean?" Addie asked.

I looked at the note. "I don't know."

"If I were you, I'd go back to America," Frank said.

"But what about the necklace?" Addie asked.

"Is it worth your life?" He darted his eyes between

VIOLET BLOOD

us.

"Yeah, he's right." I touched her shoulder. "We should probably leave first thing."

She backed away with her head down. "All right."

"We'll make sure you all receive safe transportation back to Paris," I said.

"Thank you, monsieur." Fernand bowed his head and left the room.

"I have a friend who can help me charter a private plane," Frank said.

"Well?" I looked at Addie and shrugged.

"I don't care." She walked away.

"Why don't you stay here tonight? There are plenty of rooms." I called out to Fernand and told him the same thing. "We'll figure all this out in the morning. But I'm happy to leave first thing."

They nodded in agreement, just as ready to be out of here.

I turned out the lights and found Addie in our bedroom. When I shut the door, it was so dark. I tripped on my way to the bed and fumbled around until I managed to slip beneath the covers.

"Hey." I draped my arm across her stomach, pulling her back to my chest.

"I don't want to talk about it."

"Addie, I don't know what else you want me to do." I kissed her neck. "It's time to go home."

"And where is that exactly?" Her voice cracked on the last word.

"Savannah."

"Yeah."

"What's wrong?" I asked.

"I just thought by now we'd finally have some answers."

141

"Maybe we're not supposed to know." I caressed her arm.

"And what about the necklace?" she whispered.

"I think you should give it to Edmond. He'll know what to do."

"All right."

"Hey." I leaned over her shoulder to get a good look at her.

"What?"

"Everything is gonna be all right. We're married now. We're starting our life together."

"I guess I'll never know what really happened." She looked off. "Do you think there was any truth to what Valjean said? Do you think there really is a scientist who—?"

"You can't believe anything he says. He's a thief."

"I know that," she said. "But I believed him."

"Why don't you try to get some sleep?" I ran my fingers through her hair and kissed her cheek. "We're leaving in the morning. Everything is going to get better from here. Okay?"

"Okay." She squeezed my hand. "Tom? I love you."

"I love you, too."

She fell asleep wrapped in my arms.

But I could already feel her pulling away.

* * *

We left the next morning for Paris. Frank pulled through on his offer to charter a private plane. While I hesitated at first, it was better than risking something going wrong in the airport. We'd been in an airport the first time Addie saw Valjean. So flying private felt like a lesser risk.

When we took off, I felt like throwing up. The last time we'd almost died. But I'd always heard that driving on the interstate was more dangerous than flying on a plane. As far as statistics were concerned.

Addie sat quietly and looked out the window. I watched her, wondering what to say. Nothing seemed right. I reached for her hand and squeezed it. But she didn't squeeze back. She didn't even look at me.

"What's wrong?" I asked.

"Nothing."

"What's with you?" I smiled, but she kept her eyes on the clouds. "Did I do something wrong?"

"No. You didn't do anything wrong."

"Then why does it feel like you're mad at me?"

She sighed. "I'm not mad at you."

"Then what is it?" I asked.

She looked at me. "Do we have to talk about it right now?" She darted her eyes at the cockpit.

"If you want privacy, we can talk in the back."

"I don't want privacy, Tom." She crossed her arms over her chest. "I just want to get off this plane and be home."

"Well, Frank is getting us there as fast as he can."

"I know that."

"I'll leave you alone." I got up and headed for the back. "Since you don't feel like talking right now."

She folded her hands in her lap and kept staring out the window. I watched her for a minute before I went to the bedroom. It was like she was daydreaming or something. Lost in la la land. It wasn't like her.

I took a nap, because I hadn't slept well last night. Addie woke me up before we landed. But she was out of the room just as quickly as she came into it. The closer we got to home, the greater the distance was between us.

Back at the castle, things weren't much different. I thought being with family might lighten her mood. But Addie was quiet and dark. Like an alien had invaded her body. It felt like I didn't know her at all.

"There's my beautiful niece," Edmond said. He greeted us at the front door, smoking a cigar.

Ashton and Juliette were there, too. And Adeline was so happy to see us. But Addie went straight upstairs without saying a word to anyone. I stood at the bottom of the staircase and stared.

Josette found me in the foyer. "What happened?"

"Valjean got away." I looked at Jimmy as he came into the room. "It's late. I'll see you all in the morning."

I went upstairs and put my ear to our door. But it was quiet. That couldn't be good.

I knocked first. Even though we'd been sleeping here together since the wedding.

"Come in," she said.

I opened the door and saw her closing the curtains. She had already changed clothes. And it was nearly impossible to get her to look me in the eye. So I shut the door and set my bags down.

"You don't want to eat?" I asked.

"I'm not hungry." She turned the covers down and climbed into bed.

"But you've hardly eaten anything all day."

"I told you I wasn't hungry," she snipped.

I sat down and rubbed my neck, at a loss for words. I wasn't used to her acting like this. Was this what happened when you put a ring on it? I thought married life was going to be so good. And it had been so far. Apart from the shooting and the plane crash.

But something was different. My wife was different. It was all so strange.

"Okay." I left and went downstairs. She obviously didn't want me around.

Everyone had scattered. And I wondered if I'd run off too quickly. But Addie hadn't even acknowledged anyone. And that wasn't like her at all. Something was wrong.

And it was scaring the hell out of me.

The kitchen was empty. But I found leftovers in the fridge. I was so hungry, I didn't bother warming anything up. I heard footsteps and froze, hoping it was Addie. Maybe we could make up.

"There's some pie in the fridge."

I turned around as Josette walked in the room.

"Oh, thanks."

She cut me a slice and handed me a fork.

"What's going on, Tom? Tell me about my daughter."

I took a bite and then set it aside. "I'm worried."

"Why?" She pulled up a chair and sat in it.

"She won't talk to me. And I don't know why."

"When did this happen?" she asked.

"Not until we flew back today." I thought for a second. "But she was acting weird last night, too."

"Do you think she's upset about Valjean?" She cut herself a slice of pie. "It must have been traumatizing, seeing him again."

"I don't think that's it. She was actually pretty calm through the whole thing."

"Then what is it?"

I bit my nail and hesitated.

"You can tell me. I'm her mother."

"Well, maybe I should let her tell you. But

Addie..." I looked away. "She can't. I mean, they don't think we'll be able to—"

"Thomas." Edmond appeared in the room. I hadn't even heard him coming.

"Yeah?"

"We need to talk." He looked at Josette. "Now."

"All right." I smiled at Josette. "I'll be back."

She nodded, and I followed Edmond down the hall to his study.

He shut the door and I took a seat. He came around the desk and lit another cigar.

"What have I told you about those?" I said.

"Something wise, I'm sure." He took a drag and smiled.

"What's this about?" I wanted to get back in bed with Addie. Even if she hated me.

"It's about you going home to America."

"What about it?" I asked.

"I'd like to hire security to watch you at all times."

I frowned and adjusted my posture in the chair.

"It's not as bad as it sounds. You won't even know they're there. And Addie doesn't have to know."

"How does keeping it from her help?" I asked. "You really think she's not smart enough to figure it out on her own?"

"She's smart enough. But she won't like it. So give her a couple weeks of bliss."

"You mean of ignorance," I said.

"Ignorance is bliss." He leaned his head back and blew smoke up at the ceiling.

"Is this the only reason you brought me in here?" I stood up. "I'm going to bed."

"She's not happy, Tom."

I froze and turned back around. "It's probably

from all the stress."

"You know that girl wants a baby one day."

It dawned on me. "So that's it? That's why she's so upset."

"She's a woman, Tom. They all want babies."

I approached his desk. "But what is that supposed to mean? I want kids, too."

"This is not the life she signed up for."

"Well, what do you want me to do about it?" I threw my hands in the air.

"Make her see how good it can be."

"What?" I asked.

"Your life together."

He patted my shoulder and left the room. I stood there for a while, looking at the pictures on his desk. There was one of Grandpa with Antoinette. I wondered how he had been able to make her happy.

I was a husband now. There was no room for a boy. I'd already had to grow into a man.

I trudged back to the kitchen. But Josette was gone. And she'd already put up the pie.

I had no idea what to do about Addie. On my way upstairs, I thought of ways to cheer her up. But she'd never been told that she was infertile before. Even if we loved each other, didn't that change everything?

I opened the bedroom door and slipped inside. It sounded like she was crying. But she was quiet when I closed the door. I stared at her back for a long time. Then I went to the bathroom and brushed my teeth.

When I returned, she was still lying there in bed. I took off my clothes and lay down beside her.

I'd been thinking in the bathroom. And maybe it was better if I said nothing at all. She'd been trying to tell me that she needed space. At least, that's what I figured. So I decided not to push her anymore.

I lay there and closed my eyes, tired from the long day. But then I heard the bed creak. If she left the room, I wouldn't be able to stay quiet. It had been torture to feel so distanced from her all day.

Her head dropped to my chest, and I felt her arm tighten around my waist.

"I'm sorry," she whispered.

I let out a sigh of relief and took her hand. "It's okay."

"No, it's not." She sat up. "I was horrible to you today."

I threaded my fingers in her hair. She looked like an angel in the moonlight.

"I'm sorry, Tom." She bowed her head. "I'm so, so sorry."

"Come here." I adjusted the covers as she lay down beside me.

"I love you." She ran her hand down my stomach. "So much."

"What happened today?"

"I don't know," she croaked. "I just feel really sad."

"About what?"

"I don't even know. That's what's so stupid about it."

"It's not stupid." I rubbed her hand.

"It's just that we're going back to Savannah tomorrow."

"You don't want to go?" I asked.

"No, that's not it."

"Then what it is, baby?" I lifted her chin so she would look at me.

"So much has happened here. We got married

and I met my family."

"Yeah." I petted her hair and stroked her earlobe.

"It just finally feels like home."

"We can visit. It's not like you're never going to see them again."

"I know that." She looked into my eyes. "But I wish we could stay longer."

"You're not upset about something else. Are you?" I wondered.

"No, why?"

"I just thought you might be thinking about what the doctor said."

She bit her lip and sighed. Then she put her head on my chest. "I have thought about it."

So Edmond was right. But this was a problem I couldn't solve. I couldn't be her Mr. Fix It. Not when it came to having a baby.

"But I try not to think about it." She traced my ribs with her fingertips. "Because I get depressed."

"There are still so many things we can enjoy before we start thinking about kids."

"I know that." She kissed my sternum. "But I'm a woman. I can't help thinking about it. I've been dreaming about being pregnant my whole life. I've always looked forward to having kids."

That made my heart ache. How could I ever make her happy?

"But I have to believe that everything will work out." She touched my beard. "And we still have so much to look forward to. I mean, we haven't even started college yet."

"I know. And we have each other."

She smiled in the dark. "I'm sorry I got so down."

"It's okay."

"I was mean."

I chuckled. "You weren't that bad."

She narrowed her eyes at me.

"Fine. You were mean. Are you happy?"

She giggled and straddled my waist.

"I know how you can make it up to me."

"Oh, really?" She kissed me. "And how's that?"

"I think you know, Mrs. Sutton."

"Do I?" She leaned over me and kissed my cheek.

"Yes." I sat up and wrapped my arms around her. "You're very intuitive like that."

She tilted her head to the side, and I left a string of kisses there. Her fingers twisted in my hair as I rolled her over. She lay beneath me and looked up, showing me those gorgeous bedroom eyes.

"You know what the best Christmas present I ever got was?"

"What?" I straightened my arms along either side of her.

She stroked my back and purred, "You."

I made love to her in the castle. Our last night in Europe.

And it was a moment we would always remember.

Chapter 12

Addie

I woke up with a smile on my face. The sun was shining through our bedroom window. And Tom lay against me with his arm around my waist. It felt so good to be held like this.

Turning over, I put my head on his chest and sighed. I'd always loved watching him sleep. But listening to him breathe was even better. I pulled the sheet over us and looked at the luxury bedroom.

It felt like we'd just gotten here. How could it already be time to leave?

I'd never enjoyed going back to school after a long break. But this was different.

I was different.

Tom groaned and shifted beneath me. A few seconds later, the alarm went off. So he reached for his phone on the nightstand and silenced it. I buried my face in his chest and closed my eyes.

"We have to get up." He rubbed my back and shoulders. "But I really don't want to."

"Neither do I." I kissed my way up his torso until our lips met.

"Do you want to eat now or wait 'til we get to the airport?"

"Airport," I mumbled, holding on to him as he sat up.

"Okay." He tried to get out of bed. "Baby, let go," he chuckled.

"No," I whined, pouting shamelessly. "Let's stay here forever."

He stood up and pulled me into a hug. I squeezed him with everything I had in me. And when he leaned his head back, there was a spark of curiosity in his eyes. He gave me a quick kiss and asked, "Are you okay?"

"Yeah," I shrugged. "I guess. Just sad to be leaving."

"I know." He touched my cheek. "But we'll be back. And you still have me."

I smiled and he kissed me again. "I should get dressed and finish packing."

He lifted me out of bed in his arms. It felt like a fairy tale. And I loved him for that.

While I was getting ready, he took our luggage downstairs. I brushed my teeth and put on some comfortable clothes. We would be in the airport or on a plane for most of the day. So I pulled my hair back and slipped into some cozy boots.

I finished packing in the bedroom and looked out the window. It was so beautiful here—like a winter wonderland. I would miss the snow. I would miss the castle. I would miss everything.

A knock on the door snapped me out of my daydream.

"Come in." I zipped my suitcase and sat down on the bed.

"Hi." Josette came in and shut the door behind her.

"Hi." It was a little awkward. Since we'd never had a real heart to heart.

"You and Tom all ready for Savannah?" she asked.

"Yep." I nodded, crossing my arms over my chest.

"Listen, Addie." She slipped her hands in her pockets. "I owe you an explanation."

I knew where this was headed. "No, it's okay."

"It's not." She came closer and touched my arm. "You feel like I abandoned you."

"Well, you did." I forced a smile to make it seem polite. "But I think we've moved past that."

"I'd really like to tell you what happened."

I looked at the floor. "I don't want to talk about it. I forgive you, for whatever you did."

"But Addie—"

"Look, I've spent my whole life feeling like no one wanted me, like I didn't belong. And now I've finally found a family. I don't need to know all the reasons. I love you. Okay?" I gave her a hug. "And I don't think it's healthy to go digging up the past. Whatever reason you did what you did, I don't want to know. Okay?"

There were tears in her eyes. "I really think it would be better if you let me explain."

"Do you want to be in my life?" I asked.

"Yes. Of course."

"Well, I want to be in yours. So that's all we need to know."

Tom came in the room and grabbed the bags we had left. "Are you ready to go?"

"Yeah." I looked back at Josette. "Are you going to see us off?"

She nodded and walked with us down the staircase. We talked for a few minutes until it was time to say our goodbyes. I hugged them all—Josette. Ashton. Juliette. Adeline. Jimmy. He would be back home in

Georgia soon. And we made plans to see him then. But Edmond—I would miss him most of all.

"You take care of my niece," he told Tom.

"I will, sir." They shook hands, and that's when I started to cry.

"No." Edmond saw Josette tearing up too. "None of that."

I laughed and he hugged me again. He smelled like cigars.

"We'll be back to visit," Tom said. "Soon hopefully."

"I'll hold you to that," Edmond said.

We walked outside, and Fernand was waiting with a car. He opened the back door, and I slipped inside. Once Tom got in, Fernand shut the door and I felt like dying. I hated this. So much.

I waved out the back window as Fernand sped away. Josette went inside and Jimmy hurried after her. She looked upset. I rolled up the window and watched the castle dissipate into the horizon.

Tom took my hand and held it all the way to the airport. There, I had the hardest time saying goodbye to Fernand. We'd been through so much together. And I didn't know how to thank him.

"I'll never forget you," I said. "You're one of the kindest people I know."

"Well, thank you, mademoiselle." As always, his French accent was exquisite.

Tom shook his hand. "Thank you, Fernand. For everything."

"If you see Frank, tell him we said hello," I muttered. Frank was already with his family. So we'd parted ways with him yesterday.

"I will." Fernand smiled.

I kissed him on the cheek. "Goodbye."

Tom took my hand, and we headed inside. It was hard not to look back.

On the plane, I looked out the window and tried not to cry. But every minute, I was moving farther and farther away from my family. Eventually, I had to be brave and look forward to all that lay ahead.

Tom lifted the arm rest between us and pulled me into his arms. I lay against him and watched the clouds drifting by. This was one of the hardest things I'd ever had to do. I hoped I never had to do it again.

* * *

When we landed, I felt very sad. Savannah didn't feel like home anymore. It never had.

"What are we gonna do with my stuff?" I asked Tom in the car.

"What do you mean?" He signaled and changed lanes, already sucked back into reality.

"I don't have any of my stuff at your place."

He looked at me and then focused on the road. "Just stay with me tonight. And we can move everything later this week."

"Okay. That sounds fine."

"You do want to live with me," he said. "Right?"

"Of course I do." I squeezed his hand. "It's just that I'm not on the best terms with them right now."

"You can call them by their names, you know." He threaded his fingers through mine.

"I don't know what to call them anymore."

"Is that what you're worried about?" he asked. "What they're gonna say when you move out?"

"I just feel like they hate me." I felt my throat closing up. "And it's not like I've said the nicest things about them. But I hate when they make me choose between the two of them."

"Between Jeffrey and Eleanor?"

"Between my biological parents and my adoptive parents," I sighed.

"You probably don't want to hear this. But I think they all love you. Just in a different way."

"The things they've done haven't felt like love." I saw the mansion in the distance.

"Yeah, but you've forgiven Jimmy and Josette. I think Jeffrey was just jealous and hurt. And Eleanor—"

"Do we have to talk about this right now?"

He watched me, but I didn't meet his gaze. "No. I guess not."

I leaned into the door and took a deep breath.

He parked in the driveway and turned the car off. "Addie, what's going on?"

"Nothing," I whined. "I just hate being home."

"Why?"

"Because it doesn't feel like home anymore." A lonely tear streaked down from my eye.

"Because of me?" he asked.

"No."

"You don't want to live here with me?"

"No. That's not it."

"Then what is it? Tell me. Please."

I looked him in the eye. "I've been so excited to move in with you. And I'm so happy we got married. None of this has anything to do with you. Okay?"

He nodded. "Then what is it, Addie? What's wrong?"

"I don't think I can make it through this last semester."

"Addie, what are you talking about? It's senior

year. We're almost done. And then we can go off to college and—"

"No, I mean, I don't think I can live here anymore."

"What?"

"I hate it here," I said. "I've always hated it here. You're the only good thing I've ever had in Savannah."

"You're telling me that all of a sudden, you hate your hometown? The place you were born and raised?"

"It's not Savannah. It's being away from the people I love. When am I going to see them? Once a year?"

He sighed and scratched his chin. "If you miss your family, I understand that. But it's not just about you. I'm your family, too. And you want me to uproot my whole life and move to Europe?"

"I didn't say anything about moving."

"Well, you didn't have to." He got out of the car and went inside. I flinched when he slammed the door. And then I hung my head and cried. We'd rushed into this marriage. What if it was a huge mistake?

I headed inside and went upstairs. Now that we were married, I'd be sharing a bedroom with Tom. I heard him in the shower and set my bags down. Then I let myself into the steam-filled room.

He stood behind the frosted glass, letting the water wash over him. I took my clothes off and looked in the mirror. There was a bandage on my hip. And I tried not to think about what it meant.

I stepped into the shower and put my head on his back. He stiffened at my touch. And that made me pull away. But then he grabbed my hands and wrapped them around his stomach.

I pressed my cheek into his shoulder blades and breathed him in. We stood like that for the longest time until he turned around. I was about to start apologizing, but he shook his head and kissed me instead.

Then I forgot everything and ran my fingers through his hair. His lips descended my neck. And I knew that we needed this now more than ever. He leaned my body against the wall. And I lost myself in him.

* * *

Afterwards, we lay beside each other in his bedroom. It was strange—staring at the familiar ceiling. I'd spent the night here a hundred times. But we'd never done something as hot as that.

Tom took a breath and laughed.

"What?" I propped up on my elbow, watching him.

"Is this what marriage is like?"

I traced my knuckle over his cheek. And he closed his eyes to relish my touch.

"What do you mean?" I asked.

"We argue. We make love." He looked into my eyes. "And then we do it all over again."

"Lather. Rinse. Repeat."

He narrowed his eyes. "Are you saying our sex life is like washing your hair?"

"No!" I giggled, scooting closer to him.

"Then please explain before my manhood is gone for good."

I laughed again. And he curled his arm around my back, drawing me into him.

"I think relationships aren't supposed to be easy." I

swept my fingers along his brow as he stared up at me. "It's the hard ones that really mean something. And making love..." I planted a kiss on his lips.

"Yes?"

"It's our way back to each other."

He grinned and buried his face in my neck. I bucked and squirmed, because his whiskers made me ticklish. Then he kissed his way across my collarbone, and I ran my hand down his back.

"You're gonna have to get rid of this." I touched his beard. It wasn't full grown. But he'd been skipping shaves. So I'd gotten used to his stubble while we were in Europe.

"Do you want me to?" His golden eyes raked over my face.

"Hmm." I studied him. "I might have to take a closer look." I ran my fingers through the prickly hairs. Then I kissed his right cheek. And his left.

"Just admit it." He pinned my wrists to the bed and whispered in my ear. "You secretly love it."

I blushed as he hovered above me. I was so perfectly happy. And I didn't want it to end.

"It feels strange going back to school tomorrow. Doesn't it?" I asked.

"Not really." He lay down and pulled me against him. "We're about to graduate."

"Yeah, you're right. I don't know why I was so sad about it before."

He cupped my cheek. "It's probably just a shock after everything that happened in Paris."

A flash of Valjean went through my mind. It made my heart race. "Yeah."

"You're not worried about—"

"No. I know we'll be safe." But that was a lie. I was

petrified.

"Look, as long as the necklace is away from you, I'm not worried."

I swallowed and pulled the covers over us.

"You did give it to Edmond, right?"

"Yes," I said. "Of course."

"Good." He wrapped his arm around my shoulders. "Now, all we have to worry about it school."

"Yeah."

"I better set my alarm." He leaned over his nightstand. And I left kisses down his back. "Addie, I can't focus when you're doing that." I giggled and ran my hands over his pecs. "Addie." He hit the wrong button on the clock. "Dammit."

"I'm sorry," I said.

He set the alarm and rolled over. "No you're not."

His hand slid up my thigh, and I curled my hand around his neck.

"I love you." He hovered above me. "And nothing is ever going to change that."

"I know." I felt my eyes water. "I love you, too."

He kissed me. "We have to get up early in the morning."

I looked at the clock on his nightstand. "It's not morning yet."

He shut his eyes and growled.

"And besides, that's never stopped you before."

"You've got a point there, Mrs. Sutton," he smiled.

"I know. My husband says I'm intuitive like that."

He petted my hair with a smile. "You're happy here. Aren't you?"

I looked up at him in the dark. How could I tell him no?

"Yeah. As long as I'm with you."

"We'll go back soon," he whispered. "I promise."

It would be two months before we had at least a week off from school again. March felt so far away. But I'd gone eighteen years without them in the past. What was sixty days?

"Thank you. For going with me."

"Of course. Baby, I don't want to be anywhere else."

I let out a breathless sigh. "How did I get so lucky?"

He kissed me on the cheek. "I'm the lucky one."

"I just want to be with you." I touched his biceps. "And whatever happens, we'll figure it out."

"I think so, too." He left a gentle kiss on my lips. One to get me through the night.

I fell asleep with my head on his chest. We lay in the middle of the bed, tangled in each other's arms. And I felt so euphoric, because it seemed like a dream.

But when the sun came up, my nightmares came to life.

* * *

We drove to school together. But I was plagued with guilt the whole time. It was second semester of my senior year, and I haven't even talked to my parents. I'd resented Eleanor for so long. But for the past eighteen years, she'd been the only mother I'd ever had. Most of that time, I'd thought she was my real mother. But what did being a real mother even mean? I didn't know anymore.

"Hey!" Jeanine pulled me out of my daydream in the hallway.

"Hey." I gave her a hug. "Sorry we disappeared in

Paris."

"It's okay. Edmond said you were anxious to start your honeymoon."

I breathed a sigh of relief. Not everyone in the castle had known the truth.

Tom snuck up behind me. And I gave him a gentle kiss on the cheek. But that was enough to make everyone stop and stare. He tucked his arm around my back and noticed all the students watching us.

"Why is everyone staring?" I asked.

"Why do you think?" Jeanine said. "Everyone knows."

"Knows what?" Tom asked.

"That you got married."

I saw a group of junior cheerleaders walking by. One of them rubbed her stomach, and they laughed. It made me cling to Tom like I never had before. But I should have expected as much from girls who had grown up worshipping the ground Nicki used to walk on.

"What are they saying?" Tom squeezed my waist.

Jeanine looked afraid. "Nothing, just—"

"Someone started a rumor that you're pregnant," Eric said, appearing beside her.

"What?" I hissed. "Since when?"

"Since you ran off to Europe and got married," Eric said.

"But it has nothing to do with that!" I yelled. Tom tightened his grip while I caught my breath.

"Don't get mad at me. I'm the one who's been defending you." He looked at Tom. "Both of you."

"It's just because you're still in high school," Jeanine said. "And graduation is only a semester away."

Tom scanned the hallway and sighed. "Well, I'm really going to enjoy my last few months of high school."

"You got married over Christmas break," Eric said. "What did you expect?"

"What's that supposed to mean?" I asked.

"Nothing." Eric glanced between us. "It's just that you haven't made things any easier for us. You know everyone in this town still hates me because they think I killed their precious quarterback."

"Eric," I scolded. Jeanine lowered her eyes and looked away.

"I'm sorry." He held a book in his hand. "But couldn't you have waited until after graduation?"

Anger shot through my veins. I felt betrayed. Eric was supposed to be on our side.

"I don't remember you bringing any of this up when I was in the hospital," I said.

"Yeah," he muttered. "That's because I thought you were going to die."

"What's wrong with you?" I asked. "You're mad that we got married?"

"No."

"Then what is it?"

"I just think you should have waited a little longer." He put his arm around Jeanine. "For all our sakes."

"You have no idea why Addie and I got married," Tom said.

"No, I don't." Eric looked at me. "So why did you?"

I searched Tom's eyes and swallowed. What could we say?

Eric watched me. And when he spoke, it was like Tom wasn't even in the room.

"Are you pregnant?"

Chapter 13

Tom

I don't know what happened over the next three seconds. But watching your wife almost die will do strange things to you. And I hadn't exactly recovered from the trauma.

Maybe it was jet lag. Maybe I was pissed that we had to go back to school. Maybe I couldn't stand the thought of anyone pointing fingers at Addie under the guise of a rumored teenage pregnancy.

Or maybe it was something much worse. Something deeper. Something I'd tried to bury.

Like the fact that if Addie were pregnant, it would be a miracle, not a curse.

Maybe it was the sting of disappointment—a reminder that Addie would never be with child.

For whatever reason, I punched Eric in the face, cold cocked him right there in the high school hallway. He touched his jaw and looked at me, scared, shocked. And of course, Principal Caldwell—whose wrath I thought we'd finally escaped—witnessed the whole thing.

I was ready for Eric to defend himself. Truth be told, I wanted to fight. It was the only way out of this hellish cycle my life had become.

How could Addie escape the longing for a child when the whole school thought I'd gotten her pregnant?

"Come on." I stepped back, egging him on. "Let's go."

"Tom." Addie reached out for me, but I pulled away. "Stop! What are you doing?"

"You think I knocked her up?" I shoved Eric in the shoulder. "Is that it?"

Eric balled his fists and came towards me. "Yes. You're gonna make a fool out of her. Hasn't she been through enough? Addie's like a sister to me. And I won't let you ruin her life."

"Oh my god!" Addie shouted. "I'm not even pregnant! This is stupid!"

"Come on," I said. "Hit me."

"Tom!" Addie yelled.

Jeanine stood beside her. "Eric, don't! This is crazy!"

Spectators gathered to watch. The same ones who'd been staring us down. I was so sick of life not going as planned. And I wasn't about to let a stupid rumor keep Addie from enjoying her last few months of high school.

Savannah was supposed to bring her peace. It was home to me.

But now it felt like I'd brought her back to hell.

Eric swung at me and I ducked down. Then I popped him right in the nose. And that's when he started bleeding.

"Tom!" Addie grabbed my arm. "Stop! Please stop!"

I saw Caldwell marching down the hall and felt like a fool. What was wrong with me?

"Tom! Look out!" Addie screamed.

I looked back and Eric punched me in the face. It

was such a strong blow, that it brought me to my knees. I collapsed on the floor as blood ran down my chin. My ears were ringing, and I felt terrible.

For starting a fight—especially with Eric. We were friends. And I couldn't believe what I'd done.

"Tom!" Addie touched my cheek. "Tom, oh God. Are you okay?"

I held her hand. "I'm sorry, baby."

"What has gotten into you?" she cried.

"Mr. Kent. Mr. Sutton. My office. Now."

I cringed at the sound of Caldwell's voice. I'd managed to escape his office for a year.

"Tom," Addie whimpered as I got up.

I saw Eric following Caldwell down the hall. There was no point in putting it off. Might as well pay for the damages and move on. So I put one foot in front of the other and staggered my way after them.

"Tom!" Addie cried. "Tom!"

I didn't turn around, because it was too painful. I hated myself for what I'd just done to Addie. She'd already been through so much. And everything still felt like my fault. If I'd been there in time... If Valjean had shot me instead... If the bullet had missed her hip...

I was a terrible husband. And I didn't deserve her.

In Caldwell's office, the door slammed shut behind me. Eric was already there, so I took a seat beside him. The last time I'd been reprimanded, Ricky had been here with me. That was exactly a year ago.

"Well, Mr. Sutton." Caldwell arranged some papers on his desk. "I'd been wondering when I'd have the opportunity to have you in my office again."

"It's my fault, sir," Eric said.

"I saw who threw the first punch, Mr. Kent. And it wasn't you."

167

"I know that. But it's not Tom's fault. He was provoked."

I swallowed and wiped my nose. It was still bleeding.

"Why did you provoke him?" Caldwell asked.

"There are rumors going around school," Eric said.

"About what?"

"Everyone is saying that Addie is pregnant," Eric said.

Caldwell eyed me like a hawk. "Yes, I've heard."

I played with my wedding ring and looked down.

"Mr. Sutton, is this true? Were you provoked?"

I looked at Eric. And he was innocent in all this. If anything, he'd only been trying to protect Addie. I didn't want him to get in trouble. Why should he be punished for my momentary rage?

"I threw the first punch," I confessed. "It's not his fault."

Eric was in shock.

"He was just defending himself." I took a breath and let it go.

"Is that how it happened?" Caldwell asked.

I stared at Eric until he let me take the blame.

"Yes, sir," Eric said.

"All right." He filled out a form. "But fighting is against school policy. I'm going to have to suspend you both."

My heart sank. I'd never been suspended before. Even when I got in that fight with Ricky.

Eric gulped. "For how long?"

"Three days," Caldwell said. He gave each of us a form. "You'll have to get it signed."

"What about our assignments? We have tests this

week," Eric said.

"You'll have to take zeros on them. For every day you're suspended."

I gritted my teeth and glared. Caldwell was doing this just because he hated me.

"Zeros!' Eric shouted. "Do you have any idea what that's going to do to my GPA?"

"Yes." Caldwell smiled. "It should be one hell of a lesson for you. Isn't that right, Mr. Sutton?"

Eric shook his head and freaked, leaving his office in a hurry.

"What is this?" I asked. "Revenge?"

"Well, you did contribute to the disappearance of my daughter."

All this time, and he still couldn't accept the fact that Nicki was dead.

"You know I don't have anyone to sign this." I held up the form.

"Maybe you could use your wife's signature," he said.

"Thanks for your gracious understanding," I hissed, turning to walk out.

"I'd like to remind you, Mr. Sutton, that if your wife is pregnant, she will no longer be allowed to attend Maple Creek High."

I froze in my tracks.

"We have standards. As the principal, I will not condone such behavior."

"What?" I turned around. "You can't expel a student for being pregnant. That's sexist and discriminatory."

"Would you like to call the board and see what they have to say?" He picked up his phone.

"First of all, Addie isn't pregnant. She never was.

And if she were pregnant, you couldn't just kick her out on the street and deprive her of an education. She's one of the smartest students you have here."

He sighed. "Let me make myself clear, Mr. Sutton. If Addie is pregnant, I'll have both of you removed from the premises for disorderly conduct. Is that clear?"

"Disorderly conduct?" I couldn't believe him. "Really? We're married!" I showed him my ring.

"It doesn't matter. A pregnant student would be a disgrace. And I'm not going to let you tarnish this school's reputation. I've worked too long and hard to keep it that way."

"Yeah." I thought about all the times he'd covered up for his daughter and Ricky. "You sure have."

I left his office and found Eric waiting for me in the hall.

"I'm sorry, man." He walked beside me. "I don't know what I was thinking."

"It's my fault. Don't worry about it."

"I wouldn't have said anything. But you've got to understand how it looks. I mean, you just run off to Europe and get married without telling anybody."

"I know."

"I knew it didn't sound like you. But with everyone talking, it gets in your head. I was starting to believe it, you know? I started thinking, maybe Addie was pregnant."

"Well, she's not." I stopped and looked him in the eye. "That's impossible."

"Okay. I didn't know. I'm sorry about what I said."

"Don't worry about it." I opened my locker. "I'm sorry I hit you."

"It's okay. I can't imagine what you've been

through with Addie getting shot in Paris."

I closed my eyes. I was having a hard time remembering my locker combination.

"I don't want to talk about it and neither does she."

"Right man. I'm sorry." He walked away. "I better get to class."

"Yeah, me too." I finally got my locker open. There was a picture of Addie taped to the door. I took it down and put it in my backpack. I didn't want anyone having personal insight into our relationship. Better to keep her photo in a frame at home.

I closed my locker and headed down the hall. As I passed the girls' bathroom, someone grabbed me and pulled me inside. I recognized her perfume and sighed in relief. It was only my wife.

Once I was inside, she locked the door and checked under the stalls. Then she smacked me upside the head.

"Ow!" I rubbed my head. "That hurt!"

"Why did you do that?" She was angry. "Eric is one of our best friends."

"I know."

"Then what the hell is wrong with you?" She was steaming, but she had a right to be.

"I don't know." I watched her wet some paper towels at the sink. "I'm sorry."

"Come here."

I walked over, and she wiped the blood off my face.

"The school nurse let me borrow her first aid kit." She cleaned my face and then applied a bandage. "It doesn't look like Eric broke your nose." She closed the kit. "But maybe he should have."

"Addie, I'm sorry." I touched her back. "How

many times do I have to say it?"

She hung her head and took a few staggering breaths.

"What are you doing here? You're missing class."

"Someone asked me when I was due. In front of the whole class." She looked at me. "And I just..."

"Baby." I pulled her into my arms. "I'm sorry. I should've been there."

"That's not even it," she sniffled. There were tears running down her face. "I don't care what they say."

"Then what is it?" I cupped her cheeks in my hands.

"I wish I was pregnant." Her lower lip trembled. "I wouldn't care if they teased me. I could handle all of that. It would be worth it for the baby. But now, it's just a reminder of what I can never have."

It was painful to hear. This would always haunt her. And these next few months could end up being torturous.

She cried into my chest as I petted her hair. Times like these, I didn't know what to say. What could I possibly do that would make her feel better? And how could our marriage ever be right with that looming overhead? It would always be there, just off in the distance, waiting for us.

She couldn't think about the future. Because she couldn't imagine one without kids.

"You know, I can always go in there and kick their ass," I offered.

But she didn't laugh. "No, don't. You're in enough trouble already."

That felt like a kick in the gut. Even if it was true.

"What did Caldwell say?" she asked.

"Three days of suspension."

"In school or out of school?"

"Out of school." I hated to see the disappointment in her eyes.

She buried her face in her hands. "Tom." And then she just cried.

"I'm sorry, baby." I held her close. "I'm so sorry."

She dried her eyes and leaned back. "I don't want to be mad at you."

"Then don't." I lifted her chin and looked into her eyes. "Everything will be all right."

"Stop saying that." She pushed away and grabbed her things. "I hate it when you lie."

I stood there wounded. And she ran out of the bathroom. Then I looked in the mirror and punched the glass. So much for those stitches I got in Paris.

* * *

So far, the semester wasn't getting off to a great start. Addie and I didn't have as many classes together. But since she hated me right now, maybe that wasn't such a bad thing.

Everyone kept staring at me. And I heard what they were whispering.

They thought I'd knocked up my girlfriend and then been forced to marry her.

While we had eloped, I don't remember a shotgun being present at the wedding ceremony. And yet, that's what everyone kept saying. They wanted me to feel ashamed for fornicating and conceiving an illegitimate child.

Many times, I wondered what they would have said if I'd revealed the truth. That Addie and I had both been virgins on our wedding night. That we'd only just begun having sex as man and wife. And that the prospect of children in the near or distant future was actually an impossibility.

But I kept my mouth shut. Because they didn't deserve to know the truth.

And Addie needed to have her privacy.

By seventh period, I'd learned to tune out the evil eye. Especially when our teacher reminded everyone that UGA was sending out acceptance letters this week. I checked my email, since I'd elected to be notified electronically. And there it was in black and white. I'd been accepted to the University of Georgia as a freshman in the fall.

It was the best news I'd heard in weeks. I was so excited that I couldn't wait to tell Addie. But on the drive home, she was reserved and quiet. She was still mad at me. And it didn't help that I'd have to sit out the next three days of school. She would have to endure Maple Creek High without me.

When we got home, she went straight upstairs to take a shower. Usually, I would have joined her. But it felt like she needed some space. So I stayed in the kitchen and made lasagna for dinner. It was time to celebrate.

"What's all this?" She came into the kitchen with wet hair. She'd already changed into one of my shirts and sweatpants.

"Oh, umm." I turned the burner off. "I've been accepted at Georgia. They emailed me."

"Really?" She lit up. "Tom, that's great!" She gave me a hug.

"I know. I wanted to tell you as soon as I found out."

"Congratulations." She kissed me on the cheek. "This looks good. I'm starving."

I pulled out her chair and served her plate. Then we talked about what it would be like living in Athens. Part of me thought it would be a nice change. Since Paris, she didn't feel the same way about Savannah anymore.

"So have you checked yet?" I asked.

"Umm, no." She cut through a few layers of lasagna. "I thought I'd look at it tomorrow."

I wished she would just look now, so we would know for sure.

"Today has just been too much for me," she said.

"I understand."

"But I'm so proud of you." She reached across the table and squeezed my hand.

I got up and led her into the den where we could relax. She sat down on the couch while I lit a fire. When I looked back, there was worry and frustration swimming in her eyes.

"Are you okay?" I sat down beside her and pulled her into my lap.

"Yeah." She put her head on my chest. "I'm just tired."

"When do you want to get your stuff?" I tugged the hem of her shirt. "You can't just keep wearing my clothes."

"I know. But I'm not ready to go over there yet. I don't want to see them."

"Why not?" I asked.

"Because. It's just too weird right now. I feel like they hate me."

"Addie, they don't hate you. But you're living with me now. And I want you to have everything you need."

She sighed and ran her fingers through her hair.

"Unless you're planning on living with them?"

"No, of course not. I'm just not ready, okay? Just give me a few days."

"Okay." I rubbed her back, but she felt so tense. "Do you want me to give you a massage?"

"Why?" She sat up and stared, like she couldn't understand why I would offer to do something for her.

"Because I know it's been a rough day back. And it's my fault. I want to make it up to you."

"All right," she said. "But I'd rather go upstairs."

"Want me to carry you?" She loved when I did that.

"I don't care. You can if you want."

"Are you sure you're okay?" I asked.

"Yes, I'm fine! Stop asking me that."

I followed her up the stairs. And it became incredibly clear that she wasn't.

She took off her top and got in our bed. I wondered if I should get some oil or lotion—something to calm her down. But we didn't really have anything, so my bare hands would have to do.

I watched her for a minute, lying there with her face turned. Maybe she didn't want me to touch her. But then why had she shed her clothes just as quickly as we'd come up here?

I sat down beside her and pushed her hair out of the way. Her skin was soft and smooth beneath my touch. I pressed my thumbs into her shoulder blades. She had so much tension, it must have been painful.

"Do you feel tense?" I asked.

"I don't know," she said. "I guess."

I kissed her neck and then ran my hands down her arms. Her eyes were closed, so I hoped she would be able to relax. My knuckles hurt, and they still hadn't healed since Paris. But I wanted to make Addie feel good. She deserved this. She needed this. And I couldn't imagine anyone else touching her but me.

Her breathing deepened, so I smoothed my fingertips across her ribcage. But then her back heaved and I looked at her face. She was crying.

"Baby, what's wrong?" I stopped touching her. "Did I hurt you?"

She cried so hard that she couldn't form complete sentences. But I was patient, giving her time.

She mumbled something. But I couldn't make out the words.

"What?" I leaned down to hear her.

"I didn't get in."

Chapter 14

Addie

I'd been disappointed as soon as I got my schedule. For the first time, Tom and I had fewer classes together than we had apart. I tried not to be too torn up about it, because it wasn't that big of a deal.

But it ended up being a blessing in the end.

I went to the library during class and found a vacant computer. My hands were clammy, and I was more than a little shaky. As I logged into my email account, my heart pounded in my chest like a drum.

Sure, it wasn't my dream college. To be honest, I'd much rather attend a liberal arts school. But that would mean giving up Tom. And while I wanted an education that celebrated art, I wanted him more.

I waited for the screen to load, my mouth a little dry. It didn't usually take this long. But I always found that to be the case when I wanted something in a rush. What took a minute felt like an hour.

But then my inbox popped up. And there it was.

An email from the University of Georgia. I'd always fantasized about receiving an acceptance letter in the mail. But we'd both elected to be notified electronically. No need to kill any more trees. To a certain extent, it gave us an extra layer of privacy. Because no one could access the information but us.

I held on to the mouse and let it hover. The

pointer was on the email. All I had to do was click.

I looked around the library and then stared at the screen. Why was I so nervous?

After this hellish return to Savannah, it would be nice to finally hear some good news.

I closed my eyes and smiled, making a wish. It wasn't my birthday. I didn't have candles to blow out on a cake. But it felt like rubbing a rabbit's foot—an extra touch of luck. Turns out, I would need it.

I clicked and opened my eyes. And that's when my whole world caved in. My insides collapsed like a sink hole, and I felt like throwing up. They regretted to inform me that I hadn't been accepted.

I sat back in my chair. Then I read it over and over again. It was still there. My rejection letter.

I felt sick for the rest of the day. And Tom seemed to sense my unease. He was quiet on the car ride home. And I wondered if the same thing had happened to him. Maybe he didn't want to talk about it either.

But then he cooked dinner, and his excitement was undeniable. Tom had been accepted. And why not? He was brilliant in chemistry and math. He could compute equations and rattle off algorithms at the drop of a hat.

While I was just a girl with a paint brush.

Maybe I should've poured more of myself into my art. But with the trauma in my life, it had taken a back seat. If I'd worked harder, maybe I could have applied to SCAD and even been accepted.

I felt way more confident in my paintings than my knowledge of books. It wasn't that I hadn't tried. I'd been making straight A's for years. But I had to slave away studying to get them. Academic success had never come easy for me. Like it always did for Tom.

All this was racing through my mind over dinner. But he was just so happy. How could I let him down?

As we lounged in the den, I couldn't stop thinking my future was uncertain. We were married now. Living in different cities wasn't optional. That wasn't a marriage. That was long distance. We'd never attempted that kind of relationship when we were dating. Why start now?

When Tom offered to give me a massage, I couldn't say no. I loved the idea of his hands on me. But it also felt like there was a huge elephant in the room. I'd lied when I said I would check my email tomorrow. It was wrong. I should have told him right then. But I didn't want to break it to him. Not before I'd had the chance to process it myself.

I lay down in bed and closed my eyes. It wasn't the end of the world. Right? We could figure something out. We always did. But as he rubbed my shoulders, I just didn't know anymore. It scared me.

I wasn't too sure Tom even wanted to go to Georgia. He was math and science. I was liberal arts. Really, we'd be better off attending separate schools. Maybe a place like Georgia Tech catered to his strengths, while SCAD encouraged mine. But one was in Atlanta, and the other in Savannah.

What kind of marriage was that? Wasn't that the reason we'd picked Georgia together in the first place? So we could not only be together but stay together? It wasn't about me or him anymore. It was about us. And I'd gone and blown everything by getting rejected at the one college that suited us both.

"Baby, what's wrong?" he asked. "Did I hurt you?"

I was ugly crying now. And it was so

uncontrollable, I couldn't remember when I'd started. But my mind wouldn't stop racing. There was one tear, and then another. I couldn't hold it in anymore.

"I didn't get in," I croaked.

Concealing the truth was eating a hole inside of me. So I had to get it off my chest.

"What?" he asked.

I hated when we kept secrets from each other. Even though it was typically a sign of defense.

I sat up and pulled the sheet over my chest. Then I took a breath and looked him in the eye. "I didn't get in."

"What are you talking about?"

"UGA. I didn't get accepted."

His eyes were wide with shock.

"I didn't tell you, because you were so excited about getting in." I swiped at a tear and looked up at him. "And I'm happy for you. I really am." Now the tears were coming down like rain. "But... I'm so sorry."

He drew me into his arms. "I'm sorry."

I put my head on his chest and squeezed him tightly.

"But I don't understand." He dried my eyes. "Your GPA is higher than mine."

"I know." I nodded. "But your test scores... you know I suck at those."

"Yeah." He grabbed my shoulders. "But Addie, your scores weren't that bad."

I stared at him, wondering what he was thinking. The wheels were turning in his head.

"I just can't believe you didn't get in," he said.

That made me feel like crap. "I can't believe I didn't get in either."

His face lit up. "Maybe it's a mistake. Maybe they have you confused with someone else."

"I doubt it."

"Addie, come on." He squeezed my arm. "You should call them and check."

"Tom. I'm not gonna call the people who clearly don't want me."

"Well, what about Jimmy? He works in higher education. Maybe you could ask him—"

"He's a professor, Tom. And he doesn't teach at Georgia."

"Yeah, but still. Couldn't you at least ask him?"

I gave him a stern look, because I was angry.

"He might know someone. And maybe they could pull some strings."

"Pull some strings?" I asked.

"Yeah."

"You think I've killed myself studying for four years to get in because of some favor?"

"Addie, it wouldn't be like that. You deserve it. You know you do."

I got up and tied my hair back. "Well, if I deserved it, I would've gotten in."

I went into the bathroom to brush my teeth. Then I washed my face in the sink. Tom hovered the whole time, thinking of a million different things I should do to get in.

It made me resent him, because he was trying to play Mr. Fix It with my future.

"Why can't you just accept it?" I said.

"Accept what?" He was leaning against the bathroom door.

"Accept that I didn't get in!" I was in his face now. And we'd been yelling at each other for half an hour.

"Because I don't believe that."

"Oh my God!" I ran my hands over my face. "Can't you just accept me for who I am?"

He slid his hands in his pockets and looked down.

"I'm sorry that I didn't get into the college we picked out for us. Okay? *I'm sorry*! But there is nothing I can do about it! And I won't let you make me believe that this is my fault."

"I never said that."

"Well, you're sure acting like it!" I yelled.

"I never said that!" he boomed.

His voice sent shivers down my spine. I sat on the edge of the bed and cried.

"I'm sorry," I said. "I didn't mean to yell at you."

He knelt down and wrapped me in his arms.

"I hate it when we fight," I said.

"I know." He touched my hair. "I hate it, too."

"Are you mad at me?" I asked.

"No." He circled his thumb over my cheek. "I'm not mad at you."

"Well, maybe you should be. Everything is my fault."

"That's not true." He cupped my face in his hands.

"But I'm the one who didn't get in." I found solace in his amber eyes. He looked so sweet.

"That's not your fault." He kept touching my face. "And I still say it's a mistake."

I buried my face in the crook of his neck, feeling safe in his arms. "What are we gonna do?"

"We'll figure something out." He turned down the covers. "Let's go to bed."

"Okay." I lay down beside him, pressing kisses into his chest.

"You know one thing you're forgetting?" he said.

"What?"

"Just because I got in, doesn't mean I'll be able to go."

"Why not?"

"I got a three day suspension. I have to take zeros on everything."

I took a breath and wrapped my body around him.

"I might end up with a rejection letter before you know it."

I clung to him and closed my eyes. "Why is everything so hard?"

"I don't know." He caressed my back. "But at least we have each other."

I feared that one day, that might be all we had left.

* * *

Tom drove me to school the next day. Even though he wasn't allowed to come.

I had lunch with Jeanine and she graciously failed to mention Georgia. I'd heard students in the hallway asking seniors if they'd been accepted. I had my fingers crossed that no one would ask me, because I had no idea what to say.

When Tom picked me up after school, I told him I was ready to face the music. But I wanted to do it alone.

So he dropped me off at my childhood home. And I let myself inside.

It was the afternoon, so I didn't expect anyone to be home. Maybe it would be easier to officially move out when Eleanor wasn't breathing down my neck. I took my time walking through the living room and kitchen. I'd never stayed in a place where I hadn't developed an attachment. I kind of liked the fact that it was only a stone's throw away.

I heard footsteps in the kitchen. And then my eyes landed on Jeffrey.

"Hi," I said.

"Hi." He smiled. "I was just in the office doing some work. Your mother is at the hospital."

Of course she was. But I liked being alone with Jeffrey. It gave us a chance to talk.

"So how's married life?" he asked.

"Good." I pointed upstairs. "I just needed to get some things from my room."

"Yeah, I guess you never got around to moving out."

"No." I forced a smile as he walked into the living room. "I wanted to apologize—"

"I'm sorry I—" I laughed, because we were talking over each other. "Sorry, you go ahead."

"No, ladies first."

"Well, I just wanted to say that I'm sorry," I said.

"Addie, you don't have to—"

"No, listen." I moved closer. "I never meant to exclude you. Not really. And I had no idea Jimmy was going to be there. He just showed up at the last minute. And we never planned on getting married in Europe. It was something we decided on the spur of the moment."

"I know that. But Jimmy is your father. And he was the one—"

"You're my father, too."

He grinned. "Well, I wasn't expecting that."

I gave him a hug. "I just wish we could all get along. Can't I love you both?"

He put his hands on my shoulders. "I can't bear the thought of anything happening to you."

"Well, I'm fine now. Really. And everything is going to be okay. But I can't have my parents hating each other. Could you just try to get along? For me? You don't have to compete for my love."

He lifted my chin. "I know it's my fault. Your mother and I are never around. But Jimmy has really taken the time to bond with you. I never did that. I wish I had."

"You still can. I want all of you in my life. Stop making me choose."

He gave me another hug. "Do you need help packing? I've got some extra boxes lying around here somewhere."

"That would be great."

For the next hour or so, we talked and filled boxes with my things. I was leaving the furniture here since there was nowhere to put it at Tom's. And I wasn't sure if it was mine to take anyway.

Tom showed up later and helped us pack the car. Jeffrey was really nice to him, which was such a relief. Right now, I wasn't sure if Tom had one or two father-in-laws. It had to be a lot for him to take in.

"Why don't you join us for dinner?" Tom asked.

"Yes. Tom is a great cook." I put my hand on his chest.

"I know he is. But your mother will be home soon."

As we stood outside, she pulled into the drive.

"Speak of the devil," Jeffrey said.

Eleanor went straight into the garage. So we talked to Jeffrey for a few more minutes. To my surprise, she came out on the front porch to greet us.

"When did you get back?" she asked.

"A few days ago."

"Hi, Mrs. Sutton," Tom said, waving at her.

"Tom." She nodded, always so formal and abrupt.

"Would you like to come over for dinner?" I asked.

"Well." She looked at Jeffrey. "I don't see why not."

I couldn't believe it. But they were actually being nice.

We went back home and unpacked the car. I didn't know where to put everything yet, since we were staying in Tom's room. So I left the boxes in the hall and then went back downstairs to help Tom.

"What do they like to eat?" he asked.

"Just a nice meal really." I set the table. "I could roast some vegetables. And you could grill chicken or steak?"

"That sounds good. I just hope they like it."

"They will." I kissed him on the cheek. "You know, I don't think they've ever been here before."

"Hmm." He got an apron out. "Well, I better get started."

He was really putting on the dog when that apron came out of hiding. I heard the doorbell ring, and my stomach did a somersault. I couldn't understand why Eleanor was being amenable all of a sudden. It felt too good to be true. Then again, maybe my near death experience had led her to a change of heart.

"Come in." I opened the front door and gave Jeffrey a hug. Eleanor was being stand-offish. Then again, that wasn't unusual for her. She'd always been cold. "I was just helping Tom in the kitchen."

They followed me in and sat down at the bar. "Wow," Jeffrey said. "This is really nice."

"Yes, Addison." Eleanor set her purse down. "It

really is beautiful."

She smiled, and I couldn't read her. Surely, she was displeased or jealous or something.

"Dinner will be ready soon." I checked on the vegetables. "I think I'll make a salad."

"Mr. Smith," Tom said, shaking Jeffrey's hand. "Mrs. Smith."

"Nice to see you again, Tom," Eleanor said.

"Hey," Tom whispered, grabbing my elbow. "I put some bread in the oven."

"That sounds great." I gave him a quick kiss. "I'm starving."

"So what are you planning to do with the house when you leave for college?" Eleanor asked.

Jeffrey got up and walked around the dining room, looking out the window at the forest.

"Umm..." Tom looked at me.

"We'll come home during breaks and check on it," I said.

"Yes," Tom jumped in. "And it will still be here when we graduate."

We hadn't really talked about it, but that was probably what would happen.

"Oh. Well that's nice." Eleanor saw Jeffrey staring out the window. "Do you have any wine?"

"Mom," I chuckled. "We're underage."

"I know. But do you have any?"

I looked at Tom and nodded. Edmond had given us a bottle of sherry while we were in Paris. I poured Eleanor a glass and asked Jeffrey if he wanted any. But he shook his head in silence.

"Where did you get this?" she asked.

"Edmond gave it to us," Tom said.

"As a wedding present," I added.

"Oh." She took a sip. "I'd rather have a glass of red wine, but—"

"This is all we have," I said.

She nodded with a pompous roll of her eyes. "It's fine."

Tom and I exchanged a look. So much for a change of heart. She was ornery as ever.

When it was time to eat, Tom pulled my chair out for me. I sat down and smiled at the feast before us. It was so nice to have guests over for dinner. I thought the table looked beautiful. And we truly were fortunate to be given a home like this at such a young age. All of a sudden, I felt hopeful.

"No, that's fine." Eleanor took her own seat, even though Jeffrey had tried to pull her chair out for her.

I looked at Tom, and his jaw ticked. We hadn't even broken bread yet. And there was already tension in the room.

"So..." Jeffrey stabbed a potato with his fork. "How is school?"

"Fine." I took a sip of water and averted my eyes.

"What happened to your face?" Eleanor asked.

When I looked up, she was giving my husband the death glare. I sat back and sighed, remembering why I'd been making an effort to avoid her. She always saw the worst in people.

"It was just a misunderstanding," I said. "More sherry?"

"No, I'd like to hear it from Tom."

I was surprised this hadn't come up earlier. But Jeffrey was so nice. And he didn't like confrontation. So he'd ignored the bruises on Tom's face to keep him from feeling uncomfortable. But Eleanor thrived on drama. And I wondered if she'd already gotten a phone call from Eric's mother, telling her everything.

"Well." Tom set his silverware down. "I punched Eric Kent in the face."

Jeffrey looked like his eyes were about to pop out of his head. But Eleanor wasn't so shocked.

"And he was just defending himself," Tom said.

"It's really just a big misunderstanding," I butted in. "But everything is fine now."

"Why did you punch him in the face?" Eleanor asked.

"Do we really have to talk about this right now?" I turned to Jeffrey for help.

"Because he wanted to know if Addie was pregnant," Tom said.

A migraine hit me right in the forehead. It was a sharp, painful sensation.

"Well." Eleanor put me in the hot seat. "Are you?"

"No," I hissed. "Why does everyone keep saying that?"

"Oh, I don't know. Maybe because you went to Europe and got married without even telling me. I thought we were planning a wedding. And you completely cut me out," she said.

"Well, you've cut me out of your life for as long as I can remember!" I shouted.

Eleanor glared at me, and I gave it right back to her. Tom took my hand and squeezed.

"We got married because we didn't know if we'd live to see the summer," he said. "So if you're thinking Addie wrecked your plans for a June wedding in Savannah, you're wrong."

"Tom," Jeffrey said. "Why would you think you wouldn't live to see the summer?"

I wanted to scream at the top of my lungs, *Where*

have you been?

But Tom stayed calm. "Ever since we met, we've had nothing but danger in our lives. So we got married, because we wanted to be together. In case this Christmas was our last."

Jeffrey nodded. "You're eighteen now, Addie. You certainly don't need our permission."

"I still would've liked to be invited to your wedding," Eleanor said.

I sent daggers in her direction. I couldn't count the number of times she'd left me out.

"It was a spur of the moment thing," Tom said. "She never meant to purposefully exclude you."

"No." Her dark eyes looked black. "I think she did."

"This is great steak," Jeffrey said. "What did you season it with?"

While Tom talked, I studied Eleanor. She'd never been the nicest person. But she was being exceptionally rude tonight. When it came to the wedding, I hadn't thought she would care. Was she really so offended that I hadn't invited her? It was at the last minute in Europe. With her workaholic schedule, would she have even been able to come?

"I didn't tell you we were getting married," I admitted. "Because I didn't think you'd approve."

Eleanor finished her sherry. She hadn't eaten much, just staring at the food on her plate.

"I hope you'll always let us be a part of your life," she said. "That's all."

"You are if you want to be," I told her. It was how I'd always felt.

She nodded. "Thank you."

She was the poster child for quicksilver tonight. I

couldn't figure out what kind of mood she was in.

"I'm sorry I was never there for you," she said. "I'd still like to stay in touch."

"Stay in touch?" I laughed. "We live next door! You think just because I'm married now that I'm never going to talk to you again?"

"It was starting to feel like it," Jeffrey said. "When you do have kids one day, I hope you'll let me come visit. I'd like to see them."

Here, I had an OBGYN at the table who suffered from the same malady. But I couldn't tell her.

It still hurt too much. So I pretended that babies were a natural course of action for us.

"Of course you can," I said. "I didn't realize you wanted to."

Jeffrey lowered his head and set his fork down. He hadn't eaten much either.

That's when I looked at Eleanor. She was pouring herself another glass of sherry.

Something was off about them tonight. And I couldn't put my finger on it.

But then Jeffrey cleared his throat, like he was about to say something important.

Eleanor was taking quick little sips of sherry. And that's when I realized her wedding ring was missing.

"Your mother and I are getting a divorce."

Chapter 15

Tom

I looked at Addie, because all I really cared about was how this affected her. If the universe dropped any more bombs on us, she'd have a stroke. And that wasn't exactly what I'd planned for our senior year.

"What?" she gasped. "Where did this come from?"

"The truth is, we've been growing apart for a long time," Eleanor said.

"Dad," Addie said. "Why didn't you tell me about all this?"

"Well, honey, you haven't exactly been here," he said.

Addie set her hands on the tablecloth and took a deep breath. She looked pale.

"Hey." I nuzzled her hair to whisper in her ear. "You okay?"

She gave me a look I'll never forget. I guess it was the wrong thing to say.

"We're selling the house," Jeffrey said. "And the land, too."

"Why?" Addie asked.

"Because I'm moving to Atlanta," Eleanor said. "The Kents put in a good word for me. They have a friend who's retiring. She has a huge practice. And she'll be turning it over to me."

"What about your patients?" Addie said.

"Dr. McClean is going to take them on."

Addie covered her eyes with her hand. I rubbed her back, but she stiffened at my touch.

"I'm staying in Savannah," Jeffrey said. "And after we sell the house, I'm moving into the apartment in town."

"So who's filing?" Addie asked.

"It's a mutual decision between me and your mother."

"Yes, but one of you has to file the papers," she said. "Isn't that right?"

"Your father is filing," Eleanor said. "But I'm actually relieved."

"Relieved?" Addie raised her voice.

"Yes, relieved," Eleanor repeated. "Our lives have been moving in different directions for so long. I can't even remember what it was like before."

"We've talked about this for a long time," Jeffrey said.

"How long?" Addie asked.

"Six months," Jeffrey said.

"So it's over." Addie snapped her fingers. "Just like that?"

"No part of this has been easy, Addison," Eleanor said. "I care about your father, but life's too short to go on being unhappy."

"We made this decision for both our sakes. And with you married and out of the house now." Jeffrey gestured at me. "The divorce shouldn't affect you as much as if you were still living at home."

Addie was on the verge of tears. "You've been married for over twenty years."

"It's not like we didn't try," Jeffrey said.

Eleanor looked at her. "Sometimes, it's just time to move on."

"This is too much," Addie cried. "I can't do this anymore." She got up and ran out of the room.

"Addie." I walked out of the kitchen, but she was already on the staircase. "Addie!"

She slammed the door to our bedroom, and it shook the house. If this week kept getting any worse, she might jump off the deep end. And that was the last thing I wanted for my new bride.

"Sorry." I came back to the dinner table. "She's just upset."

"Oh, it's fine," Jeffrey said. "Don't worry about it."

Eleanor got up and grabbed her purse. "Thanks for dinner, Tom."

"You're welcome." I looked at her plate. She'd hardly touched her steak.

She gave me a side-hug and then left without her husband. When I heard the front door slam, Jeffrey came over to say goodbye.

"Thanks for dinner." He shook my hand. "The steak was great."

"Thanks, Mr. Smith," I smiled.

"Why don't you call me Jeff?"

"Don't you go by Jeffrey?" I asked.

"No, that's just Eleanor. Everyone else calls me Jeff."

I nodded. I wasn't sure if Addie even knew that.

"I know you'll take care of her," he said on our way to the front door. "Be a good husband to her. But I'll always be around. I don't have any plans on leaving Savannah any time soon."

"Good. I think Addie will like that."

"Well." He nodded and reached for the door.

"Wait, Mr. Smith. I mean, Jeff." I reached into my pocket. "Do you think you could sign something for me?"

"Sure." He turned back. "What is it?"

"Eric and I got suspended for the fight. I have to get this signed by a parent, but... I don't have one."

Jeffrey looked at me. "No legal guardian either, I suppose."

"No, sir."

He took a pen out of his pocket and signed it.

I felt so relieved. Before that, I didn't have a clue what I was going to do.

"There you go." He handed me the form.

"Thank you so much."

"If you ever have a problem with something like this again, just give me a call. Okay?"

"Okay." I watched him walk out the door. "Jeff?"

"Yeah." He turned around.

"Can a school kick someone out for being pregnant?"

He looked intrigued. "What are you talking about?"

"Does it break some kind of law? If a girl gets pregnant in high school."

"No." He shook his head. "That would be discrimination. A good way to get sued."

"But suppose a school did it. They actually kicked someone out for being pregnant."

"Yeah."

"Well, what if you were that girl? What would you do about it?" I asked.

"Find a good lawyer," he smiled. "Try not to get in anymore fights, okay?"

I nodded. "I think I've learned my lesson."

"Good." He unlocked his car. "You're a husband now. And your wife needs you."

Once he drove off, I realized that they'd taken separate cars. I thought that was strange, since they'd come from the same place. But I guess they both weren't going back to the house. While we were in Europe, maybe one of them had already moved out.

I found Addie upstairs crying. But she wasn't in our room. She was out on the balcony connected to her room—the one I'd filled with her art. As I walked in, everything was as I'd left it. She probably hadn't been here since the night I surprised her with it. I wondered why she'd chosen this place to hide.

"Addie." I opened the French doors that led to the balcony. "What are you doing out here?"

She wasn't even wearing a jacket. Just a thin sweater and jeans.

"You must be freezing." I wrapped my arms around her from behind. She took my hands and leaned her back into me, resting her head on my chest. "Your hands are cold." So I warmed them up with mine.

"Did they leave already?" she asked.

"Yeah." I smelled her hair.

"I just listened to a message Adeline left me."

I saw her phone on the ledge. "What did she say?"

"Everyone misses us. And Edmond wants to know when we'll be back."

"I guess that means our first family visit went pretty well." I kissed her neck.

"Yeah." She looked up at the stars. "I miss them."

I wanted to say something about the divorce. But knowing Addie, she probably didn't want to talk about it. At least not now. She would come to me when she was ready.

"Tom."

"Hmm?"

"How come you don't play the guitar anymore?" she asked.

I chuckled. "I still play the guitar."

"But not like you used to."

I couldn't figure out where this was coming from.

"I don't know," I said. "I guess I've just been busy."

"What about me?" She stared at the horizon.

"What do you mean?" I got a glimpse of her face.

"I don't really paint anymore," she said.

"Baby, there's been a lot going on."

"I know, but..."

"But what?" I craned my neck so I could see her whole face.

She pulled out of my arms and turned around. "What if that's what marriage is?"

"I don't understand."

"What if we're pulling each other away from the things we really love?" she said.

I looked at the moon. Then I put all my focus on her. "You're what I really love."

Tears were streaming down her face. "I know I said all those horrible things about them. But I always thought they'd be together. And what if one day, we decide that—"

"Hey." I touched her cheek. "We're nothing like them, okay? You can't say that."

She nodded. "Promise me that no matter what happens, we'll always have each other."

I tucked a streak of hair behind her ear and gave her a kiss. "I promise."

She kissed me back. And before I knew it, we were making out on the balcony.

"I hate that you have to be here for the next two days."

I trailed a string of kisses down her neck.

"All by yourself," she said breathlessly.

"I know." I slid my hands around her lovely rear. "I wish I had you here with me."

She let out an adorable yelp as I nibbled at her ear. "I wish I could do that, too."

I looked her over, loving how hot and bothered I'd made her. She bit her lip and ran her nails down the back of my neck. There was this electric heat between us. There always had been. And I loved it.

I scooped her up in my arms and carried her to our bed. "Maybe you should call in sick."

She lay back as I undressed her, those emerald eyes glazing over. I took my clothes off and climbed into bed. She made room for me, coiling her legs around my back. "Maybe I should."

* * *

Addie was dozing in my arms when my phone went off. I tried to move, but she had all of her body weight on me. So I did a hug and roll and ended up on the floor.

Thankfully, I hadn't woken her. But if my cell phone kept buzzing that might do the trick.

So I grabbed it and darted out of the room, closing the door behind me. I hurried down the hall and answered it. Then I went inside Addie's art room.

"Edmond?" I croaked. "It's eleven thirty." And I was exhausted. I hadn't even been to bed yet.

"Yes, but it's five thirty in Paris. And I'm an early

riser."

In my famished state, I'd forgotten about the six hour time difference.

"What's going on? How is everybody?" I opened the French doors and walked out on the balcony.

"Good. Adeline is anxious to talk to Addie."

"Oh, she's already asleep."

"I don't mean right now," he said. "That's what she told me yesterday."

"Oh. I think Addie listened to a voicemail from her. She'll call her back tomorrow."

"Good. That will make my granddaughter very happy."

I leaned against the railing and saw Addie's phone on the ledge. It was blowing up all of a sudden.

"Is that the reason you called, Edmond? To make sure Addie calls Adeline back?" I reached for the phone. But it was vibrating so much that it reminded me of a crab on the beach, scuttling away.

"No. I have news. Have you heard?"

"What?" I almost had the phone and then it fell, dropping two stories below. "Dammit!"

"Thomas."

"What?" I went back inside and ran down the steps.

"Are you all right?"

"Sorry. I just dropped something. You were saying?" Once I was outside, I ran around the back of the house until I saw it. "Finally."

"So you already know?"

I picked her phone up and dusted it off. It was so cold out here, I could see my breath. But I also wasn't wearing anything except for my boxers. So there's that, too.

"Know what?" I looked up and saw something in the woods. It was glowing.

"Valjean got convicted. He'll spend the rest of his life rotting away in a French prison."

"Can I call you back?" It looked like a light from a distance. And it was getting closer.

"I thought you'd be pleased."

"I am." I hurried inside. "I'll call you back."

I checked Addie's phone to see what all the fuss was about. It was text after text from her French relatives. Ashton. Josette. Adeline. And they all wanted to talk about Valjean's conviction.

Any other night, I'd have been jumping up and down myself. They had finally arrested the man who'd tried to kill my wife. He was a ruthless criminal who deserved to be locked away for good.

But I couldn't celebrate. Not when there were strangers lurking in the woods.

I went upstairs and got dressed. Then I reached under our bed and grabbed a gun.

"Tom." Addie stirred awake in the dark. "What's going on?"

"Nothing," I said. "Go back to sleep."

"What are you doing?" She sat up in bed.

"Nothing." I grabbed a jacket. "Don't worry about me."

"Then why do you have a gun?"

I'd almost made it out of there. But of course, my clever little wife had to notice everything.

"I'm just going to check something, okay?"

"Check what?" She was wide awake now. "Tom."

"I just thought I saw something in the woods," I said.

"What did you see?"

"I don't know," I grumbled.

"Well then, what did it look like?"

"A light." I still couldn't figure out what it was.

"I'm going with you." She got out of bed and put her clothes on.

"Addie, no. You'll be safe here."

"If you think I'm just going to let you go into the woods by yourself in the middle of the night after everything that's happened to us, then you must be crazy." She tugged on her jeans and slipped a sweater over her head, lacing up her boots.

"I think you should just let me go," I said.

"Why?" She braided her hair back. "So you can be the next one to get shot?"

"It's probably nothing," I said so she wouldn't worry. "I just want to check."

"If it's nothing, then why can't I come?" She put on a jacket and grabbed her phone.

And I didn't have a great rebuttal.

"Let's go." She pulled the hood up on her jacket as we headed downstairs.

I thought about calling Jeff for help, since he wasn't too far away. But with the divorce, I didn't know who was staying in that house. So I told Addie to stay close, and we entered the woods.

Chapter 16

Addie

I wasn't afraid of dying anymore. That's what happens when you've slipped off the edge a few times.

I had to silence my phone, because texts kept coming in. Valjean had been sentenced to life in prison. Deep down, I knew Edmond had something to do with it. But that wasn't the problem.

Now that he'd been convicted, Valjean might retaliate. What was to stop him from hiring a hitman? He could easily send one after us. There was no telling who he'd met in his career as a thief. Crooks like that always owed each other favors. And the light we were chasing could very well be one of them.

I stayed behind Tom. Only because he was walking so fast that I could hardly keep up. It was strange to see him with a gun. Whatever he'd seen in the woods must have been pretty bad.

"Where was it?" I whispered after ten minutes of silence.

He sighed. Then he looked left to right. "There." He pointed east.

"And you saw a light?" I asked.

"Yes," he hissed. "It was glowing. At least, I thought I..." He trailed off, his eyes racing.

"Hey." I grabbed his face. "I believe you, okay?"

"You don't think I'm losing my mind?" He looked like a sick puppy.

"No," I said. "You know what you saw."

"But that's just it." He darted between the trees. "I don't."

We walked another twenty minutes before he spoke again. "Do you hear that?"

I stopped to listen. But there was nothing. "No. What?"

"Shh." He walked in a different direction.

"Tom, where are you going?"

"Come here." He grabbed my hand as we plunged deeper into the wilderness. We hadn't been out here in the dark in so long. It gave me the creeps. But maybe that was just déjà vu.

Suddenly, I heard it. And it nearly stopped my heart.

Someone was whistling Brahms' Lullaby.

"Tom." I clung to him. "I'm scared."

He hid behind a tree and tucked my head under his chin.

Slowly but surely, the sound got louder. They were getting close.

"Someone's here," he whispered.

I shut my eyes and held Tom tightly. Then I prayed that the whistler would simply go away. Within a few minutes, my wish was granted.

"Are they gone?" I asked.

"I don't know." Tom wrapped his arm around me as we followed the sound.

There was a river that ran through the woods. When we reached it, I saw a bright light in the distance. It was so strong I had to shield my eyes. But Tom went after it, tripping on a rock.

He fell down and the gun went off.

"Tom!" I knelt down beside him on the ground. "Are you okay?"

"Yeah." He let me help him up. "I'm fine. You?"

"Yeah." I brushed his clothes off as he stared into the distance.

Slowly, the light faded away. And the music stopped.

"What *was* that?" he said.

"I don't know." Something on the river bank caught my eye. So I squatted down to take a look.

"What are you doing?" he asked.

It looked like a candy wrapper. I used the light on my phone to check. Then I grabbed a stick and turned it over. It was made of foil—like something you might wrap a bon bon in.

"Bavarian chocolate," I read.

"What's that?"

"Bavaria is in Germany."

"So?" He shrugged his shoulders.

"You don't remember what Valjean said?"

"He said lots of things." He helped me up. "Come on, let's go."

"When we were in Switzerland, Valjean said there was a German scientist who believed the necklace could heal people. He thinks it's some kind of universal elixir."

"And your point is?"

I grabbed his arm, so he would take me seriously. "You remember what he said, Tom. Valjean is in prison now. And he wants that scientist to heal his daughter with the necklace."

"Well, that's not going to happen."

"What if he sent him here looking for it?" I asked.

"Bavarian chocolate? Brahms' Lullaby?"

"Okay, so he likes German chocolate and whistling the world's most famous lullaby. That doesn't make him a chemist." He walked into the woods, tired and defeated.

"Tom," I gritted my teeth. "You're not listening to me."

"No, you're not listening to me!" He got in my face. "You live for this. All this drama. You've been like that since I met you. Valjean is in prison. Edmond has the necklace. It's over."

I stood there while he walked away. "But Edmond doesn't have the necklace."

He froze.

"I do."

"What?"

"Tom please don't be mad." I grabbed his arm, but he wouldn't look at me.

"You lied to me."

"He told me to take it. Just in case."

He looked into my eyes. "Oh my God."

"What?"

"You believe in it."

"Tom, what are you talking about?"

"You believe Valjean. You believe what he said. That it's some sort of magic."

"I do not."

"Then why did you take it?" he asked.

"Because what if he's right?"

Tom pulled away and stormed off.

"Tom." I ran after him. "Tom, what are you doing?"

"Did you know Edmond wanted us to have personal security?"

I furrowed my brow.

"Yeah. And I almost took him up on it, too. But I knew you wouldn't like it. Especially since he wanted me to keep it from you. So I called him and made him cancel it."

"Is that what this is about?" I asked. "You think I betrayed you?"

"You did!"

"Well, if that isn't the pot calling the kettle black. How many times did you keep things from me in Paris? Like the fact that I'll never be able to have a child!" My voice cracked on the last word.

I felt my throat closing up as tears welled in my eyes. He saw the look on my face and came towards me.

"Don't." I moved past him and trudged back to the house. I didn't hear his footsteps behind me. And I was too angry to look back. So I went to the kitchen, because I had a terrible headache.

A glass of water helped. But I didn't have a clue how I was going to get any sleep.

I changed into a t-shirt and climbed into our bed. Then I called Edmond. It was already morning in Paris, since they were six hours ahead. I wanted to talk to him, because he was the only one who would understand.

"My favorite niece," he said. I could hear him grinning in his office.

"Hello, Uncle Edmond."

"Did Tom tell you the news?" he asked.

"Hmm?"

"About Valjean?"

"Oh yes. I heard he's in prison."

"Are you pleased?" he said.

I got up and looked out the window, waiting for Tom. "I don't know what I am anymore."

"What are you doing up so late?" he asked. "I wasn't expecting your call until this afternoon."

"Have you ever heard of Gustav Lehmann?" His name came to me on the long walk home.

"I don't believe so. Why?"

"He's a German scientist who believes the necklace has healing properties. In Switzerland, Valjean said he had a dying daughter. And the scientist could heal her with this magic cure."

"It sounds a little farfetched to me."

"I know. But the scientist, do you think he's real?"

"I'll have someone look into it."

"Thank you."

"How is your man?"

"Fine." I saw Tom standing in the doorway. "I have to go. But I'll call you later."

"Au revoir."

"Who was that?" Tom took his jacket off.

"Edmond. I told him about the scientist. He's going to look into it."

Tom nodded and finished getting undressed. He took a quick shower while I lay awake in bed. I hated the tension between us. There seemed to be so much of it lately. I wanted the madness to end.

When he came out of the bathroom, I sat up in bed. But he put his boxers on and ignored me.

"I'll show you where it is."

He stopped, but wouldn't turn around to face me.

"I never wanted to keep it from you."

He didn't say anything.

"I just wanted us to be safe." I stared at his back.

"If it means that much to you, then don't show me.

It's probably better if I don't know where it is." He sat down on the edge of our bed. There were a few droplets of water running down his back.

"I don't want you to be mad at me." I slid my hands down his chest.

"I'm not mad at you." He touched my arm. "I just wish everything was easier."

He had a point. There had been way too much going on lately.

"Maybe Mercury is in retrograde."

He laughed, and I breathed a sigh of relief. Then he turned back and pulled me into his lap.

"Why can't I ever stay mad at you?" He touched his nose to mine.

"Because you love me."

He smiled and lay down with me in his arms. I kissed his chest and wrapped my body around him, as he pulled the covers over us. Then I closed my eyes and curled into his strength.

"You're always so warm." I drifted off in his arms, trying to put peaceful thoughts in my head.

But then I remembered Valjean's note in Switzerland.

And his words suddenly make sense.

I won't return. I'm not the one looking for you now.

* * *

When the alarm went off, I felt like a zombie. I'd only gotten a few hours of sleep. But I couldn't miss school. And I had lunch planned with Jimmy. It would be the first time we'd met since Paris.

"No." Tom pulled me back into bed. "Stay with me."

It was tempting, believe me. But I had to be a responsible adult. As much as one can be at eighteen.

I kissed him. "I wish I could. But I've got to go. I'm gonna be late."

I got dressed and grabbed my car keys. We usually drove to school together. But it was nice to drive my car for a change.

Maybe it was lack of sleep. But I felt kind of sick. So I skipped breakfast.

School wasn't so bad. It was the third day back. And most people were getting bored with bullying me. I guess that's the beauty of a two-second attention span. I still heard whispers in the halls, but it was nothing I couldn't deal with. Besides, I was so drained from the night before, that I didn't really care.

During lunch, I drove to a restaurant a few minutes away. Jimmy already had a table waiting, so I was able to order right away. Thankfully, my appetite had returned. But now it meant that I was starving.

"I have some exciting news," he said.

"Oh." I munched on my salad. "What is it?"

"Your mother is coming to visit for a week."

"Really?" I was beaming. "Oh, I'm so happy."

"Yeah, me too." He smirked.

The waitress brought a plate of eight chicken quesadillas with a side of fries.

"Oh, thank God." I slid a couple onto my plate. "Could I have some honey mustard?"

"Sure." The waitress set an extra plate down for Jimmy.

I took a few bites of salad and then stuffed my face with quesadillas. Our waitress returned with a cup of honey mustard, and I thanked her for it. Then I dunked four fries into the sweet sauce and took a bite.

"You have some kind of appetite," Jimmy said.

"Well, I didn't exactly eat breakfast this morning."

"How come?" He put a quesadilla on his plate.

"It's a long story," I talked around my food.

"So how's Tom? I thought he would be here."

"Well." I swallowed and gulped down my water. "Something came up."

"At school."

"No." I shook my head, stabbing my salad with a fork.

"Then what came up?"

"He got suspended for a few days."

"Tom?"

"Yeah." I poured more dressing on my salad.

"That doesn't sound like him."

"It's really just a big misunderstanding. The kids have been teasing me at school." I munched on a fry. "Because we got married, everyone assumes I'm pregnant."

"Well, with the way you're eating, I'm not so sure you aren't."

"Hey!" I threw a fry at him, and he caught it with his mouth.

"It's just a joke. Maybe try to eat breakfast next time."

"I will." I thought about telling him that there would never be any grandchildren. But he seemed so happy, and I didn't want to break it to him yet. So I let him go on believing that it was possible.

"What really happened with you and Josette?" I asked.

"She said she tried to tell you, but you wouldn't listen."

"I know. I wasn't ready."

"You're stubborn," he said.

I ate slower now that I was getting fed.

"Wonder where you get that from." He winked at me and ate his quesadilla.

I wanted to tell him lots of things. Find out if he'd heard about Valjean. Or the fact that my parents were getting divorced. Or the crushing blow of getting rejected by a major university.

But I didn't. He was on cloud nine, and I wanted to keep him that way.

Especially since the love of his life would be here soon.

That afternoon, I had plans to study with Jeanine in the library. It was weird without Tom and Eric around. But it gave us a chance for some girl time. Just one more day, and we'd have our men back.

"Hey, Addie." Jeanine touched my arm. "Are you okay?"

A wave of nausea hit me like a gust of wind. "I don't feel good."

Jeanine shut her textbook. "You're white as a ghost."

"I'll be right back." I left the library and ran to the bathroom. Every stall was empty, so I went into the first one and keeled over. I pulled my hair back and threw up. When it was over, I flushed the toilet and came out of the stall. I felt clammy and weak as I washed my hands, splashing cool water on my face.

Jeanine came into the bathroom. "Are you feeling okay?"

I rinsed my mouth out in the sink. "I don't know."

"Didn't you have lunch with your dad?" she asked.

"Yeah." I looked at her reflection in the mirror. "Maybe it was the quesadillas."

"There was a stomach bug going around. But that was a month ago."

"Hmm." I looked at myself in the glass. I really did look like a ghost.

"Unless..."

"What?" I turned around.

"Well..." she hesitated. "You don't think you could be... pregnant. Do you?"

"No." I shook my head. "Of course not."

"It never hurts to check."

"Jeanine," I smiled. "I can assure you that I'm not pregnant." I dried my hands off on some paper towels. "Now, let's get back to studying. Midterms will be here before you know it."

"When was your last period?"

"What?" I stood in the doorway.

"Your last monthly cycle," she said. "When was it?"

"Jeanine, this is stupid."

"Just tell me when it was, and I'll drop it." She crossed her arms, those blue eyes bright with ferocity.

"Fine," I huffed. "My last period was..." I thought back to December and everything that had happened in Paris. The wedding. The shooting. The hospital. "Umm. I don't remember."

"Think Addie."

"I don't know." I stomped my foot. "It might've been the first week of December."

"Are you sure?" She pulled a calendar up on her phone.

"I think so." Now she had me biting my nails. "Jeanine, this is ridiculous."

"You're late."

"What?" I looked at the dates on her phone.

"By a whole week." She showed me the proof. "We're usually on the same cycle. And you're never late."

I gulped. The doctors in France had said I might see a change in my period. But they said nothing about it completely going away.

"It's just a week," I said. "No big deal."

"I think you should take a pregnancy test."

"What?" I hissed.

"Just to be sure. Don't you want some peace of mind?"

And that's how I found myself at the drug store searching for a pregnancy test. It felt like such a waste of time. There was no way I could be pregnant. But Jeanine didn't know that.

"Okay, most of these look the same." She picked up a box. "Should we get a dual pack? Then you can take the test more than once."

"Oh, just give it to me!" I grabbed the box and marched to the register. There, I saw a pack of chocolate brownies. And I was so nervous that I made the cashier ring those up too.

"What are these for?" Jeanine picked up the brownies.

"I'm stress eating."

"Are you're sure you're not pregnant?" she asked.

I rolled my eyes and she grabbed a travel size bottle of milk.

"To eat with your brownies," she said. But really, she just wanted to make sure I would pee.

A couple underclassmen from school walked in, and I wanted to crawl under a table. If they saw me buying a pregnancy test, it would confirm all the rumors that had been going around. I'd never be able to live this one down.

I paid in cash and grabbed the bag, rushing for the exit. To avoid my peers, I wasn't watching where I was going. So I ran right into them. And the pregnancy test toppled out of the bag.

One of them looked at me. A gangly boy with acne. He pointed his finger at me. "I knew it!"

Jeanine grabbed the test and pushed me out the door. Then I drove to her house, eating brownies and sipping milk the whole way there.

"No!" Jeanine growled when I parked in her driveway. "What's Mom doing here?"

"Well, it's not like we can go to my place."

"Don't worry." Jeanine got out. "I'll tell her we're studying."

So I told Mrs. Travis hi and followed Jeanine up the stairs. I needed to head home soon or Tom would worry. But Jeanine had gotten me this far, and she wasn't about to quit now.

"Girls!" Mrs. Travis knocked on the door. "Do you want anything to eat?"

"No, Mom!" Jeanine opened the box. "We're fine!"

"Okay."

Jeanine handed me one of the tests.

"My massage got cancelled," Mrs. Travis said.

"We have to study!" Jeanine yelled.

I laughed and covered my mouth. It had to be so obvious that we were hiding something.

"Okay. I'll be downstairs. Actually, I think I might go for a run."

"That sounds great!" Jeanine said. "Have a good time!"

We waited in her room. And then Jeanine opened

her door to make sure that Mrs. Travis was really gone. I looked out the window and saw her stretching in the drive. Then she hopped onto the street and started to run.

"Okay." Jeanine put her hands on her hips. "All you have to do is go in there and pee."

"I still say this is a complete waste of time."

"Addie, would you just do it!" she begged.

"Fine!" I went in the bathroom and did as I was told. The good thing was, I actually did have to go. I blamed it on the milk. But it was better than Jeanine making me chug juice beforehand.

I set the test on a tissue over the counter. Then I washed my hands.

For a second, I really studied myself. My face. My complexion. I even lifted my shirt and searched for signs of a baby in my belly. But I looked the same. Just a little tired from getting sick today.

Jeanine knocked on the door. "How's it going in there?"

"Fine." I came out of the bathroom. "Now what?"

"The box said wait three minutes." She grabbed her phone. "Let me set the timer."

I walked into her room and sat down on the bed.

It was the longest three minutes of my life.

"What happens if it's positive?" I asked.

"It will have two pink lines."

"I know that." I looked down. "I mean, what happens?"

She put her hand over mine. "I don't know."

The timer went off and I jumped. Jeanine silenced her phone.

"I can't do it," I said. "You go look."

So she walked into the bathroom without a word. I

waited on her bed, twiddling my thumbs. In a few seconds, she was back. But she still hadn't said anything. She sat down and handed me the test.

I glanced at her, searching for a clue in her eyes. But she had her poker face on.

I took a deep breath and looked at the test.

And there they were. Two pink lines.

"This has to be a mistake." I stood up. "Don't these things put out false positives all the time?"

"Not that brand." Jeanine emptied the box. "How about round two?"

I drank a bottle of water and peed on the stick. Then I set it on the same tissue on the counter.

This time, as I was washing my hands, I thought about how amazing it would be if I actually were pregnant. Ever since the shooting, I thought I'd never be able to experience this part of womanhood. Taking pregnancy tests and waiting to see the results. In that sense, it was actually kind of fun.

"I want to look this time."

"Okay." Jeanine checked the timer.

When it was up, I went into the bathroom and set the first test on the counter.

Now there were four pink lines. And I didn't know how to feel about it.

So I grinned like a fool and cried, bringing my hand to my mouth.

"What does it say?" Jeanine peeked inside.

I watched the expression on her face as she saw the results. She looked surprised.

"Well." I dried my eyes. "What do you think?"

"You're pregnant."

Chapter 17

Tom

I slept in late. And when I woke up and reached for Addie, I hated that she wasn't there.

It was ten thirty, which made me realize that being suspended wasn't half bad. I had plenty of school work to keep me occupied. And now that I'd been given zeros for three days straight, I'd have to study like hell to keep from losing my admission to Georgia.

I put a shirt on and went downstairs. Then I cooked breakfast for myself. And I'll admit, it wasn't the same being alone in this big house. I missed Addie. I needed her here.

Thinking of her, I called Edmond to make plans. I knew Addie wasn't happy. I could see it in her eyes.

She'd finally been reunited with her family. And now the one in Savannah was splitting apart.

"And then we could go to Italy for a few days," I said.

"You're welcome to use my plane."

"Thanks Edmond. Addie really misses Europe. She hasn't adjusted that well since we got back."

"She told me to look into a Gustav Lehmann."

I hadn't even remembered the scientist's name. Addie must have been listening.

"There is a chemist living in Munich by that name. He teaches at the university."

I held my breath. "Did you talk to him?"

"No. Apparently, he's out of the country."

Bavarian chocolate. Brahm's Lullaby.

"Tom, is there something going on?" he asked.

"I think he was here last night."

"Who?"

"Lehmann. The scientist."

"And what would he be doing there?"

"I think Valjean hired him."

"Valjean is locked up."

"I know." I went upstairs. "But in Switzerland, Frank found a note from Valjean." I went through my drawers. "I know I kept it." I dumped my socks out. "What did it say?"

"I think Valjean was the only one you really needed to be worried about."

"I found it!" I opened the note. "It says, 'I won't return. I'm not the one looking for you now.' What does that mean? Valjean must have known he was going to prison. And what about the last part? That could be talking about the scientist."

"When they found Valjean, he was getting on a train headed for Germany."

"That can't be a coincidence," I said.

"Let me find someone who can tell me more about Lehmann."

"And what do we do in the meantime?"

"Do you still have the gun I gave you?" he asked.

"Yes."

"Keep it loaded."

He hung up, and I knew Addie was right. I felt bad about everything I'd said to her last night. Maybe a trip to Paris would be just the thing to cheer her up. It wouldn't be for another couple months. And then I'd surprise her with a few nights in Italy. The honeymoon I'd promised, but never been able to deliver.

I went for a walk and then spent the rest of the day doing homework. Late in the afternoon, I got my guitar out and played for a little bit. Addie's comment had rubbed me the wrong way last night.

I hadn't given up the guitar. It's just that I had something else in my life now. Something that meant more to me than anything. *Her.* And she should know that more than anyone else.

When five o'clock came, I started to worry. She'd texted me that she was going to the library with Jeanine after school. But they didn't usually study for more than an hour.

Maybe she was still mad about last night. Maybe she didn't want to see me.

I was about to call when I heard someone at the front door. I ran down the stairs as she let herself inside. She didn't look happy. And while I didn't want to overwhelm her, I was so happy to see her.

I'd missed her.

"Hey." I approached her in the foyer. "How was your day?"

"Fine." She shut the door and stumbled. "Can you take that?"

"Sure." I grabbed her backpack and set it on the floor.

She yawned and went into the den, collapsing on the couch.

"What do you want for dinner?"

"I'm not really hungry." She rubbed her stomach. "I might be sick."

I knelt down and felt her forehead. "You do feel kind of warm."

"I had lunch with Jimmy today. And then when I was studying with Jeanine, I threw up."

"What did you eat?" I threw a blanket over her and took her shoes off.

"Quesadillas."

"Hmm. Maybe you had some bad food."

"Jeanine said there was a stomach bug going around."

I went into the bathroom and ran hot water over a washcloth. Then I came back and placed it on her forehead. "Well, I hope you don't have it."

"I hope so, too."

"Do you want me to make you a cup of tea or some hot soup?"

"Okay. I don't know how much I'll be able to eat."

"That's all right. You can eat it later if you're not hungry."

"Thank you." She grabbed my hand when I turned to leave. "Tom?"

I sat down on the couch. "Yeah, baby. What is it?"

"What did Dr. Laurent tell you about me when I was in the hospital?"

I brushed her hair out of her face. I had no idea why she'd brought this up.

"I mean, about being able to have a baby. Am I completely infertile?"

"No." I frowned. "There is a very small chance. But even if you were able to get pregnant, it would be too dangerous."

"Why?"

"Didn't you hear what the doctors said? In your condition, childbirth could kill you."

She swallowed and looked away.

"Did they say something to you at school again

today?"

"No. Nothing I couldn't handle. I was just curious."

"You're sure?" I cupped her cheek in my hand.

"Yes." She gave me a gorgeous smile.

"Good." I kissed her. "I'll go make your soup."

I went to the kitchen and whipped up some vegetable soup. I made it with plenty of broth, so she could drink a cup if she wanted to. She felt cold. Even though her skin was clammy. It worried me.

"You feelin' any better?" I brought her a dinner tray with a cup of chamomile tea and a bowl of soup.

"A little bit." She sat up with the blanket in her lap.

I helped her with the tray, and she ate a little soup. Then she sipped at her tea.

"I remember the first time I ever drank this," she said. "It was in the kitchen with you."

I leaned in and kissed her a few times, leaving the last one on her forehead.

"I'm sorry I yelled at you last night. I've been thinking about it all day. I feel terrible."

She giggled. "It's okay. I don't think we'll ever be one of those couples who never fight."

"But is that normal?" I asked.

"I think so." She drank her tea. "I forgot to call Adeline today."

"You could call her now."

She shook her head. "It's too late. I'll just call her tomorrow."

"I talked to Edmond today."

Her eyes lit up.

"There is a scientist living in Munich named Gustav Lehmann."

"So it's true," she said. "Valjean wasn't lying."

"He said Lehmann was reported to be out of the country."

"Do you think it was him?" She finished her tea.

"I don't know. But when they found Valjean, he was on a train headed for Germany."

"That has to be the reason." She tried to move the tray off her lap, but she was too weak.

"Let me." I set it on the end table and sat back down. "I hope you feel better soon."

"Me too." She leaned against my chest and closed her eyes.

I wrapped my arm around her and tucked her head under my chin.

"I think I want to take a bath," she said.

"Okay." I picked her up in my arms, because she was so tired.

When I made it upstairs, I set her down in the bedroom and ran a hot bath. Then I helped her take her clothes off and pulled her hair back. She gained a little energy as I helped her into the bathroom. And then she eased into the tub on her own.

"Ah." She leaned her head back. "This is nice."

"Do you want me to put another washcloth on your head?"

"No, I'm fine." She closed her eyes. "But I am kind of thirsty."

"I'll get you some water." I grabbed a bottle downstairs and she drank most of it.

That was a relief. I hoped it was exhaustion from last night, not a virus that was making her feel lousy. The last thing she needed was to be sick when school had just started back.

"Will you stay in here with me?" she asked.

I was surprised she wanted me to. "Yes, of course."

"I want to talk." She relaxed in the tub. "I feel like we never talk anymore."

"What do you mean? We talk all the time."

"But not like we used to. Now all we talk about is the necklace and Valjean. It's stressful."

I chuckled because she said it like a little girl. "Yes, it is."

"I want to talk about us."

"Okay." I sat down. "We can do that."

"I remember when you came to Maple Creek High. I had the biggest crush on you."

"You did not. I thought you hated me."

"I thought you were hot," she said.

I laughed. "What else?"

"I thought, there's no way someone who looks that good can't be a jerk."

"Why would you think that?" I asked.

"Hot guys. They kind of have a bad reputation."

"I didn't know that."

"Well, that's why I'm here to educate you." She opened her eyes and smiled.

I smirked, resting my knuckles under my chin.

"I never knew someone could care about me as much as you do."

"Well, I've spent most of my life loving you," I said.

She sat perfectly still as she stared at me.

"Sometimes, I still can't believe your mine. If I'm awake at night, I just lie there and watch you. Even now, it still doesn't feel real. I can't believe you said yes. I can't believe you're my wife."

A tear streamed down from her eye.

"I got lucky somehow. I got you."

"Are you trying to seduce me?" she asked.

"You're the one who wanted to talk. I'm just being honest."

"Get over here." She gave me a come hither stare.

I took my clothes off and stepped into the warm water. Once I was submerged, she lay against me with her head on my heart. And we sat like that for the longest time—just the two of us in the tub.

"I think that there is one person for everyone."

I cradled her in my arms and kissed her cheek. It was nice to listen to her voice in the night.

"And if you're lucky—only if you're lucky—you get to spend your whole life with them."

"So you think we were destined?" I asked.

"I don't know. But it sure feels like it."

"I believe that there's one person for everyone, too." I tucked a lock of hair behind her ear.

She leaned her head back to look at me. "I should hope so."

I touched her cheek and gave her a kiss. Then I ran my fingers down her back.

"You're pretty romantic." She grinned. "You know that?"

"Is that a good thing?" I wondered.

"Yes." She kissed me. "A very good thing."

* * *

Once we got out of the tub, I worked on homework at my desk. I tried to stop thinking about these three days of nothing but zeros. But it was hard. How could I ever recoup the damage?

Addie had wandered off about an hour ago. And she seemed to be feeling better. I walked down the hall in search of her, hoping she would be ready for bed soon. Because real men like to cuddle.

The door to her art room was cracked. So I knocked, and she told me to come in.

She was drawing a picture of the necklace. It was still black on white—no green yet. But she would come back and fill the emerald with color when the time was right.

"That looks great." I leaned against the wall. "When did you start it?"

"Tonight." She put her pencil down. "It's been so long since I've drawn anything. I miss it."

I saw the necklace in her lap. She caught my eye and picked it up.

"Just using it for inspiration," she said. "It's always easier to model after the original."

"I'm not going to take it away from you." I held my hands up. "I promise."

"I didn't think you would." She stared at the emerald in the palm of her hand.

I was about to ask her to come to bed, but I saw her lips move.

"I know it doesn't make any sense. But somehow, it makes me feel safe. Like I'm closer to her."

"To your grandmother?" I asked.

"To all of them really. My family in France."

I watched her smile at the stone.

"Edmond won't admit it, but even he must sense that there's something special about it. He always sends it with me like a good luck charm. I know you think it's done nothing but cause us danger. I used to feel the same way. But after everything that's happened, I'm still alive. Maybe it's not the killer." She looked deeply into my eyes. "Maybe it's what saves me. Maybe it's the reason why I'm still alive."

I couldn't think of the right thing to say. So I didn't

say anything at all.

"I know it sounds crazy."

"No." I circled my arms around her until she was right in front of me. "It's not."

"Hmm." She pressed her nose against my cheek. "Let's go to bed."

I swept her off her feet and carried her to our room. She brushed her hair and then climbed between the sheets. I got in with her and turned the light out, pulling her against me in the dark.

"I forgot to tell you," she said. "Jimmy said Josette is coming to visit."

"When?"

"Next week."

"That's great." I caressed her arm.

"I know. I'm so excited to see her."

"I'm sure she's excited to see you, too."

She looked at me. "You really think so?"

"Absolutely. She loves you."

She snuggled closer and curled her leg around my hips. I kissed her hair and sighed, glad that we could finally get some sleep tonight. But when I woke up several hours later, she was gone.

"Addie?" I saw the light on in the bathroom. And then I heard her.

It was five a.m. and she was hurling in the toilet. I opened the door and saw her on the floor. She was holding her hair back as she puked. I got down beside her and held it for her.

"It's okay, baby." I rubbed her back. "I'm here."

She took a breath and flushed the toilet. I wet a new washcloth with warm water and wiped her face with it. She moaned and lay down on the floor, pressing her cheek against the tile.

"Addie." I was getting scared. "Tell me what you want me to do."

"Help me rinse my mouth out," she said.

I helped her to the sink where she brushed her teeth. Then I ran a hot bath and helped her inside. She sank down in the tub and shut her eyes. I hated to see her like this. It made me feel helpless.

"Maybe you shouldn't go to school today." I touched her cheek.

"But I can't miss—"

"You're sick. And you need to stay home until you get better." I put the warm washcloth over her head. "It's my last day of suspension. I'll be here to take care of you. I'll get you whatever you need."

Her eyes were glazed over. "Okay."

I knew she felt awful. And there was no way I'd let her go to school like this.

"Hey Tom?"

I splashed warm water over her arms and shoulders.

"I think I might be..." She was struggling with something, trying to get the words out.

"You're sick," I said. "It's a stomach bug."

"No, I think..." She shut her eyes and reached for my hand.

"I know you feel bad, baby." I squeezed her hand and grabbed a towel. "I'm going to warm up some soup and bring it up here. I'll bring a lot of water, too. I'll be right back."

"Tom, wait," she cried. "I don't think that's it."

Tears streamed down from her eyes. But I couldn't figure out what she was saying.

"You just feel bad, honey." I lifted her chin. "Okay?"

228

She nodded, her lower lip trembling.

"I'll be right back." I turned to leave.

"I could be pregnant."

I stopped in my tracks. And I had to grab the doorframe to brace myself.

"This could be morning sickness."

I turned around. And I saw it in her eyes. She wanted it to be true.

"Addie, you know that..." I felt the daggers she sent my way.

She looked angry.

"Well, I'll be right back." I went downstairs and heated the soup.

Her longing brought tears to my eyes. I turned off the burner and sank to the floor.

The truth is, Addie could never be pregnant. It just wasn't possible. But I knew how badly she wanted it to be. It made me realize that no matter how hard I tried, I might never be able to make her happy.

What if I wasn't enough?

I dried my eyes and made her a cup of tea. Then I took it upstairs with the soup. Addie had already gotten out of the tub. She lay in bed with a washcloth over her head. And she wouldn't even look at me.

I knew this would always cause tension between us. And there was nothing I could do about it. She probably thought I never wanted to talk about the possibility. Since it only conjured up pain.

She would be right. And it wasn't because I didn't want her to be pregnant.

I didn't want to give her false hope. She'd only be more devastated in the end.

But now she thought I was the bad guy, squashing her dreams.

But I was also a realist. And I couldn't let her live a life of eternal disappointment.

Still, there was a part of me that I'd hidden from her. Deep down inside, I longed for a miracle. I'd fantasized about having children with her, too. But we had to accept what the fates allowed.

It's not that I didn't want it to be true. I just knew that it couldn't be.

Because if she really were pregnant, it would've been amazing.

Chapter 18

Addie

Now that I knew Tom's true reaction, it was plain to see that he'd never be happy about this. But it cast shadows of doubt on my certainty. After all, how could I possibly be pregnant?

It's why I didn't want to believe it at first.

Because it was too good to be true.

I mean, could you fake a pregnancy test? Twice?

I didn't know, so that's why I took a step back. I hadn't been entirely positive when my last period was. And there was no guarantee that the calendar Jeanine had mapped out for me was accurate. In two weeks, I'd know for sure. In the meantime, I distracted myself with the news that Josette was in town.

She arrived on a Friday. And we all went to the airport to greet her.

In the last week, my relationship with Tom had gotten weaker. It was his blunt reaction that had truly killed me. The fact that there was no doubt in his mind that I was destined to be barren forever.

To be honest, it kind of pissed me off. He was supposed to be my husband, someone who I could share my hopes and dreams with. Clearly, his aspirations weren't lining up with mine.

"You look beautiful!" Josette gave me a hug, kissing my cheeks at the airport.

"So do you." It was nice to be with my mother. "I'm so glad you're here."

She had a lovely French accent. And I thought she looked like a super model.

I couldn't believe she was my mom. She was just so cool—classy and elegant. I was proud to be her daughter, even if we hadn't exactly figured out what that meant yet.

"We're taking you out to dinner," Jimmy said.

"That sounds wonderful." She wrapped her arms around us. "Let's go."

Since it was Friday night, we had to wait for a table. But not too long. Jimmy and I had thought about making reservations. But her flight had been delayed. So it was just as well.

"Let's order a bottle of wine," Josette said. "To celebrate."

"We won't be able to drink any of it," Tom said.

"Oh, that's right. I'm sorry. Then never mind."

"No." I smiled. "You two go ahead. It's all right."

"Are you sure?" she asked.

"Yes."

"That sounds perfect, because we actually have something to tell you," Jimmy said.

"Oh, really?" I wondered. "What?"

Jimmy admired Josette and then looked at us. "Your mother and I are getting married."

She showed me the diamond engagement ring on her finger.

I was so excited I couldn't contain myself. "Really?"

"Yes." Josette put her hand on Jimmy's chest. "We've been wanting to tell you."

"When did this happen?" I asked.

Jimmy looked into her eyes. "Do you want to tell them?"

"Okay," she beamed. "It was his last night in Paris."

"And it was just the two of us," Jimmy said.

"We've been apart for so long. I didn't know if he would ever love me again. But he said he did. And that we had the rest of our lives to spend together. I was just so happy, I said yes right then!"

"Wow." I couldn't believe it. "So you're getting married?"

"Yes," they said together.

"When is the wedding?" I asked.

"This summer," Josette said.

"I'm so excited." I got up and hugged them both, fighting the tears that would come.

I felt Tom's eyes on me. It was weird because things weren't the best between us right now. At a moment like this, he was the one person I wanted to be celebrating with. But I couldn't.

"I've already turned in my resignation letter," Jimmy said. "But I'm finishing out the semester."

I sat back down as the appetizers came. "What are you talking about?"

"I'm moving to Paris."

A wave of emotions hit me all at once. My parents were getting married. And I couldn't be happier. But if they were both going to be four thousand miles away, then where did that leave me?

"Oh." I didn't know what else to say.

"Well, with you and Tom headed off for college," Jimmy said. "I figured it was better to wait until after you graduated."

Tom put a couple onion rings on my plate,

because I'd failed to touch the appetizers.

"But we plan to come visit," Josette said. "And you can come see us as much as you like."

I picked up my fork and knife. Even though that wasn't necessary to eat an onion ring.

"It's just that I didn't realize you'd be moving to France," I said.

"It's not like you're never going to see us," Jimmy smiled. "And you have Tom."

I hated being mad at my husband. But we hadn't bounced back to normal since the night he told me there was no way I could ever be pregnant. I'd wanted to apologize for being so cold. But he'd hurt me.

Tonight, I'd been excited to see my parents. But now they were the ones letting me down.

After dinner, we made plans to see them again soon. Josette was staying with Jimmy. But she wanted to see the mansion, so I invited them to come over the next day. It would be a nice chance to catch up and have that conversation with my mother that was long overdue.

I was finally ready to hear the truth.

We drove home in silence, and I looked over at Tom. He kept his eyes on the road, but his jaw was taut. He was still mad at me. There was no doubt in my mind. And I wasn't so sure that I'd stopped being mad at him either.

It was a silent drive until we reached the house. I got out and went inside, perpetuating the silence between us. Then I took my shoes off and sauntered into the kitchen. I opened the fridge and wondered if I should stop by the grocery store tomorrow. I had no idea what Josette liked.

"You didn't eat much at dinner."

I felt him behind me, looming and smoldering.

"Well." I shut the fridge. "I wasn't very hungry."

I crossed my arms and moved in front of the counter.

"Don't you want to talk about it?" he asked.

"About what?"

"Oh, I don't know. Maybe the fact that Jimmy is moving to another continent."

"He's a grown man," I said. "He can do whatever he wants."

"So you're saying it doesn't bother you?"

I turned around to face him. "What doesn't bother me?"

"Eleanor and Jeffrey are getting a divorce. And she's moving to Atlanta. Jimmy and Josette are getting married. And he's moving to Europe. Before you know it, the only parent you'll have left is Jeff."

I bit my lip as tears filled my eyes. Tom saw them and reached out. But I dodged him and hurried out of the kitchen.

"Why won't you argue with me?" he yelled.

"Because I don't want to argue with you!"

He grabbed my arm and pushed me up against the wall. I looked up at him and trembled. Secretly, I wanted him to say he was sorry and put his hands all over me. We hadn't stood this close to each other in what felt like a long time. I felt his body heat and smelled his cologne. It made me blush.

"Why not?" He put his hands on the wall, caging me in with his arms.

I looked at his eyes. They were scorching amber. And he was smoldering like never before.

"Because I'm too upset."

He cupped my cheek in his hand. "Baby."

It felt so good it made me shudder.

"Don't." I pulled out of his grasp and ran up the stairs. I had to regain control from him. He couldn't just put those brown eyes on me and think all of our problems would go away.

"Addie!" He was on my heels, but I wasn't surprised. I knew he would come after me.

"Just leave me alone, Tom." I went into our bedroom and slammed the door. But that didn't do much good. Because he walked right in. So I headed for the bathroom next.

"Addie." He grabbed the door before I could shut it in his face. "Stop it!"

My arms were getting tired. So I gave out from the exertion.

He just stood there and looked at me, standing in the doorway.

I slid down to the floor and burst into tears, burying my face in my hands. It was all too much.

My biological parents were getting married.

And my adoptive parents were getting a divorce.

Apart from feeling abandoned, my one source of strength had gotten away from me. I needed Tom. He was my rock. He always had been. And I felt so lost without him, drifting from day to day.

He knelt down and touched my face. "Talk to me, baby."

I saw the look in his eyes. And I couldn't take it anymore.

"I hate this."

"I know." He brought his forehead to mine. "I hate it, too."

"I don't wanna fight anymore," I said.

"Neither do I."

"I'm sorry." I dove into his arms. "I'm so sorry."

"I'm sorry, too." He rubbed my back.

"And I am upset," I cried. "I just got him back."

"I know." Tom pulled me into his lap as I buried my face in his chest.

It felt so good to be held like this. One of the things that had drawn me to Tom was the fact that he was always so warm. I liked to be petted and comforted by him. It was one of the many things he was good at.

"I'm so sorry about what I said." He ran his fingers through my hair. "I know I hurt you. But all I'm trying to say is that I want you in whatever way I can have you."

"You do have me, Tom." I stroked his face. "You always have."

He smiled and we kissed. It was soft and sweet. But just as good as the first.

"They say the first year of marriage is the hardest." He tucked a lock of hair behind my ear.

I looked into his eyes and smiled. "Then let's go make up."

He gave me that crooked grin. The one that made my skin tingle. I stood up first and stretched out my hand. He took it and got to his feet. Then I led him into our bedroom and we made up.

* * *

"You really don't have to do all this," I said.

Tom stood in the kitchen with his apron on. Since he was the better cook, I'd commissioned him for the day. Jimmy and Josette were coming over in the afternoon and then staying for dinner. And Tom had prepared a menu that was making my mouth water.

"We cooked a nice meal for Jeff and Eleanor," he said. "It's only fair."

He had a point. I munched on pistachios as he cooked.

"Why have you been calling him Jeff lately?" I wondered. Last night was the first time I'd heard it.

"Well." He set a pair of tongs down. "Apparently, that's what everyone calls him."

"What?"

"Yeah, the only one who harps on calling him Jeffrey is Eleanor."

"Hmm." I grabbed a handful of almonds. "I didn't know that."

"Yeah." He finished chopping steak. "I didn't think you did."

"This looks delicious." I rubbed my stomach.

"Hungry already?" he asked. "It's only two thirty."

"That means they'll be here soon." I clapped my hands together and circled the room.

"You excited?" He dumped the steak chunks in a tub and seasoned them with teriyaki sauce.

"Yeah." I nodded, jumping up and down like a little girl. "I'm just so happy to see them."

He put the steak in the fridge. "That needs to stay in there for a few hours."

"I bet it's going to be delicious." I ran my hands down his torso and put my head on his back. He turned around and gave me a kiss, braiding his fingers through mine. "How did I get so lucky?"

He tapped my nose. "I'm the lucky one."

"Ooh! Can we start making the cake?" I asked.

He looked at his watch. "We're gonna have to. What time will they be here?"

"Around four."

"But first." He picked me up and set me down on the counter. "We have some more making up to do."

"Tom!" I giggled, lightly hitting his arm. "We have guests coming!"

"And don't you want to be in a good mood when they arrive?"

He gave me a look that sent delicious shivers down my spine.

"I'll take that as a yes."

"Tom!"

He picked me up again. And this time, I landed on the couch.

"I thought we were going to bake a cake." I shut my eyes as he kissed my neck.

"We will." He slid his hands under my top. "But first..."

I tried to argue. I really did. We needed to have everything ready for when Josette and Jimmy arrived.

"You have the softest skin," he whispered in my ear.

But I'm a sucker for sweet talk. So I lay back and relaxed, running my fingers down the back of his shirt.

"Okay," I said. And I felt his smile against my lips.

He savored every kiss and looked down at me in awe. "You're so beautiful."

I wrapped my arms around him and we made up again.

* * *

I was on cloud nine when Josette arrived. Jimmy was with her, and I couldn't have been happier.

We all sat in the den and talked until it was time to eat. Tom cooked wild rice and steamed green beans to go along with the steak. And it was all so delicious that

I went back for seconds.

There was a chocolate cake for dessert. And it was nice to have something to contribute. Lately, it felt like Tom had done all the cooking. And I'd just been the one to make a salad.

When the sun went down, Tom lit a fire. We lounged in the den while Josette told us stories about her life in Paris. Then Jimmy brought up tales from their courtship, when they'd first met and fallen in love.

I leaned against Tom and swooned, feeling sleepy. It was so good to see my parents together. And even better to have them in my life. How had I gone all these years without them?

"It's getting late," Tom said. "Why don't y'all just stay?"

"Oh, no." Josette got up. "We wouldn't want to impose."

"No, you wouldn't be imposing at all." In fact, I was pretty ecstatic about the idea and thrilled Tom had brought it up.

"Well." Jimmy looked at her. "It's the weekend. Why not?"

"We have plenty of room," I said, trying to sell them on a sleepover.

"Okay," Josette agreed. "I don't see why not."

I was so happy I could've screamed. Instead, I changed the sheets in the guest room downstairs and prettied the place up as much as possible. I put towels out in the hallway bathroom and grabbed a couple spare toothbrushes, since we always kept extras on hand.

"It's been ages since I've been in this room." Josette found me making up the bed.

"I remember the first time I stayed here. I'd just met Tom."

"Where did Papa sleep?" she asked.

"In there." I pointed to the room down the hall.

She turned back and stared, like it haunted her. Then she crept in that direction and opened the door. I stayed behind, not knowing what to say. She looked at his bed and the pictures on his nightstand. Then she saw a collection of paintings we'd left in there to remember him by.

"He always loved to paint," she said. "That must be where you got it from."

"Josette?" I leaned against the doorframe. "How come you never came to visit him?"

She looked down and pressed her lips into a fine line.

"I'm not judging you or trying to make you feel guilty. I just always wondered why."

She took a seat. "Why don't you close the door?"

I did what she said and sat down on the bed. "What happened back then?"

Tears were already coming down as she struggled to rein in her emotions.

"Do you know what really happened to Antoinette that night?" I asked.

She dried her eyes and nodded. "Yes."

"Will you tell me?" I knew she'd tried in the past. But now, I was finally ready to hear the truth.

She licked her lips and looked out the window. "It all started with the necklace."

Chapter 19

Many moons ago, Antoinette Beaumont left Paris for the first time. Her father had business dealings in Georgia. So Antoinette departed for America with her elder brother, Edmond and their parents.

They took a summer home in Savannah. And Antoinette felt free at last. Her bedroom faced the garden, where she spent time planting roses. In no time, the family was attending movies and barbeques, mingling with the local residents. Until one day when Antoinette felt someone watching her.

He was a shy boy who never said much. He stood in the corner every weekend at dances. And on Sunday mornings, he sat with his parents at church. She felt his warm stares from a distance. And nothing had ever disturbed her more. So when school started that autumn, she decided to do something about it.

"Why are you always staring at me?" she asked.

He stood at his locker, completely petrified.

"Well." She had no patience at fifteen. "Aren't you going to say something?"

He turned to walk away.

"Wait." She grabbed his arm. "I didn't mean to be rude."

He tried to breathe, but she made him so nervous.

"My name is Antoinette Beaumont." She stuck out her hand. "What's yours?"

He cleared his throat and shook her hand. "Daniel Sutton."

"So why are you always looking at me?"

He stared into her emerald eyes. They were so unique.

"Because you're the prettiest girl I've ever seen."

She was surprised. He turned to walk away.

"Then why didn't you just come over and say something?"

He blushed. "I didn't know I was allowed to."

From that moment on, the two were inseparable. Antoinette quite liked the American boy from Georgia. He had all the Southern charm a girl could ask for. But he was gentle and sweet.

His family were wealthy land owners, descended from the Civil War era. The couple spent summers out on the lake, rowing in his father's boat. And when winter came, they cozied up in front of the fire.

As seasons changed, their love blossomed. And Daniel took up painting. It was the only way to express all the wild abandon he felt for her on the inside. Before long, they were downright mad for each other.

On her sixteenth birthday, Antoinette's father gave her an emerald necklace. It was a family heirloom, and there was no other like it. The stone hung heavy and cold against her breast. But Antoinette couldn't deny feeling drawn to the emerald. It was the very embodiment of her.

"Daniel!" Antoinette ran to keep up as he pulled her by the hand. "What are you doing?"

He took her inside while his parents weren't home. "I want to show you something."

She waited in the hall as he unlocked a secret door. They'd run up the stairs to reach it.

"Are you ready?" He turned back, guarding the entrance. He was nervous and excited all at once.

She nodded and he opened the door. Then he led her into the dusty attic he'd been bursting to show her.

Antoinette walked in and looked around. When a bat flew overhead, she screamed. Daniel wrapped her in his arms and covered her face, since she seemed so afraid. "Is it gone?" she asked.

"Yeah." He looked at the ceiling. "I still need to do something about that."

She giggled. But then she saw paintings leaned against the far wall. They were breathtaking.

"Whose are these?" she asked. Her father had been an art collector for years. She loved it.

"Well." He took a breath. "They're mine."

She smiled. "Really? You never told me you liked to paint."

"I've only taken it up recently." He watched her eyeballing his work. It made him agitated. He wanted her to love it as much as he did. "So what do you think?"

"They're so beautiful." She put her hand to her heart. "Where did you paint this?"

"By the lake." It was a landscape with water, trees and a setting sun. There was a girl in the painting. Her hair was blonde, but her back was turned to the viewer. She appeared to be out of reach.

"Who is that supposed to be?" she asked.

"You."

"And what does it mean?" She felt him moving closer. "The perspective of the painter?"

"I think it's fear that the object of his affection might disappear."

Antoinette spun around. "Leave?" She found it

absurd. "I'm not going anywhere."

"Not yet." He looked out the window. "Your father's business here isn't permanent."

"It could be," she chimed, hopeful. "If he wanted it to."

As she approached him, he turned and slid his hands around her waist. Then he kissed her. What started out soft, gentle and sweet quickly turned passionate. So she put her head on his shoulder.

"I don't know what I would do if I never saw you again." He touched her hair.

"You don't need to worry about that." She caressed his face with her hands. "I promise."

They kissed and frolicked in the back yard. It was a summer spent in each other's arms. Bicycle rides and trips to the beach. Neither had ever been happier. But their summertime bliss was about to come to an end.

"Moving?" Antoinette shouted. "Back to France?"

The countess was packing her bags in the master suite. "Yes, you're father's work here is done."

"But what about my schooling? I'm about to start my last year at Maple Creek High."

"You can finish up in France. You know the schools are much better in Europe."

Antoinette began to cry. She couldn't hold back. She couldn't hold it in.

"Antoinette, darling." The countess comforted her. "It will all be all right."

"No, it won't." She pulled away, drying her eyes. "What about Daniel?"

"You haven't been intimate with him yet. Have you?"

"No, Mama." She felt accused. "Of course not.

We wanted to wait."

"Wait for what?" The count entered the room. He was a strong, tall man who often favored cigars and cognac to real people. The only exception, of course, being his beloved daughter, Antoinette.

"Papa." She took his hands. "I made a promise to Daniel. I can't leave."

The count looked at her. "My pretty little Antoinette all grown up." He patted her hand. "The boy is rich for sure. But he's not French. And he doesn't have royal blood."

She jerked away from him, backing into the wall. "I won't go back to France! You can't make me!"

"Darling." The count lit a cigar. "Be a dear and talk some sense into your foolish daughter."

Antoinette couldn't breathe. The count slammed the door. And she felt the walls closing in.

"Come now, Antoinette. It's all right." The countess hugged her close. "It's not unusual to have a summer love. But that's all it is. You'll forget him in time. And there are plenty of fine gentlemen in Paris. When we return, I'll have dozens of suitors lined up for you in no time."

"I don't want dozens of suitors!" She stormed out. "I want Daniel."

She lay in bed awake that night, waiting for the house to fall asleep. As soon as the clock struck midnight, she grabbed a bag and filled it with her things. Then she opened her bedroom window and dropped the bag. It fell to the ground with a muted thud.

She'd never been the biggest fan of heights. Thankfully, there was a rather large oak tree by her window. So she took a deep breath and made the leap, closing the window behind her. Then she scaled the branches and landed on the ground where she collected her bag.

Antoinette walked her bicycle down the lane and looked back at the summer house. It had been a pleasant home for the past two years. But it would mean nothing if they took it away from her.

She mounted her bike and strapped the bag to her back. Then she rode the four miles to Daniel's house. She was thirsty and out of breath by the time she reached the mansion. It was the middle of the night, and she was covered in sweat. But she hid her bike in the woods and snuck around the house.

Blood was pounding through her veins. She'd never done something so thrilling.

She picked up a rock and tossed it at his window. Then another. Then another.

Daniel got out of bed and saw her outside. Then he opened his window and stuck his head out. "Antoinette, is that you?"

"Yes!" she whispered. "Please, come down."

Daniel put some clothes on and climbed the tree outside his window. Antoinette ran into his arms and cried. He held her close and ran his fingers through her hair. She was sobbing uncontrollably.

"What's the matter?" He cupped her face in his hands.

"We're going back to Paris." She choked on the words, barely able to get them out.

"What?"

"Papa just said we're leaving before the summer's over. You were right."

His eyes widened in terror, as he wrapped her in his arms. "I can't lose you."

"I won't go," she cried, burying her face in his neck. "I won't go. They can't make me. Not without you."

"Why don't you come inside?" he asked, leading her around the front of the house.

"What about your parents?"

"They left this afternoon on a business trip. They won't be back until Monday."

She nodded and went with him into the house. Then she took a shower to wash away the grime of the bike ride. But all she really did was cry.

When she came out in clean clothes, he was pacing in the den. She didn't want to squander these moments. She was afraid her parents might take them away forever. She would have to bottle up every last one until she saw him in her dreams.

"Why don't we get married?" he asked.

"What?" She was shocked. It had never occurred to her that they could do something like that.

She was sitting on the couch. So he got down on both knees and grabbed her hand. "Do you love me?"

"Yes."

"And do you want to be with me?"

She nodded with tears in her eyes. "Very much so."

"Then let's just get married." He reached into his pocket. "I already bought a ring."

"When did you do that?" she asked.

"A while ago." He opened it. "I wanted to have your father's permission first but..."

Antoinette put her hands to her chest as she looked at the delicate creation. It was an exquisite white diamond centered between two emeralds. It looked like no other ring she'd ever seen.

"I picked this one because of the emeralds," he said. "Because they match your eyes."

She plunged into a kiss and wrapped her arms around him. "Yes," she said against his lips.

"Wait," he chuckled. "But I haven't even asked you yet."

"I don't care." She kissed his face. "My answer is yes."

He took the ring out of the box and slid it on her finger. "Let's do it tomorrow."

"What? Get married?"

He nodded.

"But I don't have anything to wear."

"My mother's wedding dress is in the hall closet. You're about the same size." He got up and started digging around in there.

"Daniel."

But he returned in a flash, holding the dress up as proof.

"Daniel." She stood up. "I can't wear your mother's wedding dress."

"Why not?"

"Because it would be wrong. She's not even here."

"She won't mind. I promise. She loves you. And she already knows about the ring."

"Who else knows about it?" she asked.

"Just Mom. She helped me pick it out."

Antoinette gave in and went upstairs to try the dress on. It fit perfectly, but Daniel had to help her with the buttons. "It's bad luck to see the bride before the wedding," she said.

"I don't believe that." He looked at her in the mirror. "It's just an old tradition."

She leaned into him as he wrapped his arms

around her. They watched each other in the mirror.

"Then why don't we make a new one?" She shut her eyes, reveling in his warmth and touch.

"I have an idea." He turned her around. "A wedding portrait."

"What? Daniel, I'm so tired." She yawned just thinking about it, her eyes glazing over.

"I want to remember the way you look tonight," he said. "Forever."

She liked that so much it made her shiver. "Okay."

He grabbed her hand to lead her into the attic.

"Wait." She went through her bag until she found a jewelry box. "I want to wear this."

Daniel opened the box and saw an emerald necklace inside. "Wow."

"I love it," she said. "But it's so gaudy that I never feel right wearing it out."

"If this is real..." Daniel picked the necklace up. "Then it has to be worth a fortune."

"It's a family heirloom. Papa says I can never get rid of it."

"I've never seen anything like it," he said.

"Papa said there isn't another one like it. He believes there is magic inside."

"Magic?" Daniel said.

"*Oui.* But who knows what he is talking about?"

"Well, I think you should wear it." He unclasped the necklace. "Turn around."

Antoinette obeyed, and he moved her hair out of the way. He kissed the back of her neck and then put the necklace on. Her skin was tingling by the time his fingers swept over her collarbone.

"Are you ready?" He turned her around and extended his hand.

She nodded, following him into the darkness. Truth be told, she would have followed him anywhere.

Daniel put a chair at the center of the room. Antoinette made herself comfortable, while he arranged his canvas and stool. Then he prepared the proper paints, mixing a few new colors.

"How long do I sit here?" she asked.

"Until I tell you to move."

She smirked. "You're not even my husband yet and you're already so bossy."

"Like that." He got up and fixed her posture. "Lift your chin. Now look at me."

Her heart was beating so fast. Here in this dark room, even his gaze felt like a caress.

"Now just keep looking at me like that for as long as you can."

"I'll do my best, Mr. Sutton." For her, everything about tonight felt intimate.

It took him until morning to finish it. But when he was done, Daniel had never been prouder of a painting. They took it with them on their drive to the Justice of the Peace. And Antoinette placed it on the count's front door just as the sun was coming up. It was her version of a wedding announcement.

Daniel drove a few hours away, so they could get married in a different city. Antoinette wanted privacy and a way to prove herself to the count. She was going to be Daniel's wife. And there was nothing her noble father could do about it.

They bought matching wedding bands at a jewelry store and then went to the courthouse. The ceremony didn't last very long, and they were both glad. Daniel said his vows with absolute certainty. Marriage was between the two of them. Even his parents didn't need to know right now.

Antoinette felt the same. It was so special to have it so private. She knew her father would never forgive her. She'd left the portrait at his front door so he wouldn't worry about where she was. He would know by now that she had run away with Daniel. And that her new husband would keep her safe.

After the wedding ceremony, they drove to the nearest hotel. Daniel got a room and carried her over the threshold. She closed the curtains and he locked the door. And then everything slowed down.

He helped her out of the dress, caressing her soft skin along the way. When she turned around, he couldn't keep his eyes off her. He'd never seen a naked woman before. And he liked what he saw.

Antoinette swallowed and helped him out of his jacket. Then she unbuttoned his dress shirt. He took his shoes off and unbuckled his belt. And she watched him drop his pants.

Nervous excitement swept through her. It seemed marriage was a new world they had to discover.

They looked at each other, feeling a bit like Adam and Eve. And he reached out to cup her cheek.

"I've never done this before," he admitted.

She smiled into the curve of his hand. "Neither have I."

He looked at her, and she shut her eyes. Then he captured her bottom lip as she wrapped her arms around his neck. He picked her up and lay her down on the bed. And he was scared to death.

"Feel my heart." She moved his hand over her breast. "It's beating so fast."

He took her hand and put it against his chest. "So is mine."

She knew he was afraid, because she was petrified.

"It's okay." She ran her thumb across his bottom lip. "I'll follow you anywhere."

He kissed the palm of her hand and then gazed into her eyes.

They made love for the first time. And it was everything Antoinette could have hoped for. Daniel was nervous, because he wanted so badly to please her. But Antoinette just wanted to be with him.

When the sun went down, they lay tangled in the sheets. He held her hand as they stared at each other. She put her head on his chest and shut her eyes. Was it possible to have so much happiness?

He smiled and kissed her forehead. Because all of his dreams had come true.

But when they returned to Savannah, the count was beside himself. Antoinette sat on the couch with Daniel. And he held her hand through the whole thing.

"If you stay here with him, then I will disinherit you!" he yelled.

"Fine!" she cried. "Then do it! You can't control me anymore."

He stormed out of the mansion, and she never saw him again.

Her brother arrived later that day. He brought the portrait of Antoinette with him.

"Does Papa hate me, Edmond?"

"No." He touched her arm. "When he learned what you'd done, he went to his room and cried."

"Oh, Edmond." She leaned on him. "I never meant to hurt him."

"It will be all right. You're all grown up now."

But everything wasn't all right. Daniel's parents

never returned from their business trip. They were killed in a car accident just days after the wedding. Now the mansion and all the land went to Daniel.

Newlywed and orphaned, Daniel was a nervous wreck. But Antoinette was the glue that put the pieces back together again. And they developed an intimate bond stronger than anything else.

Antoinette became estranged from her family. Because Edmond was the only one who would talk to her. It was a heavy burden to bear. But Daniel helped her carry it.

That is, until Tony DeMilo enrolled at Maple Creek High.

He'd heard rumors about the beauty from France. And some part of him couldn't stand that another man had already made her his wife. But beyond that, there was a deep obsession with her past.

A mystical necklace with a universal cure. He wondered how much it would sell for.

On December 21, 1963, Tony kidnapped Antoinette and stole the necklace. He'd put a crew together to help him do the job. So they held Daniel at gunpoint and dragged his wife to the river.

"Tony," he begged. "Stop. Please. You're going to kill her."

"I just want to see if it's working." He tapped the emerald. "This damn thing is made of granite."

The men held Daniel back. Even though he'd fought and scratched along the way. They had roughed him up pretty bad. But he had to do something. Only, with the way they had him restrained, he couldn't.

Tony pushed Antoinette under the water again. And Daniel fell to his knees. He simply couldn't take it anymore. "Stop! Please! No more! You can have the damn necklace! I don't care!"

He pulled her out of the water but she already looked blue. Then he put the necklace on her.

"Tony!" Daniel screamed. "She is a mother. Please let her go."

Tony smiled. "Okay." And then he dropped Antoinette into the bone cold water one last time.

Daniel dove in after her. But the current was too strong. He lost her in a matter of seconds.

He came up for air and ran down the river bank, shouting her name. But she was gone.

Tony and his men were nowhere to be seen. And Daniel didn't know what to do.

So he ran home and called the cops. Hours later, they found her lifeless body floating in the river.

Paramedics pulled her out of the water and tried to defibrillate her heart. But it was too late.

Daniel lay beside her body and touched her hair. Then he said her name over and over again.

She was only twenty one. She wasn't supposed to die. Not like this.

At the funeral, Daniel was a basket case. He wanted to jump in her casket and let them take him instead. She had a son and a daughter who loved her, who needed her, who would never know her.

Daniel thought about throwing that necklace in the river. But he hated to destroy something that had been so precious to her. So he placed it in a photo album with all of their wedding photos. And he went through them every night. Right before he got started on a fresh six-pack.

A few years later, Wesley—their only son—died of a rare blood disease that no one had been able to cure. And that was the last straw. Daniel completely lost it.

And Edmond flew in from France to take Josette.

Daniel was so spaced out that he didn't even care.

The count died of a massive heart attack the day after he heard about what happened to Antoinette. A few months passed, and the countess was right behind him. Edmond was the count now, and he knew Josette needed a family. So he took her home to Paris to raise her himself.

Given Daniel's condition, he knew it was what his sister would have wanted.

Josette loved growing up in France. But she missed her father and resented him for sending her away. As the years passed, Daniel improved. Painting was the only way to stabilize the trauma.

So she began spending summers in Savannah, where she could know her father again.

That was how she met James Blake—one of her father's art students. It was a passionate love affair. But there was more to it than hot summer nights and sex. They cared for each other. And from those scorching passions, they made a child.

Josette was terrified at first. An unplanned pregnancy could tarnish the family.

But then she realized how happy it made her. She loved Jimmy. And he loved her.

She was on her way to tell him the news when a white van pulled out in front of her. Her car crashed into the guard rail. And when she woke up, there were tubes in her arms.

Panicking, she pulled them out and blood gushed everywhere. A man with copper hair tied her up and put them back in. That's when Josette got a good look at the place she'd thought was a hospital.

It was an underground basement with no windows.

The man with copper hair was there at all times. And every now and then another man would show up. One with black hair and dark eyes.

This was a testing facility. And she was his lab rat.

They ran experiments on Josette all nine months of the pregnancy. Where she was held prisoner.

When the baby came, the man with copper hair gave her nothing for the pain. Josette saw her daughter for the first time lying on a hospital bed in that dungeon. And when Tony DeMilo tried to take that innocent newborn and run tests on her, Josette unleashed her inner mother.

She hit DeMilo in the back of the head with testing equipment, and he hit the floor. When the copper-haired man came after her, she scratched his face with her fingernails. And then she pushed him up against the concrete wall. There was a scalpel on the equipment table. One he'd been using on Josette. One he planned to use on the baby.

Josette took the scalpel and stuck it straight through his heart. When he pulled it out, she found a bigger one and sliced his throat. He collapsed on the ground and bled out in minutes.

In a state of panic, Josette washed the blood off her hands and grabbed the baby. Then she broke out of the back door entrance using the dead man's keys. It was pouring outside. But she ran through the rain and kept her baby warm in the night.

She walked barefoot for three days before she collapsed in the street. A Good Samaritan took her to the hospital, where she was diagnosed with pneumonia. She was in and out of consciousness for days, wondering what they were giving her. But one thing was for sure. The baby was missing.

Someone had drawn up papers for a closed adoption and forged Josette's signature. It was the perfect plan to get the baby away from its mother. Then they could run tests on it as much as they wanted.

When she asked about the baby, a nurse told her it had died.

Josette was completely distraught. So she ended up on the streets again.

And that's when DeMilo found her. "Give me the necklace."

"What necklace?" she asked.

"I'll tell you where your kid is if you'll give me the necklace."

Josette broke down crying. "She's dead. You killed her!" She hit him in the chest until he twisted her arm. Then he threw her on the ground, bringing her up by the hair of her head.

"Where is it, Josette? Just tell me where the necklace is, and it will all go away."

"I don't know about a necklace! Okay? I don't even live here anymore."

Seeing that she could no longer be useful to him, he jerked her to her feet. "It's okay. I don't need you. Not anymore. But if you ever step foot in this country again, I'll kill your father."

Scared to death, Josette knew she had to get out of there. Or he would kill Daniel.

So she found a payphone and called Edmond. He was on the first flight to Savannah. And then they hopped right on a flight to Paris. Josette was exhausted and depressed. So she went to the bathroom and wept.

She longed for Jimmy and their child who'd died.

But she knew contacting him would be too

dangerous. It broke her heart.

In Paris, Edmond devised a plan for her security. They died her hair and changed her name to Genevieve Beaumont. She would become his long lost daughter, not his niece. And it would keep her safe.

Every night, she thought about her father in America. She'd spent most of her life without him. But now, it pained her more than ever. And yet, she knew it was the only way to protect him.

And all the men she loved.

The nurse who'd told Josette her child had died was the same one telling a well to do doctor and attorney that the birth mother of their adopted child had died. She'd been planted by DeMilo and paid very well. It's no wonder that in no time, Daniel believed Josette was dead, too.

But then something amazing happened. Daniel heard about DeMilo's orphaned grandson. And it felt like the greatest form of payback. He could adopt him out from under the family. Only, then he met Tom and heard about how his parents had just died in a car accident. Both of them.

With all of his family dead, Daniel expressed a strong interest in adopting Tom.

And he became the grandson he never knew he needed.

Years passed, and Daniel wondered what had happened to Josette's child. By the time he learned about the adoption, it was too late. So he did everything he could to make sure The Smiths bought the house closest to him. He didn't want to interfere with the child. After all, he had no legal right to her.

It wasn't until DeMilo's syphilis diagnosis that he was hungry to find the necklace again. After the news of his death spread to Europe, Josette was eager to return to America. But by then, Daniel had already died.

Heartbroken, she poured her heart and soul into remembering what had happened when she gave birth. It had been coming back in pieces for years. But she had a faint memory of talking to a couple who couldn't have kids. Had they planned on taking hers?

The experimentation had left her body so awash with the side effects of the drugs, that she hadn't been coherent in the hospital. Since it troubled her so, Edmond hired a private detective to track down the couple and the baby they might have adopted. When Josette learned the truth, she couldn't reconcile her destiny. Maybe the rich doctor was a better mother because of what she could provide.

And she didn't know if it was entirely fair to put her child in that position.

Then she found out it was a girl. And she had more of those flashbacks.

Her daughter. With Jimmy. It felt like another life.

Josette was scared of being rejected by her daughter. So Edmond invited Addie to Paris himself. And Josette had kept her secret identity because it was a defense mechanism. What if Addie hated her for being given away? Even though the adoption had never been processed on grounds of consent?

It had taken time to get to this place. Pain and misery spread out over three generations.

But as Josette sat there, explaining it all to her long lost daughter, she'd never felt more at peace.

Chapter 20

Addie

I'd been wanted—not tossed to the wayside like a piece of garbage. I couldn't believe everything Josette had been through. And I felt so guilty for resenting her in the past. Now I knew the truth.

"I love you, Mama." I gave her a hug as we cried together. "I've missed you so much."

"I've missed you, too." She ran her fingers through my hair and squeezed me tightly.

I showed her Antoinette's portrait and we cried some more. Then we stayed up for hours looking at old photos Daniel had saved. We talked and laughed, sharing memories we wished we'd made together.

Around one in the morning, I went upstairs to get ready for bed. I was so tired that I brushed my teeth, took a quick shower and slipped into bed with Tom. He was in a deep sleep. But I watched him and thought about Antoinette and Daniel. What they'd had was special. And what we had was special, too. That's why I would never let it go to waste.

"Hmm." Tom pulled me against him. "You girls must have had a lot to talk about."

I put my hand on his chest and snuggled closer. "She finally told me everything."

He inhaled. "I'm glad you finally gave her a chance to."

"You were right," I said. "It's a good thing I listened to you."

He ran his hand down my back and gave me a sloppy kiss. "I'm glad you're spending time together."

I tucked my head under his chin, wrapping my arms around him. "Me too."

It had been one of the best weeks of my life. I'd bonded with Josette in a way that I'd never bonded with anyone. But when it was time for her to leave, we were in tears at the airport.

"I'll be out there to see you soon," Jimmy said, giving her a soft kiss.

There was something pleasant in observing their PDA. I'd never witnessed Jeffrey and Eleanor being affectionate. And look where that had gotten them. Maybe these parents were in it for the long haul.

"I will miss you," Josette said, cupping my cheek in her hand.

We hugged for a long time, but then she really had to leave.

"My beautiful daughter," she whispered. "You're glowing."

I looked into her eyes, not quite following.

Then she turned discreetly to whisper in my ear. "Are you expecting a little one?"

I gaped at her level of intuition. "I'm not sure yet."

"Well, be sure." She tucked my hair behind my ears. "Then call and tell me all about it."

"Okay." I went to Tom for comfort. And he rubbed my back as we watched her leave.

She turned around and waved. And I was so happy we'd been able to spend time together. She was the coolest mom in the world. And she was mine.

On the drive home, Tom held my hand. "You

okay?"

"Yeah," I sighed. "Just a little sad."

"I've got something that might cheer you up."

I looked at him. "Tell me more."

"How would you like to spend Spring Break in Paris?" he asked.

I froze because I was so shocked he'd want to go there too.

"I'd been waiting for the right time to tell you. Edmond and I already made all the arrangements."

"Oh, Tom!" I hugged him across the console. "That would mean so much to me."

He smiled, drawing me into a kiss. "I wanted to surprise you. But I couldn't keep it from you anymore."

While I was over the moon, my smile quickly faded. It was what he'd said at the end.

Because I'd been keeping a huge secret from him. And even Josette had divulged her suspicions.

Two weeks had gone by, and there was still no sign of my period.

Which meant there was a 100% chance that I was late.

I took two more pregnancy tests without Tom's knowledge. Because now I was starting to believe that Jeanine might actually be right. And the last time I checked, you couldn't fake four tests in a row.

When they both came back positive, I was happy and sad. I was pregnant. We were going to have a baby, which was what I'd always wanted. The one thing I desired most that I'd been told I could never have.

But then there were all the risks. In the back of my mind, I knew that if I really was carrying our child, it wasn't going to be a normal pregnancy.

So I turned to Eleanor—Ms. OBGYN Extraordinaire. And she squeezed me into her busy schedule.

"Didn't I give you a lifetime supply of condoms?" she asked.

The way she said it was so funny, I almost laughed.

"We quit using them when we thought I couldn't get pregnant."

"And when was that?" She sat in front of a computer, trying to calculate the moment of conception.

I thought about it and rattled off the date. She typed a few strokes, recording it in the system.

"I believe you conceived the first time you had intercourse without a condom."

I put my hand on my stomach, feeling a wave of nausea.

"That would put you right around four weeks. Would you like to see?"

I nodded and she gave me an ultrasound. It was so small. Like a tiny little bean.

"The baby is right there. In your second trimester, I'll be able to determine the sex."

"It's so small." I looked at the screen. And I wanted that tiny little bean.

"Addie, I've read over your file. Dr. Laurent sent it to me from Paris."

I looked down and nodded, not liking where this was headed.

"In your condition, childbirth puts you in a great amount of danger."

"I know." I'd known all along. It was why I'd been in denial.

"I really think you should consider other options."

"What are you talking about?" I asked.

"If you carry to full term, baring this child could kill you."

I looked her in the eye and swallowed. "I know that."

"Does Tom know about this?" she asked.

"No. I haven't told him."

"You need to. Carrying this baby puts your life at risk."

I drove home. And Tom was so happy to see me. But the elephant in the room was back.

"Are you okay?" he said at dinner. "You look a little pale."

There was no point in stalling. Might as well get it off my chest.

"I'm pregnant."

He gave me a strange look. "Addie, I don't think—"

"I took a pregnancy test two weeks ago," I said. "With Jeanine. I took two, because we didn't think the first one was right. They were both positive."

He furrowed his brow and narrowed his eyes.

"I wasn't sure, so I didn't say anything. But I saw Eleanor today. And she said I'm four weeks pregnant."

He set his fork down and folded his hands. "How is that possible?"

"I don't know," I cried. "Dr. Laurent said there was still a small chance."

"And what about the risk involved? Do you remember him saying anything about that?"

I swallowed and looked at my plate.

"I thought if you had a child, it put you at a risk. You could—"

"Die?" I stared at him. "Yes, I know." I touched

my stomach.

"So what are you going to do?"

"I don't know yet," I said. "I haven't decided."

"What did Eleanor say?"

"She thinks I should eliminate the pregnancy. Because it could end up taking my life."

"And what about me?" he asked. "Do I get a say?"

"What?"

He raised his voice. "Do I get a vote when it comes to my wife putting herself in danger?"

"I'm not the one putting myself in danger."

"So you're just going to go through with it? Even though it could kill you? You don't remember what Dr. Laurent said in Paris. You have a 98% mortality rate if you choose to have this baby."

"I know."

"Do you have any concern for your own life?" he shouted.

"Look, it's not like I did this on purpose."

"How did it happen?" he asked. "I'm still trying to figure out how the hell—"

"Because you made love to me *over* and *over* again!" I yelled.

He didn't say anything for a few minutes. He was too busy steaming.

"So this is my fault now? Because I like being with my wife?"

"No. But you know how often we have sex. How do you think it works?"

He got up and threw his plate across the room. "You can't do this to me."

"Do what?" I cried. "What did I do?"

"You intentionally excluded me from all your secret pregnancy tests. Why?"

"Because I knew what you would say!" I burst into tears. "You think I don't remember what the doctor said? I'm sorry, but a 98% mortality rate is pretty freaking high. I don't think I'd forget that."

He leaned against the wall. "I don't know what you're doing. What are your plans?"

"I don't know!" I shouted. "Okay? I don't know."

"It wasn't supposed to be like this," he said. "We just got married."

"I know." My lower lip trembled. "But we have to be responsible adults and deal with it."

"Responsible? How are you being responsible? You've excluded me from everything."

"I know and I'm sorry. But I didn't think you'd be too excited about it."

He watched me get up to leave.

"Now I can see why." I left the room and went upstairs to cry.

When he found me, I was lying under the covers in bed. He'd calmed down since the argument. But it felt like he hated me. At a time like this, I really needed his support more than ever.

"How are you feeling?" He leaned in the doorway.

"Fine."

He sat down on the edge of our bed. Then he twisted his wedding band around on his finger.

"I'm not mad about the baby," he said. "And I'm not even mad at you."

"Then why are you so angry?" I asked.

He turned around with tears in his eyes and touched my hand. "Because I don't want to lose you."

I swallowed and clenched my jaw, staring at the most beautiful man.

"If you died, I don't know what I'd do." He broke

down crying, vocal and unrestrained.

I put his head on my breast as he lay down beside me. "I don't want to lose you either."

"It's not fair," he sobbed. "You're so young. We just got married. It's not fair."

"I know." I wrapped my arms around him. "It never is."

"It's not that I don't want a baby, Addie. I know that's what you're thinking."

I dried the tears from his face. "No, it's not. I know why you're upset."

"If you wanted to... How long do you have to decide?"

"It's pretty early on. I'm only about four weeks along."

"So we have time?" he asked.

"Yeah." I nodded. "We have time."

He lifted my shirt and kissed my stomach. "I love you, Addie. I love you so much."

I lay there and cried. "I know. I love you, too."

He flattened his hand on my stomach. "It's kind of amazing. Isn't it?"

"What?"

"The one thing the doctors said we'd never be able to do. And we did it."

I showed him the ultrasound, and he was in disbelief. The baby was so tiny. But it was there. It was growing inside me. And somehow, I felt a sense of peace knowing that no matter the outcome, I would have been given the chance to experience this part of life. Even if it ended far too soon.

He stroked my cheek. "I'm sorry for what I said. But I'm really scared."

"I'm scared, too," I confessed. "But it's what I've

always wanted."

I took his hand and placed it on my stomach.

"Whatever you decide," he whispered. "Well, it's your choice, not mine."

I took a breath and put his hand on my face.

"But haven't you had enough danger in your life?"

"I don't know what I'm going to do." I looked into his eyes. "But until I decide, I think we should enjoy every part of this pregnancy. It's not the baby's fault. And who knows if we'll ever be able to do this again."

"You're right." He ran his hands down my stomach. "I feel like it's my fault."

"Why?"

"I should have known better. We'd been told there was a small chance of pregnancy. And we knew how dangerous it would be for you. I should have been more careful. I should have—."

"Tom, I love this baby. And I know this baby already loves you."

He kissed my face and put his head on my stomach.

"I don't know what's going to happen. So I think we should just enjoy every moment of this experience."

"Okay." He ran his fingers down my neck. "I'm sorry."

"It's not your fault. And maybe everything will be all right."

"I'm sorry I was so cruel before," he said. "But I'm here for you. And I'll support you."

"I know how hard this must be for you. But it's hard for me, too."

"Then why don't we forget about it for a while and pretend like it's a normal pregnancy?"

I smiled and touched his warm cheek. "That's exactly what I want."

"Okay." He covered my face in kisses. "Then that's what we'll do."

* * *

We flew to Paris at the start of my second trimester. And for the past five weeks, my pregnancy had been an easy one. I was sleeping well, and my morning sickness had waned. It was a pleasant relief.

Jimmy met us at the airport, and we all stayed at the castle. I was so happy to be back. Being in Savannah, I'd felt half a world away. But now that I was surrounded by family, it felt like home.

On our third day in Europe, Tom surprised me with a trip to Italy. It was the honeymoon we'd never had. And I couldn't wait to pick up where we'd left off.

Frank took us to beautiful Italy on Edmond's private plane. And it was so good to see him again. He told us his wife was pregnant, and that felt like a good omen. So I was bubbling over the whole way there.

Since it was a short trip, we spent the first day in Rome and the second in Naples. I loved touring each city. The museums and cathedrals alone were enough to take my breath away. And what made it all so sweet was having Tom, my loving husband, exploring it all with me.

We had gelato every day. And I was happy Tom let me splurge. My pregnancy cravings were off the charts. Maybe because I'd finally overcome the early stages of morning sickness.

Either way, I was just so thrilled to be alive. Having his baby inside of me made me feel different. Like there was more to this life than just the two of us. So on our last day in Italy, I made my decision while lying on a beach in Florence. Tom was in the lounge chair beside me, looking like a male model.

"Hey." I kissed his neck as he stirred awake.

"Hey." He lifted his sunglasses and looked at me.

I climbed on top of him and lay down, resting my head on his stomach.

"Are you having fun?" he asked.

"Yes. I love Italy."

"I'm glad." He touched my back. "At least we were finally able to make it."

"Tom?" I sat up and stared into his golden eyes. Even now, they mesmerized me. They were just so hypnotic and beautiful. I wondered if the baby would have eyes like him.

He smiled. "What is it?"

"Everything has been going so well with the pregnancy." I rubbed my stomach. "It feels like a really good sign."

"A sign?" His smile disappeared. "A sign of what?"

"Well, I think everything is going to be all right. I want to have this baby."

He clenched his jaw. "Just like that?"

"I've put a lot of thought into this decision, Tom."

"But it's only been a few months. I mean, what if something changes? What if—"

"This is never going to work if you keep putting out all this negative energy!"

He smoldered but didn't say anything.

"What I mean is, I think it would be better for the baby if we just believe in her."

"It's a girl?" he asked. "How do you know?"

"I had a dream."

"Dreams, feelings, that's all this ever is for you."

He stood up. "What about facts? What about science?"

"I believe I can have this baby and survive." I gritted my teeth. "So that's what I'm going to do."

"You have that kind of confidence from a two percent survival rate?"

I looked at the sand. "You told me that you would support me, no matter what I decide."

"Yeah." He grabbed his towel. "That's before I knew you'd already decided without me."

He went back to our hotel room and left me alone on the beach. I looked out at the ocean and cried, thankful for the shield my sunglasses provided. I'd made the decision now, because I wanted to tell the whole family when we returned to Paris. But with the way Tom was acting, maybe that wasn't such a good idea.

When I went back to the room, he was packing our bags. It was our last day in Italy, and we were flying out at the crack of dawn. He wouldn't look at me, even though I knew he'd heard me come in.

"Tom." I let the door swing shut. But he kept on ignoring me.

He was wearing a frown. The one that always made me feel like I'd done something wrong.

"Tom." I touched his arm, and he moved away. "Talk to me."

He sighed. "I would have if you'd let me. But now you've already gone on and made the decision without me. You could have at least let me make a decent argument for your life."

"But you don't know that I'm going to lose my life," I said. "What if the baby and I are fine?"

"What if you're not?" He glared at me and then

zipped my suitcase. "I know I said I would support you no matter what. But I can't just stand by while you put yourself in unnecessary danger."

"It's not unnecessary."

"What about Eleanor? She's the doctor. For once, I actually agree with her."

"Tom, this is my body. And you're not gonna make this decision for me."

"How can I?" He grabbed his wallet and keys. "You've already made it without me."

I stood there dumbfounded as he walked out the door. Then I went out on the balcony and cried. My only comfort was the warm sun and fresh air. Until I saw Tom walking on the beach by himself. He moved slowly, putting his hands in his pockets. He wouldn't even look up.

It was a couple of hours later when he returned. I'd closed the blinds and gotten in bed, too devastated to do anything else. I heard his key click in the door and stood up to face him.

He walked into the room. And I was too on edge to let him shame me again.

"If no one is going to stand up for this baby, then I will. I'm having her. Her life is more important than mine. So if I have to lose mine in the process, then so be it. But I'm not going to let you guilt trip me for the rest of this pregnancy! We made this baby together. And if you don't want her, then fine. But I do! And what if this is the only chance I get? You think I could go my whole life without this and live with the fact that it could have been mine? That the time is now? That I want this so much, I'll do anything to keep her? Because I am a mother now! And you're not gonna tell me how to—"

He crashed into me and molded his mouth with mine. I whimpered and grew weak in the knees as he lowered me onto the bed, leaving sumptuous kisses down my neck. He took my clothes off and put his hands all over me. And when we made love, it was unlike anything I'd ever experienced before.

He didn't say anything afterwards. But I felt more bonded to him than ever.

We fell asleep and left for Paris the next day. When we landed, Fernand was waiting with a car for us on the tarmac. Tom gave Fernand my bags, and he stored them in the trunk.

"Tom." His bags were missing. "What are you doing?"

He kissed me and then got back on the plane.

Fernand helped me into the car, and I watched the jet fly away. Was he leaving me?

I cried the whole way to the castle. But Fernand respected my humanity and didn't pry.

I told everyone the news that I was pregnant. And they were over the moon. Especially my parents.

When they asked about Tom, I said he would be home later. But I didn't even know if that were true.

Luckily, I had a private moment with Edmond. And he put his arm around me. "Congratulations."

"Thank you."

"I'm surprised you aren't with Tom. I thought you would want to go with him."

"Go where?" I asked.

"He didn't tell you?"

"No."

"He's on his way to Germany."

Chapter 21

Tom

We landed in Munich at sundown. But I wasn't about to wait for the dawn.

A good husband would call his wife and tell her where he'd gone. But I was in no mood to speak to my darling wife now. I had business to attend to. And it might just end up saving her in the end.

Frank escorted me to the university where Gustav Lehmann had been teaching. It was a long shot. But right now, the best thing I could offer Addie was some piece of mind. She believed he had been at the river that night. And getting to the bottom of this prospect would help her sleep better at night.

"Professor Lehmann," I requested at the front desk.

"He is working on research in the laboratory."

"All right." I wore dark sunglasses and a business suit. Yeah, I was putting out real classy vibes.

"It is a closed laboratory."

I walked away as the receptionist yelled at me in German. Frank handed me a photo of Lehmann. And within forty-five minutes, we'd found the closed laboratory where he worked alone.

I knocked on the door. And it surprised me when he answered it.

"Are you Gustav Lehmann?" I asked.

He looked just like his photo. Broad shoulders. Long white hair. Stilted smile.

"This is a closed laboratory," he said. "No visitors."

As he went to shut the door in my face, I stuck my foot inside. "I know about Valjean and DeMilo." I took off my sunglasses for dramatic effect. "Tony was my grandfather."

And that's when he let me in.

There was classical music playing in the background. The kind that thrived on pure instrumentation.

"Would you mind if I asked you some questions?" I said.

"I don't see why not." He seemed pretty laid back.

"Valjean said that you believe the necklace has healing properties."

"Yes." He tended to a variety of potions. "I do."

"And why do you want the necklace?" I asked.

"If I can extract the compound, it could be used in my research."

"What kind of research?" I looked around the place.

"I've been searching for the cure to cancer."

"And you believe..." I showed him a picture of the necklace on my phone. "That it's here."

"Well, I don't really know. But I've always heard stories. It's a legend."

"Legend?" I put my hands on the table.

"My grandfather told me stories when I was a little boy." He penciled numbers into tiny squares on a chart. "About the alchemist who fashioned such a necklace for the Queen of France."

"You mean Marie Antoinette?" I asked.

"To escape the guillotine. That is why her hair

turned white during the trial."

"I'm afraid I'm not following you." It sounded a little out there to me.

"If administered too frequently, the elixir will activate pre-mature grey."

"Elixir?" I looked at a jar filled with chocolates. "I don't understand."

"Yes." He showed me a drawing of the necklace. "Beneath the stone."

"But that doesn't make any sense."

Lehmann grabbed a pen. "Whoever manufactured the stone sealed the outer layer with a casing. This is why the necklace is cool to the touch. Because the center is filled with the elixir."

"So what happened to Marie Antoinette?"

"Maybe it was the stress. She was rumored to want everything in excess. When it came time for her dosage, she probably kept taking it every day. But even if she had administered the elixir properly, I don't think it would have helped her. You can't bring someone back from the guillotine."

"So what will the necklace do?" I asked.

"If I could extract the elixir in a controlled environment, I might discover the right compound."

"And then what? Testing? Lab rats? That sort of thing?"

"Most likely." He put his hand on the drawing. "This necklace was not the only one of its kind. Centuries ago, they were quite popular among the alchemists. It was seen as a talisman."

"So are there others?" I asked.

"No, they were all destroyed in the name of religion. Your necklace is the only one left."

"It's not exactly my necklace," I said.

Frank cleared his throat, reminding me that it probably wasn't the right thing to say.

"How do you use it?" I asked. "How do you know if it works?"

"There is a hidden latch at the back. You can see it, but only if you're looking closely. Turn it counterclockwise three times and it should open. Then you administer three drops on the tongue."

It sounded like something out of a Harry Potter movie.

"According to legend, it can do everything from healing deadly viruses to restarting the heart."

I gave him a curious look, not wanting to buy into any of it.

"How often would you take it?" I asked.

"It depends on the ailment. For a disease, monthly. For restarting the heart, only once."

"But what is the elixir made of?"

"Nobody knows. That's why I'd like to crack the necklace open and take a look myself."

So far, this trip to Germany felt like a complete waste of time. I was tired and grumpy. He sounded like a quack. And my wife was five hundred miles away, wondering why I'd jetted off without her.

"Have you been to America recently?" I asked.

"Yes."

"Were you on a river in Savannah, Georgia by any chance?"

"I heard the necklace was hidden in that river once. So I collected a sample of the water."

"And have you tested it?" I asked.

"All worthless. Even if the necklace was kept there, the elixir is sealed with a diamond encasing on the inside. There was no possible chance it could leak out.

That emerald is unbreakable."

At least those words rang true. I remembered throwing the necklace at a mirror once.

It broke the mirror. But the emerald was unharmed.

"So why are you working for Valjean?" I asked.

He looked confused and maybe a little angry. "I'm not."

"But he was going to give you the necklace," I said.

"No. He wanted me to buy it from him for an obscene fortune. I'm doing the best I can here. But I can't go bankrupt over this. I'll have to find the cure another way, the best way I can."

"Tom." Frank pulled me aside. "We should get going soon if you want to fly back tonight. A storm is coming."

"All right." I shook the chemist's hand. "Thank you for your time."

As we headed for the door, I thought to ask something else.

"How is Valjean's daughter?" I asked.

"What?"

"The little girl who's sick. How is she?"

"Valjean doesn't have a daughter."

I stepped back in the room. "What are you talking about? I thought he wanted the necklace so he could bring it to you. And you were going to heal her with this magic cure."

"Wrong. Valjean was going to sell the necklace to me so I could use it for cancer research. He was only in it for the money. And I don't generally work with criminals. But I need that necklace."

"Why?"

He pointed to a picture frame on his desk. "For

Mira."

It was a little girl with dark curly hair.

"She was only eight years old when she died. Leukemia."

"I'm very sorry for your loss."

"That's why I won't give up. I have to end this." He looked at the picture. "For her."

"Do you believe the elixir should go to those who need it the most?" I asked.

"Of course. Imagine if it got into the wrong hands. People terrified of old age."

"Like the fountain of youth?"

"Exactly. It would be a waste of the elixir, because that's not what it's designed for."

"Why do people believe in things like the fountain of youth? It's obviously not true."

"Because everyone wants to live forever."

I thought about that on the flight home to Paris. Valjean had been the criminal all along. He'd stolen the necklace in the hope of getting a steep price out of Lehmann. Because he knew how vulnerable the man was—on some kind of life long crusade to end the cancer that had killed his daughter.

With Valjean in prison, there were no enemies left to fear. And yet, I felt more afraid.

We landed late that night. And when I entered the castle, everyone had already gone to sleep.

I went into our room and shut the door behind me. Addie slept in the middle of the bed with her head on my pillow. The streaks of mascara down her face let me know that she'd been crying.

I took my shoes off and got in bed. She grumbled and shifted, putting her head on my chest.

"I talked to Gustav Lehmann. He's real. He

teaches at the university in Munich."

She opened her eyes but didn't look at me. She just listened.

"He was never working for DeMilo or Valjean. He's just some poor guy who lost his daughter to cancer. And he's been spending his life trying to find a cure. I think DeMilo planned to use him to treat his own illness. That's why he wanted the necklace. But Valjean just wants to make a profit. He never even had a daughter."

She didn't say anything.

"So you were right about Lehmann. You had the whole thing figured out from the start."

"I don't care about being right, Tom. I'd just like to know where you are. I mean, I'm your wife. Don't I deserve to know that much?"

"I'm sorry."

"You left without even saying goodbye." She ran her hand down my shirt.

"I'm sorry. You're right."

"You're the one who's so worried about me. Well, guess what honey? If these are the last months of my life, you sure aren't doing anything to make them pleasant, are you?"

She had a point.

"And you still don't know that I won't survive. Wouldn't you want to cherish these moments with me before I'm gone for good? Or are you so mad that all you care about is yourself?"

They were the words I needed to hear. And she'd always been one for good timing.

I got out of bed and knelt down on the floor.

"Tom." She leaned against the pillows. "What are you doing?"

"I know I've been a terrible husband." I took her hand. "And you're right. About everything." I looked into her eyes and touched her cheek. "I've been so scared of losing you that I've blocked out everything else. In case these months are your last, I should be making the best of every second I have left."

She teared up.

"Because when it's over, I don't get you back. There are no second chances."

"So you support this baby?" she asked. "Because I can't get past this without that."

I put my hand on her stomach. "I love this baby. And I want you to be happy."

"So you will support me from this day forward? Until the day this baby is born?"

I opened my mouth to speak.

"You better mean it, Tom! I don't want any half-hearted attempts or this wishy-washy attitude. You're either all in or you're not. Which is it gonna be?"

"I'm all in. With you. With the baby. Whatever you want—just tell me and I'll do it."

"You promise?" She looked down at me with those gorgeous eyes.

"Yes." I wrapped my arms around her small body. "I promise."

"Oh, thank God." She burst into tears and kissed me. "I missed you."

"I missed you, too." I put my lips on her neck and she clawed at my shirt.

"Would you take your shirt off already?" she snapped, then realized her attitude. "Sorry. I don't know where that came from."

I grinned and unbuttoned my shirt. "I think I'm starting to like you pregnant."

"Good." She grabbed my collar. "Now get over here."

* * *

For the next month, life was pretty great. My relationship with Addie was better than ever. And I'd learned to embrace her killer cravings and mood swings.

As far as the pregnancy was concerned, Addie was healthy as a horse. I went with her to every doctor's appointment. And it was actually nice for it to be someone as familiar as Eleanor. She'd even agreed to delay her move to Atlanta until after the baby was born. I knew it meant a lot to Addie, to have someone deliver the baby who she had known all her life. I was proud of Eleanor for doing something so selfless. And when the big day came, I didn't want any other doctor but her.

One night, Addie called me from upstairs. I ran like a bolt of lightning, terrified that something was wrong. But when I got there, she made me sit down on the bed and grabbed my hand.

"What is it?" I asked.

She put my hand on her belly. "Do you feel that?"

I did feel it. And it lit up every part of me.

"She's kicking!"

A week ago, we'd learned that Addie's instincts were right. It was a girl.

"I can't believe she's—" Addie grabbed her stomach and keeled over in pain.

"Are you okay?" The look on her face terrified me.

"Yeah," she gasped. "Just ah. A little bit of discomfort."

It passed as quickly as it came. But my anxiety did the opposite.

"Are you sure?" I touched her forehead. She was sweating.

"Yeah, I'm fine. Could you maybe get me some water?"

"Sure." I'd like to say that things were getting better at school. We were seniors, it should have all been downhill from here. But these spikes of discomfort at home were nothing compared to what lay beyond those double doors.

In the first few months, Addie's pregnancy had been easy to hide. But now she had a baby bump that was getting harder and harder to conceal. People still talked trash and I just had to roll my eyes.

We were married. We liked to have sex. Didn't these juveniles understand how babies were made?

But then it got worse on the day Addie and I were called to the principal's office. Caldwell didn't even say anything. He just handed each of us an envelope. There was the same letter inside.

Because of Addie's "condition," we were both being asked to leave the school. And since I was the "impregnator," I had to leave too. In the last month leading up to graduation.

"What?" Addie said. "You're kicking me out?"

"I already warned your husband about this."

"What?" She looked at me. "Tom?"

"This is bull. You can't do this. In terms of the law, you don't have a leg to stand on," I said.

"You can't prevent me from graduating just because of this," Addie said. She stood up and raised her voice. But then her face clenched, and she put her hand on her stomach. "Ah, Tom."

"Baby, are you okay?" I helped her up.

"I don't know. I need some fresh air."

So I took her outside. And that's when she stood her ground.

"I can't believe he's trying to do this. It's just ridiculous," I said.

"Sounds like discrimination to me. Why don't we call our lawyer?"

I remembered a conversation I'd once had with Jeff. "Good idea, babe."

We talked to him on the phone that night for over an hour. And he told us to attend school the next day as if nothing had happened. I can't be sure exactly what he did. But all I know is, by the time Jeff was through with Caldwell, he was so terrified of a lawsuit that the school had to give us free lunch for the rest of the semester. Addie also received perks for being pregnant, such as a larger locker, extended breaks between classes and snack privileges throughout the day. It was nothing we were really interested in, and we never exploited the situation. Because we just wanted to be given the freedom to graduate.

And when that day came, I'd never seen Addie happier. All of her family came over from France. And we had a big celebration at our house. Despite their impending divorce, Eleanor and Jeff were civil with each other. And they genuinely seemed happy for Addie.

She looked so adorable—pregnant in her cap and gown. While she entertained guests, I sat back that night and watched her. My beautiful wife. The girl I'd watched for years from afar. And now she was pregnant with my child. How could it be that she was mine?

* * *

I deferred my admission at the University of Georgia. And Addie couldn't believe that I'd done it. But I couldn't miss out on the most important part of the pregnancy. I wanted to be there for her, no matter what happened. And I couldn't do that by packing up and leaving for Athens in the fall.

The baby wasn't due until September. And I needed to be there for her arrival.

Deep down, I had that nagging fear that something would go wrong. But I kept sweeping it under the rug. I had to put on a brave face for Addie. Because she deserved it.

But that was easier said than done. Especially since that summer was scalding hot. My anxiety peaked every time she put her hand on her stomach. But I had to quit freaking out on the inside, because she would know it. Addie had a sixth sense like that. Especially since she'd been carrying my child.

"I'm going for a walk," she said on one of those scorching afternoons. "I won't be gone long."

"Want me to go with you?" I grabbed a bottle of water.

"No. I'll be fine." She kissed my cheek. "Stop worrying about me."

So I stood on the front porch and watched her head for the woods. I shook my head and packed a small bag with things she might need. It was the middle of July. And I wasn't about to let her die of heat exhaustion out in the blazing sun while she was seven months pregnant. Crazy, stubborn woman.

But then my phone buzzed and I saw that it was Edmond. So I stopped to grab it.

"Hey, Edmond. Listen, I'm in the middle of

something. Can I—"

"Tom! Tom! Where are you? Where is Addie?" He sounded short of breath.

"Calm down. We're at home. What's going on?"

"I'm guessing you haven't been watching the news lately?"

"Not really. Why?" I grabbed a juice box from the fridge. She needed her electrolytes.

"Valjean escaped from prison three days ago. And the media just released the story. The police are after him. He's a fugitive on the run. And an anonymous caller already phoned in with his whereabouts."

I looked out the window. And I didn't see Addie.

"He's in Savannah."

Chapter 22

Addie

I went to the river almost every day now. And I saw the pain in his eyes every time I left.

But this was *my* problem. And I had to handle it *my* way.

I'd stayed there for hours before, sinking into the cool water. It was such a nice relief compared to the blazing sun. Being pregnant in the heat of summer was making me swell.

But that wasn't why I'd gone to the river today. I'd come here for absolution. Because I was scared.

Scared that I'd made a terrible mistake. Scared that something would go wrong. Scared that I might lose my whole life in the process of bringing another one into this world. Scared that he would never forgive me if I did.

I didn't want to die. But this baby deserved a life. And I was going to give her that.

Even if it killed me.

I dipped my toes into the water and sat down on the bank. I wondered how many more afternoons I'd be able to do this until she came. The beautiful little girl floating in my belly.

It made me giddy just thinking about it. So I leaned my head back and soaked up the sun. It wasn't nearly as hot here in the shade. And I loved being outdoors beneath the trees. I always had.

I stood up and walked across the river, balancing on stones. I was wearing a white cotton dress. It was breathable and flowy, a comfortable fit for my baby bump. I put my hand on my belly and smiled.

In that moment, I knew everything was going to be all right. I just had to have *faith* and trust in the fact that Eleanor knew what she was doing. And I would get to meet my precious little girl before long.

"Hello, Mrs. Sutton. What a lovely dress you're wearing."

My blood ran cold. I heard the cock of a gun. I'd been here before.

"You've changed since the last time I saw you."

I wanted to scream. Tom was less than a mile away. But I was paralyzed.

"Did you receive your acceptance letter from the university?"

I felt him on the bank behind me. "What?"

"The university. They were delighted to receive you. Correct?"

I turned around. And he was closer than I realized.

"You see, I have this friend. And she's married to the president of the university."

I swallowed and took a step back. My only refuge was the river.

"Or did your rich uncle already tell you that?" He approached the edge. "Because I have another friend. And he works for the FBI. Have you ever heard of wiretapping? Well, he's pretty good at it."

I wrapped my arms around my stomach. But it only drew more attention to the baby.

"What do we have here?" He looked at my bump. "Mrs. Sutton, are you pregnant?"

"Don't come any closer." I stepped back in the water. And it felt like the same thing was happening again. Only the river wasn't frozen. And we weren't in Paris anymore.

"Shut up!" He pulled out a gun. "And do exactly as I say!"

My knees were shaking so badly that I couldn't stand up straight.

"I am sick and tired of chasing you! You stupid Americans think you're so smart. But you're wrong! Okay? I am the one with the power, because I am the one with the gun. So you are going to give me that necklace. The *real* necklace. And I'm going to walk away. Because if you don't, I will kill you."

The water felt warm around my ankles.

"And it won't be like last time. You are out of second chances."

I wished the river would swallow me up whole. So my baby could have a life.

"Is that understood?" he screamed.

"Yes."

"Now, where is the necklace? I want it *now*. Or you'll never get to meet your little one."

I saw something out of the corner of my eye, but I didn't take my eyes off Valjean.

"You think I'm just going to stand here and wait all day?"

I was frozen, writhing in pain. Suddenly, I felt so cold.

"Is this what you need?" He pointed the gun at me. "Is this a good motivator for you?"

I heard the gun go off. And Valjean toppled over in the river. Tom was standing behind him with a loaded pistol in his hand.

Valjean fell face first, smashing his head on a rock. I crouched down and watched him, because my legs couldn't support me anymore. We were cautious and weary, waiting for him to move.

But if Valjean were alive, he wouldn't have been able to keep his head underwater for long. After a couple minutes, Tom pulled him out and checked his pulse. "He's dead." He looked shocked, like he couldn't believe it. "I already called the police. They should be here soon."

I shut my eyes and sighed.

"Did he hurt you?" he asked.

"No. But he was going to."

Tom waded into the river and hugged me. I was still petrified, because I didn't want anything to happen to the baby. And Tom was shaking. He sat there and threaded his fingers through my hair.

"I don't know what I would have done if I'd lost you," he said.

I rubbed his head and breathed him in. "Everything is going to be okay now."

He was crying as he looked me in the eye. "I'm glad I killed him. So he can't hurt you anymore."

"Is it over?" I asked.

He traced his knuckles against my cheek. "Yes. It's all over. No one is chasing us now."

I put my head on his chest, letting my body calm down from the panic. But then I felt a sudden stab of pain. I stood still and tried to breathe it out, not wanting him to worry. But it wouldn't go away.

"Ah," I gasped, lurching over.

"Addie, what is it?" He held me up. "What's wrong?"

"The baby." I winced and put my hand on my

stomach. "Something's wrong."

"Addie." He let me put all of my weight on him. "Addie, you're bleeding."

"What?" I held on to his neck and looked at the back of my dress. "Oh no," I cried.

"It's okay." He lifted me in his arms. "Let's just get you out of the water."

"Ah! Tom!" I clawed his shirt. "It's too early. The baby isn't supposed to come yet."

"Just stay calm," he said. "Keep breathing. Come on, baby."

That was easier said than done, considering it was hot as hell outside.

"Tom, something's wrong." I cried on his shoulder, letting the tears run freely.

"We have to get you to the hospital." He kicked in the front door and lay me down on the couch.

"Tom." I grabbed the collar of his shirt. Then I felt my eyes rolling into the back of my head. And that's when the whole world around me went dark.

* * *

Tom

"Addie." I felt her pulse. She was still breathing. "Addie."

It all must have been too much for her. Because she'd passed out on the couch.

And the bleeding hadn't stopped. In fact, it had gotten worse.

I heard sirens as the cops pulled into the drive. I ran out the front door to them.

"Where is Valjean?" the officer said. He was terse, tall and blonde.

"In the river." I pointed. "He tried to kill my wife. He's dead."

The cop looked at me, reading between the lines. "Self-defense?"

"Absolutely, but you have to help me. Please! I think my wife is having a miscarriage."

"Where is she?" he asked.

"In the house." I ran back inside and he followed me. "Please."

He saw her body lying on the sofa. There was blood on the back of her dress.

"Help her!" I begged. "Do something! Please!"

He nodded and left, rounding up the other officers to handle Valjean. Then he helped me get Addie in the back of his police car. He took off with his sirens blaring and I panicked.

"Wait! Stop the car!"

"What is it?" He came to a screeching halt.

I jumped out of the car and ran back in the house. "I forgot something!"

I hustled up the staircase and into our bedroom. Then I went through every drawer, tossing clothes everywhere. I looked under the bed. I looked in her nightstand. I looked in her jewelry box.

"Dammit, Addie!" I yelled. "Where the hell is it?"

Then I thought about the last time I'd seen her with it.

Just using it for inspiration. It's always easier to model after the original.

In the art room, months ago. It was the first time she'd drawn since we got married.

I know it doesn't make any sense. But somehow, it makes me feel safe.

I ran down the hall and opened the door, rifling

through her sketches.

I know you think it's done nothing but cause us danger.

I knocked over a box of her colored pencils.

But after everything that's happened, I'm still alive.

"Dammit, Addie." I went through every cabinet in a rush.

Maybe it's not the killer.

And then I saw it in plain sight.

Maybe it's what saves me.

I'd knocked over a tiny wooden box. And the necklace spilled out.

I grabbed both and ran down the stairs. Then the cop took off down the drive. He put his sirens on again and drove ninety miles an hour to get us to the hospital. If only he'd brought an ambulance with him.

I called Eleanor in the car. And when we got to the hospital, she was ready and waiting.

"I need a wheelchair!" Eleanor fussed until a nurse brought one over.

"What's happening to her?" I walked with them in hurried strides down the hall.

"Tom, I really think you ought to let me do my job."

"But..." I broke down, shaking and crying.

"Tom." She pulled me aside. "I'm a trained professional. You're going to have to trust me. I know what I'm doing. Just have a little faith."

I went to the waiting room and took a seat. Then I looked at my wedding ring.

I heard her laughter running through my head. The noises she made in her sleep at night.

I love you. So much. How did I get so lucky?

I twisted my hands together and cried. Life meant

nothing without her. And I'd done nothing but fight with her over this baby. I was glad I'd let her have her way in the end. It was what she wanted.

But if she died, I wouldn't be able to handle it. I wasn't strong like Daniel. He'd lost Antoinette. But he kept on going. He lived his life. And mine was the better for it.

But I wasn't noble like that. I wasn't heroic. I was greedy and selfish.

I wanted my wife. In my arms. In my bed. Every day and night.

Without Addie, I couldn't survive. I couldn't recover. I couldn't—

"Tom. You can come see her now."

I looked up and saw Eleanor standing in her lab coat.

I didn't have a clue how long I'd been sitting there.

"Is she—"

"Alive? Yes. And you have a daughter."

I hung my head and cried. And then I stood up and hugged her close. "Thank you."

She patted my back. And I heard the tears in her voice. "I was just doing my job."

"So Addie's okay?" I dried my eyes. "She's gonna be all right?"

"Yes, she's fine."

"And the baby?" I asked.

"She came early. But she's fine. I've already made sure she has everything she needs."

"Where is she?" I looked down the hall.

"She may have to spend a few weeks in the NICU. She's there now. But she's strong."

"Can I see Addie first?" I asked. "I don't want her to feel like she's alone."

"Of course." She led me to Addie's room. "We had to do an emergency C-section. I was just as concerned about the baby as I was the mother on this one. Both were at high risk."

"I can't thank you enough for telling me to get out of the way," I said.

"Well, she's my daughter." She opened the door. "And I'm a grandma now."

I saw Addie lying in the hospital bed. And it was enough to make me lose it all over again.

The nurse finished tending to her and then left. Eleanor followed her. "I'll give you two a minute."

The door closed and I walked up to her bed. She looked sleepy and exhausted. But she was still beautiful to me.

"Hi." I gazed into her emerald eyes.

"Hi," she echoed with a sweet smile.

"How do you feel?" I asked.

"Fine. Just pretty tired."

I pulled up a chair so I could sit with her. I reached out and she took my hand.

"You know, I'm starting to think Eleanor is a bad ass."

I laughed because she said it so seriously.

"I don't think I could ever do something like that."

I put my hand on her cheek. She felt warm.

"I know we've had our issues. But when it comes to this, she's pretty amazing."

I rubbed the back of her hand. "I agree."

"Have you seen her?" she asked.

"No, not yet. But I want to."

"I wish they would let me hold her."

"They will," I said. "You just need to rest first."

"Tom?"

"Yeah, baby."

"I've loved every part of my life with you," she whispered.

"Me too." I kissed her forehead. "Me too."

When she dozed off, I popped out for a second to see our daughter. She was so small, lying helplessly in an incubator. I touched my hand to the glass as a tear ran down my eye. She was wearing pink.

I wanted to hold her in my arms. She looked so beautiful. I couldn't believe we'd made her.

I checked on her every hour. And I paid more attention each time.

Every now and then, I saw her eyelids move. I wondered what she was dreaming about.

I called Jimmy and Jeff. And they both came immediately. Given the circumstances, I was a little worried they might be at each other's throats. But they were civil. Maybe they were finally getting along.

Josette had been coming to visit every month, since they had postponed the wedding. With Addie in her third trimester, flying across the country was not advised. And they didn't want her to miss the wedding.

So Jimmy had decided to stay until the baby was born. And then he was moving to Paris.

When I called Josette, she was screaming at me in French. All nice things of course.

She was just so excited, in a rush to get back over here. The funny thing was, she'd just stayed with us the week before. And then traveled back to Paris for work, since she ran a lucrative business as an art dealer.

I talked to Edmond next, and the whole family was getting on his private plane. I heard Adeline celebrating in the background. It had been a long time since there had been a newborn in the family.

Eric and Jeanine stopped by the hospital next. They were concerned about the baby. But I told them what Eleanor had said. At this stage, she had a 95% survival rate. Which was a hell of a lot higher than the one we'd worried over with Addie.

"Tom." Jimmy put his arm around me. "Aren't you forgetting somethin', son?"

I looked at my daughter through the glass as we all stood out in the hall.

"What?" I asked.

Jeanine stood beside me. And they were all on the same page.

"What's her name?" she asked.

It dawned on me that we'd skipped the most important part. We hadn't been expecting this little one to enter the world for another two months. So when it came to baby names, we were lacking.

"What should we name her?" I asked Addie that night. Everyone had already gone home. So it was just the two of us in her room. "Right now, the tag on her ankle just says, Sutton Baby."

She laughed, the first sign that she was getting her strength back.

"I've thought of a few, since I knew she was going to be a girl."

"Really?" I sat down beside her. "What are they?"

"I thought about all of our parents and grandparents. It would be nice to name her after one of them. But I love them all so much. And I kind of want her to have her own name. What do you think?"

"Yeah. I think that would be pretty cool."

"I wrote some names down in that notebook." She pointed to the small table beside her. "You were in the NICU and I wanted to jot them down before I forgot them."

I picked up the notebook and opened it.

"You can tell me which ones you don't like. It won't hurt my feelings."

I smiled and flipped through the pages. She'd written on a few.

But there were only two she'd put stars by.

"Faith and Amelia," I read.

"I thought they were pretty names," she said. "And they both sound good with Sutton."

"I kind of like them both. Which one is your favorite?"

"Well." She was propped up with her head against the pillow. "I'd really like to call her Faith."

"How about Amelia Faith Sutton? And we could call her by her middle name."

"Yeah," she smiled. "I like it."

"I like it, too." I leaned in to give her a kiss.

"I'm so happy," she breathed. "I think I might close my eyes for a minute."

"Do you want to sleep?" I asked.

"You just keep talking," she said. "I like the sound of your voice."

"Okay." I told her about all the phone calls I'd made today. Everyone in Paris was in such a hurry to get over here. I mentioned that Frank was the one flying the plane. "When I called, it was the middle of the night in Paris. They probably dragged him out of bed. I'm sure they're driving him crazy."

She was silent. And she looked very still.

I started to talk about something else, but then her heart monitor went off.

Addie was flatlining.

A nurse ran in. And thankfully, Eleanor was still

there.

I was so in shock that I backed into the wall. It had happened so suddenly.

One minute we were talking. And the next, she was gone.

The medical team did everything they could. But it was too late.

Eleanor put her hand over her mouth and looked at me. "I'm sorry."

Then she ran out of the room in tears. One by one, the nurses followed.

They were all so sorry. But I didn't want to hear it.

I got up and slammed the door. I was glad they were gone.

"No." I took her hand and kissed her face. "No. Not now. Not like this."

Her body was still warm. And her voice was in my head again.

Maybe it's not the killer.

Suddenly, I remembered the necklace in my pocket.

Maybe it's what saves me.

I stood up and pulled it out. What had the scientist said?

There is a hidden latch at the back. You can see it, but only if you're looking closely. Turn it counterclockwise three times and it should open. Then you administer three drops on the tongue.

I flipped the necklace over and found the latch. But when I turned it counterclockwise, it broke.

That's when I lost it. I squeezed the necklace in my hand and then threw it against the wall.

Everything had been taken from me. And there was no way I would ever get it back.

I put my head on her chest and cried, holding her close. And then I heard a soft drip.

I got up and looked at the necklace on the floor. It was leaking.

Alive with hope, I scooped it up and fiddled with the broken latch. Somehow, when I threw the necklace against the wall, it had opened.

I got on the bed and opened Addie's mouth. Then I held her head in my hand and poured the elixir on her tongue. It looked like water. It was clear, odorless. And I used every last drop.

I waited for a sign, but she looked the same.

"Please, baby." I kissed her and held her head in my hands. "Come back to me."

I gave up and wrapped her arms around me. They'd have to bury me with her.

I would never let her go.

But then her heart started beating again. And I saw waves on the monitor.

She opened her eyes and swallowed. "Tom. What happened?"

I touched her cheek with tears in my eyes. "Welcome back, Sleeping Beauty."

Epilogue

Addie

I'll never be sure what happened that night. All I know is, Tom saved my life.

For a few weeks, the woods by our home were a crime scene. It didn't take long for the police to prove our story was true.

And the news of a murder in Savannah, even in the case of self-defense, spread like wildfire.

I spent most of that time in the hospital, waiting for Faith to recover. The first time they let me hold her in my arms, it took my breath away.

"She's so beautiful," I said. And I cried tears of joy with one of the nurses.

When they finally let Faith go home, Eleanor came to say goodbye.

"So you're really leaving?" I asked.

"Yep." She stood at the edge of my bed. "My new job starts in two weeks."

"Can I ask you something?"

"Sure." She looked intrigued.

"Do you hate Dad? And does he hate you? Is it one of those divorces?"

She sat down and put her hand on mine. "The truth is, we've never had a normal marriage. We were each other's back up plan. We were both older. He was a bachelor. I was a divorcé."

"So you had a marriage of convenience?" I asked.

"Yeah. At the time, we were both at a point in our careers where no one would take us seriously unless we were married. Our bosses were old fashioned. That probably doesn't happen as much now."

"Did you love each other?"

She looked up. "In our own way, I think we did. We really tried. If you've ever felt neglected, it wasn't your fault. There were just some nights that I didn't want to come home."

"But I thought the two of you traveled together?"

"Sometimes," she said. "And sometimes, we got along better when we were apart."

We looked at each other, and she gave me a hug. "I hope we can still have a relationship."

"I thought you wouldn't want one," she said, tearing up. "My mother used to say, 'Eleanor, you'll be a good doctor or a good mother. But you'll never be both.' And I know I'm a good doctor."

I hugged her back. "I have felt neglected. But I still love you anyway."

"I love you too, Addie. And I really hope you'll be happy."

"You too." I dried my eyes. "Did you get everything from the house?"

"No," she groaned. "I've been waiting until the last minute. I only took what I needed in the beginning."

"Well, why don't we have a party tonight and pack?" I volunteered. "It could be fun."

"Okay," she agreed. "I don't see why not."

So Tom checked us out of the hospital and we went home. Faith looked so healthy now. Tom had cleaned the place from top to bottom while I was gone. So I sat down on the couch and held her against my breast.

"It feels strange doesn't it?" I asked.

"What?" He brought me a glass of water.

"There are three of us now."

"I know." He kissed me. "I love it."

"Jeffrey is coming tonight," I said.

"Really? Isn't that going to be awkward?"

"I don't know. I think he's still in love with her."

A few hours later, he sure looked like it. I lounged around my childhood home with Faith while the men helped Eleanor pack. To my surprise, she was leaving most of the furniture with Jeffrey. That seemed awfully generous of her, but I guess she was in a giving mood.

Before I knew it, she was all packed and ready to go. We stood out on the front porch to see her off. And I thought Jeffrey looked unusually sad considering the circumstances. What if they had been in an arranged marriage of sorts, but then he'd actually fallen in love with her?

"Goodbye, darling." She held Faith and kissed her on the forehead. "Don't forget your Grandma."

When she handed her back to me, I leaned against Tom. He shook her hand and then she looked at Jeffrey. He smiled at her. And by some miracle, she actually smiled back.

"You take care." He kissed her cheek. "Okay?"

She gave him a hug and nodded. "You too."

Then she got in her car and rode off into the sunset.

When she was gone, Tom and I sat in the rocking chairs on the front porch. Faith nestled in my arms while we watched Jeffrey just standing there. It was a full ten minutes before he moved.

"Well." He climbed up the steps and leaned

against the post. "How did you kids get to be so old?"

We laughed. And I was happy that we were here. I knew this was hard for him.

"You know what?" He looked out at the land. "I've always liked it here. I think I might stay."

"Really?" I hadn't seen that one coming.

"Yeah," he grinned. "I'm not selling this place. I just need to find a woman who likes the outdoors."

All three of us laughed and Jeffrey opened the front door. "Do y'all have plans for dinner?"

I looked at Tom. And he shook his head.

"No," I said.

"Well, why don't we eat together? I mean, I can't cook anything, but—"

"Don't worry," Tom stood up. "I'm on it."

He went inside to start dinner. And Jeffrey sat down beside me.

"You know somethin' kid?" He held Faith's hand and she wrapped her fingers around his thumb.

"What?" I looked at my little girl and then up at him.

"You're the best thing that ever happened to me."

There were tears in his eyes. So I started crying and leaned my head on his shoulder.

"Stop it, Dad!" I joked. "You know I'm hormonal."

He chuckled, and it was like music to my ears.

"If you ever need anything, I'll always be here."

"Thanks." Faith squirmed in my arms. "I think somebody's hungry."

In a few seconds, she started to cry.

"I think somebody is, too," he said. "Come on." He helped me up. "Let's go inside and see what your man's got cookin'."

So we had a lovely dinner. And cheered Jeffrey up on the loneliest night of his life.

* * *

A few months later, we fly to Paris for the big day. Josette and Jimmy were getting married at a grand hotel in the city. The wedding would take place outside in the courtyard in the early afternoon.

It was a small ceremony with less than thirty guests. But everyone important was there.

I sat in the front row with Tom. And he held my hand.

Maybe it was backwards, me being the one crying in the audience. I mean, I was the daughter and she was the mother. But I was just so happy that they had found each other again.

As much as I'd been through, Josette's experiences were far worse. She was so brave. Fearless. I hoped that, one day, I would be just like her.

Faith was very observant during the ceremony. She was wearing a pretty cream dress. And Tom held her securely in his lap. When the minister asked if anyone objected to the ceremony, Faith sneezed.

And the entire crowd laughed. I stroked my finger over Faith's cheek. And she smiled.

The reception was simple, yet elegant. They had their first dance as man and wife and then cut the cake. I danced with Jimmy, and Tom danced with Josette. And we even took Faith for a spin.

But in a couple hours, the fun and games were over. So we saw them off and said our goodbyes. They were jet-setting to Spain for the honeymoon, and I'd never seen them happier.

After they were gone, Edmond came over. "Hello,

my darling girl." He tapped Faith on the nose.

She reached her arms out for him, so I handed her over. She laughed and smiled, staring into his eyes. Tom returned from the bar and handed me a glass of water. He wrapped an arm around me and took a sip of beer.

"It would be nice to see this little one as she gets older." Edmond kissed her cheek.

"What do you mean?" I asked.

"Well, you know." He made a silly face at her. "So she can really get to know her Uncle Edmond. And all of her other French relations. I mean, look at her. Doesn't she seem like she belongs in Paris?"

"Oh." I finished my water. "I need some air."

So Tom and I put Faith in her baby carriage and went for a walk. There was a park nearby, and the city was so beautiful this time of year. I'd never been to Paris in the fall.

We stopped at a bridge overlooking the water. And I felt his eyes on me.

"It's gonna be weird without your dad around," he said.

I put my hands on the railing and looked out. He stood beside me, bumping his elbow against mine.

"What?" I grouched.

"Why are you in such a bad mood?"

"I'm not," I said. "I'm fine."

"You're going to miss them."

"Yeah. And I'm sure they'll miss me, too."

"It would be a shame." He looked at Faith. "For her to only see her grandparents a few times a year."

"What are you hiding?" I glared at him. I'd only meant it playfully.

He smiled and pulled out a brochure.

"What's this?" I took it and started flipping through.

"They have these estates for sale. Nice location. Plenty of land. Plenty of room for us."

I looked at the houses. The acreage was great. And the architecture was beautiful.

"What if I told you that Edmond has offered to buy us one?" He waited for my reaction.

"What?"

"It could be just for the summer or to vacation or to live."

"To live?" I asked. "To live?"

"Yes."

"You want to move to France?" I couldn't believe him.

"Well, I didn't tell you. But I've been applying to universities in Paris. And I got in."

"To which one?" I asked.

"Just a couple."

"But what about Georgia?"

"I can tell them I'm no longer interested, that I've decided to go somewhere else."

"You're telling me, that you've been okay with the idea of moving here this whole time?" I asked.

He shrugged and looked out at the water. "Well, yeah."

"You idiot!" I slapped his shoulder. "Why didn't you tell me that six months ago? You know I've been wanting to live here ever since we came last Christmas."

"You haven't noticed Edmond dropping hints?" he asked.

"Yes! He's been dropping hints ever since the baby was born. But I've been blowing him off, because I thought you'd never want to live here. You're the one who said Savannah is our home. That's why I've just been pretending to love the fact that Jimmy moved over here! And we can just stay in—"

He grabbed my cheeks and squeezed them together. "You're sassy when you're lactating."

I slapped his hand. But not very hard. "So you've been orchestrating this whole thing behind my back? You and Edmond! Didn't you ever think to ask me what I thought?" I took the carriage and stormed off. "Then you would have known how I felt! And here I've been thinking that you want to stay in Georgia."

"Hey." He grabbed my arm and I stopped. "Listen, I don't care where we live. I just want to be with you. But I think we could be happy here. Faith likes it."

We looked at her, and she was giggling. "What does she think of us? Two parents squabbling?"

"Let's go back to the hotel," he said. "It will be getting dark soon."

We went up to our room, and I put Faith down. She had fallen asleep in her carriage.

I was mad at Edmond and Tom for excluding me from something so important. I went into the bathroom and took my clothes off. And then I stepped beneath the warm shower. In a matter of minutes, he was behind me, kissing my neck. But I was unresponsive, frustrated and hurt.

"Look, if you don't like *any* of those houses, then fine. But I thought you—"

"I do like them." I spun around. "I love them."

"Which ones?" he said.

"All of them."

"Then what's the problem?" he asked.

"I *do* want to live here. With my family. This is my home."

"Then let's make it *our* home."

"Really?" I clung to him beneath the water.

"Yeah." He kissed me. "Why not?"

I batted my eyes and put on the charm. "You're such a good man."

He laughed. "That's because I have such a good woman. She keeps me in line."

"Is that so?" I felt his fingertips tracing my back.

"Yeah." He backed me up against the wall. "She drives me wild. But I love her."

I wrapped my arms around him and touched his lips. "She loves you, too."

FOR MR. GUSTAV LEHMANN

Dear Sir,

You once gave me a few minutes of your time. And those minutes turned into years added to my wife's life. You may not remember me. But I will never forget you.

Your daughter, Mira was a fighter. I would have liked to meet her. As a father myself, I now have an understanding of life that I never had before. I understand the necessity of protecting those we hold most dear.

Attached to this letter, you will find a package. Inside the package, you will find what is left of the necklace. The one that belongs to my wife. The one that, legend has it, once belonged to Marie Antoinette.

I'd like you to break it apart and study it.

I've sealed the necklace in an air tight case. And I'm sure traces of the elixir remain.

My wife almost died once. And what I found inside of this necklace saved her.

You were right. And my wife and I want to give you this as a token of our gratitude.

Use it for good, as I know you will. I too, believe there will be a cure one day.

I hope what you find will give you great joy. May you live a long and happy life.

Sincerely,

Tom Sutton

P.S. I've enclosed a check for one million euros. Please send me all that you find.

Tell Me Your Favorite Part!

If you enjoyed Violet Blood, I invite you to head over to Amazon and let me know your favorite part. Reviews are so important to an author's career, because they help new readers like you discover the book. Even if you didn't enjoy Violet Blood, I'd still love it if you could take three minutes to let me know what you think of the book.

Leaving a review is super easy:

1) Go to Violet Blood Book Page on Amazon

2) Scroll Down and click "Write a Customer Review"

3) Sign in to Amazon if prompted

4) Select a star rating

5) Write a few short words (or long words, I won't judge)

6) Click the 'submit' button

I thank you in advance!

Acknowledgements

I hate goodbyes. And this was a pretty epic one for me. Addie and Tom have been with me for 10 years. That's longer than any other characters I've ever written about. And I've loved every moment of their epic love saga—from the meet cute to the finale.

But what makes it so special is readers like *you*. Thank you for every compliment, email, message, comment, shout-out and review. You've stuck with me through this series, and I truly hope you've enjoyed watching it all unfold. Thank you for tweeting about this series and adding it on Goodreads and recommending it on BookBub. Watching readers talk about these characters who are so close to my heart has been kind of mind-blowing for me. Because I kept them to myself for so long before I finally hit publish in June of 2015. And now, exactly three years later, I'm sending the last book out into the world and saying goodbye.

I think what makes this so difficult is the fact that these were not only the first characters I ever published, they were also the first characters I ever wrote about. And when I look back on myself at sixteen, having no clue what I was getting into when I decided to start writing, I'm shocked. Simply because it's been so long, and yet it doesn't seem like that much time has gone by at all.

I'll miss Savannah. I'll miss Maple Creek High.

I'll miss the crazy twists and turns that even I didn't see coming.

But most importantly, I'll miss witnessing the bond between Tom and Addie. Because, for me, the love story is what I care about most. And despite all the things this series can be classified as (mystery, suspense, thriller, drama) it truly is a love story. Because love is the best part of any story. And I'm so grateful that you've let me share a few snapshots of these high school sweethearts with you.

I put off writing this final book. Because I didn't want something I'd put so many years into to finally be over. What I realize now, is that there are so many other amazing characters out there whose stories are just waiting to be told. So while I'm sad about sealing the lid on Tom and Addie, I'm also excited for all the new couples to come. And I can't wait to show you how each and every one of them fall in love.

I'd like to thank my parents for the moral support. To my mother: for your excitement every time I'm drafting a new book idea. If you were my only reader, I'd keep on writing anyway. To my father: for your wisdom and encouragement. To my grandparents: for being the coolest when I was a kid and the best babysitters ever. To my cousins: for being the little sisters I never had. To my aunt: for choosing one of my novels for your book club last year and letting me be a part of it. And to my other aunt: for the constant supply of books as a child from Barnes & Noble.

Thank you to all the author friends and bloggers I've met along the way. None of this would be possible without you. Thank you for the advice, chats and support. I love being a part of this community.

Lastly, thank you to the fans. When I started out, I had no idea how any of this was going to go. I never imagined that in a few short years I'd have fourteen books out. And it's not really about the number.

I just want to tell love stories in as many ways as I can. Even if platforms for independent writer/authors didn't exist, I'd still be writing. Because I can't really make myself stop.

So thank you for sticking with me for all these years. It's time to tell Tom and Addie goodbye, because they have their own life to live. And I can't try to write the rest of their story for them. But that just means it's time to discover new characters. And I've already been anxious to do that.

I've had a lot to say, so if you've read this far I applaud you :)

I don't know what stories will pop into my head next. But I can promise you that I'm going to keep challenging myself as a writer. I'm not trying to replace Tom and Addie. I'm just adding some new members to our little family tree.

As always thank you for the love and support! It means the world to me.

Happy Reading!

Lindsay x

About the Author

Lindsay Marie Miller was born and raised in Tallahassee, Florida, where she graduated from high school as Valedictorian. At sixteen, she started writing her first novel, *Emerald Green*, after being inspired by Stephenie Meyer's International Bestselling *Twilight Saga*. During her time in college, Lindsay wrote 5 more novels and over 100 songs. After graduating Summa Cum Laude from Florida State University, she put her B.A. in English Literature to good use and published her debut novel, *Emerald Green*. An author of over 10 Romance Titles, Lindsay currently resides in her hometown of Tallahassee where she is always working on her next novel.

VISIT THE WEBSITE
https://www.lindsaymariemillerauthor.com

NEWSLETTER SIGN UP
http://bit.ly/2wHeWsR

FOLLOW ON BOOKBUB
https://bit.ly/2rtMMzd

LIKE US ON FACEBOOK
facebook.com/LindsayMarieMillerAuthor

JOIN THE VIP GROUP
http://bit.ly/2EKmZcn

FOLLOW US ON TWITTER
twitter.com/Lindsay_MMiller

FOLLOW US ON AMAZON
http://amzn.to/2BZnWdP

FOLLOW US ON GOODREADS
https://bit.ly/2JpmRAK

WANT MORE TOM & ADDIE?

FIND OUT WHERE IT ALL STARTED

The Girl in the Woods: A Novella

AVAILABLE NOW